# This was no way for a Pinkerton agent to behave,

Anna reminded herself as she rushed along.

It was no way for a self-respecting woman to behave, either. To be so flummoxed by a kiss. To have her legitimate and quite serious concerns turned into frilly bows and butterflies by a man's mouth on hers. And it wouldn't happen again.

Jack Hazard came to a halt. His dark face glowered down on her. "I apologize," he snarled. "It won't happen again, Mrs. Matlin. Mrs. Hazard. Whoever the hell you are." He let go of her arm to drag his fingers through his hair.

Had the kiss affected him, too? There was a definite flush to his face that Anna had never seen, and his fingers trembled as they threaded through that shiny black hair. Jack Hazard, master spy, seemed nearly as unsettled as she...!

Dear Reader,

Welcome to Harlequin Historicals. Whether you're a longtime fan of Mary McBride or have just discovered her, we know you'll be delighted by her new book, *Darling Jack*, the touching tale of a handsome Pinkerton detective, driven by revenge, and the steady, unassuming file clerk who poses as his wife for an assignment. Don't let this terrific story slip by you.

*Dulcie's Gift*, from Ruth Langan, is the prequel to the contemporary stories in the Harlequin cross-line continuity series, BRIDE'S BAY. When a boatful of women and children seek refuge on his island, Cal Jermain isn't pleased with the added responsibility, especially when he finds himself falling for their secretive leader, Dulcie Trenton.

This month's books also include a new medieval novel from Claire Delacroix, *My Lady's Champion*, the story of a woman who must marry in order to protect her holdings, and a Western from newcomer Carolyn Davidson, *Loving Katherine*, about a lonely woman who has struggled to keep the family horse farm, and a drifter who teaches her that there's more to life.

We hope you'll keep a lookout for all four titles.

Sincerely,

Tracy Farrell
Senior Editor

Please address questions and book requests to:
Harlequin Reader Service
U.S.: 3010 Walden Ave., P.O. Box 1325, Buffalo, NY 14269
Canadian: P.O. Box 609, Fort Erie, Ont. L2A 5X3

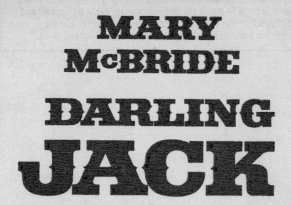

# MARY McBRIDE

# DARLING JACK

*Harlequin Books*

TORONTO • NEW YORK • LONDON
AMSTERDAM • PARIS • SYDNEY • HAMBURG
STOCKHOLM • ATHENS • TOKYO • MILAN
MADRID • WARSAW • BUDAPEST • AUCKLAND

ISBN 0-373-28923-5

DARLING JACK

## MARY McBRIDE

is a former special education teacher who lives in St. Louis, Missouri, with her husband and two young sons. She loves to correspond with readers and invites them to write to her at:

P.O. Box 411202
St. Louis, MO 63141

With deep affection to my friends in The Lounge

# Prologue

Anna Matlin was invisible.

As a child in the grim coal-mining hills of southern Illinois, she had learned her lessons well. In a family of thirteen, the squeaking wheel got backhanded and burdened with extra chores. In any forest, it was the tallest tree that suffered the lightning.

So Anna, early on, had decided to be a shrub.

She had blossomed once—and briefly—at the age of sixteen, when she eloped to Chicago with Billy Matlin. But Billy had soon looked beyond her, to Colorado and the promise of gold.

"I'll send for you," he'd said. But Billy never had. He'd died instead, leaving his young widow pale and even more invisible.

Under bleak winter skies, in her somber wools and black galoshes, Anna Matlin was barely distinguishable from the soot-laden banks of snow along Washington Street as she made her way to number 89, the offices of the Pinkerton National Detective Agency, where she had been employed for six years, filing papers and transcribing notes and more or less blending into the wainscoting.

In summer, in her drab poplins and sensible shoes, she seemed to disappear against brick walls and dull paving stones.

Whatever the season or setting, Anna Matlin was—by her own volition—invisible.

But every once in a while, particularly in summer, when the sun managed to slice through the smoke-dense Chicago sky, it would cast a rare and peculiar glint from Anna's spectacles, a flash that for an instant made her seem exceptional and altogether visible.

As it did on the morning of May 3, 1869...

# Chapter One

*Chicago*
*May 3, 1869*

"I need a wife."

"That's impossible, Jack. Entirely out of the question." Allan Pinkerton leaned back in his chair. He raised both hands to knead his throbbing temples, then closed his eyes a moment, wishing—praying, actually—that when he opened them again both the headache and Mad Jack Hazard would be gone.

But—damn it—they weren't. The nagging pain was still there, and so was his best and bravest operative. The man was a headache in human form, slanted back now with his arms crossed and his brazen boots up on the boss's desk.

"I need a wife, Allan," Hazard said again, in that voice that still had a touch of English mist, even after all these years.

The founder of the world's largest, most successful detective agency sighed as he continued to massage his forehead. "You work alone. Damn it. You've worked alone since the war. It's the way you've wanted it."

"Not this time."

Something in the man's tone made Pinkerton lean forward. Jack Hazard made demands. He didn't plead. But now there seemed to be a tentative note playing just beneath the usual bravado.

"If it were possible," Pinkerton said. "But it's not. Right now all of my female operatives are assigned. There's no one—"

Hazard cut him off, jerking his thumb toward the closed office door. "There's a roomful of females out there, and you bloody well know it."

"Secretaries." Pinkerton dismissed them with a wave of his hand. "They always gather when you come. You know that. They flock like silly pigeons at a popcorn festival."

"Surely one of them—"

"No." Pinkerton banged a fist on his desk. "Absolutely not. They're clerks, not operatives. None of them has been trained or is qualified."

"They're women, for God's sake. That qualifies any one of them to play the part of my wife. It's not as if you're asking them to use a gun, or to wrench a confession out of a counterfeiter."

"I understand that, but . . ."

"What you need to understand is this, old friend." As Hazard's voice lowered, his eyes lifted slowly to meet Pinkerton's straight on. Gray to Gray. Steel to stone. There was a spark. And then it died. "I can't do it alone. Not this time."

Suddenly Pinkerton did understand. He understood all too well, and his voice softened considerably. "Perhaps I ought to assign someone else...."

"No." In one swift and fluid movement, Jack Hazard's boots hit the floor and he was out of his chair, towering over Pinkerton's desk. "She's mine. If anybody's going to bring Chloe Von Drosten down, Allan, it's going to be me. Nobody else. Me. You owe me that, damn it."

Pinkerton didn't answer for a moment. He studied his folded hands, then let his eyes drift closed. When he spoke, it was quietly, with calm deliberation. "The woman did you considerable damage, Jack. More than I had imagined."

"I'm over it," came the terse reply.

"And the drinking?"

"That, too. It's been five months." Hazard yanked his watch from his vest pocket and snapped it open. "Five months. Hell, it's been a hundred twenty-two days, ten hours and thirty-seven minutes."

Pinkerton sank back in his chair, out of Hazard's towering shadow. He massaged his temples a moment before asking, "You don't believe you need more time?"

"I've had time. Now I need something else."

"Revenge?" Pinkerton lifted a wary brow. "I won't have one of my agents rolling around like a loose cannon, bent on nothing more than wreaking havoc."

Hazard shook his head. "No, not revenge. That isn't it. What I need, Allan, is redemption." He smiled grimly as he closed the watch and jammed it back into his pocket. "And a wife."

And then his voice didn't break so much as it unraveled, coming apart in a thready whisper.

"Allan. Please."

The commotion down the hall had drawn Anna Matlin to the door of the file room. She stood there now, shaking her head and watching two more secretaries as they attempted to enter Allan Pinkerton's anteroom simultaneously. After a collision of shoulders, a collapse of crinolines and a good deal of elbowing and hissing, the women somehow managed to squeeze through and to join the throng already inside.

It didn't take a Philadelphia lawyer or a Pinkerton spy to figure out what was happening. *He* was back. It happened once or twice a year. The arrival and departure of Johnathan Hazard sent the entire office into a tizzy, a frenzy of swishing skirts and sighs and giggles. Last spring, Martha Epsom had broken her ankle racing down the hall. Today, Judith and Mayetta had nearly come to blows while wedged between the doorjambs. All for a glimpse of Mad Jack Hazard. All for the sake of a fluttering heart. A fleeting sigh.

Such silliness.

Anna was about to turn and go back to her filing when someone grasped her elbow.

"Come along, Mrs. Matlin." Miss Nora Quillan's voice was brisk and efficient. Her grip on Anna's arm was secure. "There's a batch of expense sheets somewhere in there." The woman cast a dour glance at the door of the anteroom. "Perhaps you'd better get them before they're trampled."

There was no refusing Allan Pinkerton's steel-willed longtime secretary. Not if one had a thimble-ful of sense, anyway, or if one prized one's employment at the agency, which Anna most certainly did.

"Yes, ma'am," she said, even as the tall, broad-shouldered woman ushered her down the hall.

"I'm glad to see at least one of our young ladies has a sense of decency," Miss Quillan muttered. "Some modicum of pride."

They had reached the door to the anteroom now. Beyond the threshold was pandemonium—the sighing, simpering and swooning of a dozen or more of Johnathan Hazard's devotees.

Miss Quillan clucked her tongue in disgust. "I'm helpless. Mr. Pinkerton insists this...this frenzy is good for morale, although for whose, I really couldn't say. Certainly not mine!" She narrowed her eyes on Anna now, and her mouth crimped in a small smile. "I'm glad to see you're immune, Mrs. Matlin."

"Well, I'm not exactly..."

"Yes. Well. You're a sensible girl. You'll find the expense sheets over there by the window. I hope. Good luck." Nora Quillan sniffed and waded into the feminine melee, clapping her hands and shouting, "Ladies! Ladies! Could we have a little order in here, please?"

It wasn't that she was immune, Anna thought as she made her way to the window. That wasn't the case at all. It was rather that she didn't believe in expending useless emotions. She wasn't the sort of person who wasted dreams. Not that she had any. But if she had...

She gave a little shrug, and was reaching for the sheaf of papers on the library table when the door of Allan Pinkerton's office opened. There was a last-moment jostling in the anteroom, a flurry of movement followed by a communal sigh that dwindled to a breathless hush as Pinkerton's most illustrious spy appeared.

Anna's hand halted in midair. Her heart, like countless others in the room, gathered speed, bounded into her throat and then plummeted to the pit of her stomach.

Johnathan Hazard—Mad Jack—was the most beautiful man in the world. From his jet-dark hair to the tips of his high glossed boots. He was broad of shoulder, narrow of waist, and perfectly tall. His bearing was straight and military, although Anna knew he had never been a soldier. His air of command was that of a duke or baron, even though he was the fourth son of an earl. Still, he was beautiful. Hazard was fashioned, Anna thought suddenly, not as a man at all, but as a model for what a man might be, if all the gods could agree on a single definition of masculine beauty. Or if they consulted her.

Which they hadn't. Anna reminded herself quickly and firmly, redirecting her gaze to the stack of papers and the task at hand.

"Well?" Allan Pinkerton stood at Jack Hazard's shoulder. He spoke with the hushed tone of a conspirator. "That's the lot of them. A bevy, if you will. Take your pick, Jack. And be quick about it. I'd like to get back to business."

"It doesn't matter." Hazard shifted his stance and crossed his arms, surveying the roomful of women. "I'll need her for a month or so. Which one can you spare?"

"None of them, damn it." Pinkerton shot back. Then he demurred. "Well, anyone but Miss Quillan, I suppose. The whole place would come undone without her."

"I don't want your ramrod, Allan. God forbid." Hazard laughed as his gaze cut to the dark-haired secretary, who was poised like a pillar of salt behind her desk. And then, just at the edge of his vision, there came a sudden flash of light, a glint of gold that made him turn toward the window.

"What about her?"

"Her?"

"Over there. The little mouse. The one in the brown dress and the spectacles who's doing her best to blend into the woodwork."

Pinkerton squinted. "Oh. Mrs. Matlin."

"Mrs. Matlin?" A frown creased Hazard's forehead. "Is she married?"

"No. At least I don't believe so. She's a widow, as I recall. Been here for years."

"I never noticed her."

"I don't suppose many do."

Jack Hazard grinned. "A widow ought to do nicely. See that she's on the train tomorrow morning, will you?"

Pinkerton cleared his throat. "I'll ask her, Jack, but I can't promise—"

"Don't promise, Allan. Just do it."

Then, with what seemed like a gust of audible sighs at his back, the Pinkerton National Detective Agency's most illustrious spy walked out of the room.

Nora Quillan already had her hat and gloves on. As on most days, she had worked late. Today in particular, with all the commotion, she had been hard-pressed to get the agency back to some semblance of order. Having done that, Nora was ready to go home to a cold supper, a single glass of ale and a good night's sleep. Still, she knocked on her employer's door and walked into his office before he was able to call, "Come in."

"You're making a dreadful mistake, Mr. P.," she said.

"Another one, Nora?" Allan Pinkerton turned from the window, hands clasped at his back, an indulgent grin upon his lips. "And just what is this dreadful mistake?"

"I know you think the world of Johnathan Hazard, but—"

"He's the best man I have," Pinkerton said, interrupting her.

"He *was*." Nora sighed now as she crossed the room and settled on the arm of a chair. "His imprisonment during the war changed him. And now, after that Von Drosten woman sank her claws into him—and probably her fangs, as well—he's worse. Much worse." She narrowed her gaze on the man at the window. "Frankly, I'm surprised you haven't noticed it. And I must say I'm shocked that you'd risk letting him fall into her clutches again."

Allan Pinkerton was accustomed to his secretary's candor. He valued her opinions. Nora Quillan was rarely wrong. In this instance, however, he prayed she was. Dead wrong.

"Did Jack say anything to you?" he asked her.

Nora sniffed. "He didn't have to. I've known him for over ten years. Nearly as long as you have. The changes are obvious, although I must say he's done his best to mask them."

Pinkerton nodded—in agreement, in dismay. He was remembering his detective's uncharacteristic plea earlier that day, the way the man's voice had shattered, the tremor in his hands that he'd been hardpressed to disguise. But Hazard had, damn it. He had.

"He isn't drinking anymore, Nora."

"That doesn't mean he won't. Especially if he's under *her* influence again. That woman is evil, Mr. P. Surely you recognize that now if you didn't before. The Baroness Von Drosten is the devil in silk and ermine."

"She's a fake," Pinkerton said through clenched teeth.

A harsh laugh broke from Nora's throat. "It doesn't seem to matter, does it? Fake or not, she still manages to cast her evil spell on—"

"That's enough, Nora." Allan Pinkerton sagged into the chair behind his desk and began massaging his throbbing temples. His own worries about Jack Hazard were legion; he didn't need Nora's to aggravate them.

"Hazard has a plan," he said, attempting to put an end to the discussion.

"He had a plan *before*," Nora shot back, as soon as the words were out of her employer's mouth. "He was going to seduce her last year, wasn't he? But instead, the baroness seduced him. And worse."

"This time he won't be alone."

Nora rolled her eyes. "That's the other mistake I was intending to bring to your attention. To send little Mrs. Matlin along on this . . . this devil's business . . . is like sending a lamb to the slaughter.''

''She agreed, Nora. We spoke at length this afternoon,'' he muttered. ''The woman even seemed rather pleased.''

''She wants to keep her job! How the devil else would you expect her to behave?'' Nora shot up from the arm of the chair now, planting her fists on her hips. ''You're determined to carry through with this, aren't you?''

Allan Pinkerton closed his eyes and slowly nodded his head.

Nora threw up her hands. ''I knew it. Sometimes I don't know why I bother wasting my breath,'' she muttered on her way to the door. ''Nothing good will come of this. You mark my words. Jack Hazard will be lost forever, if he isn't already. And God only knows what will happen to poor, unsuspecting Anna Matlin.''

''Is that all, Nora?'' Pinkerton asked wearily.

''I should think that would be quite enough,'' she said with a sniff. ''Good night, Mr. P. I'll see you tomorrow.''

After his secretary slammed the door, Allan Pinkerton leaned forward, cradling his aching head in his hands, praying that for once in her life the infallible Nora Quillan was fallible—and dead, dead wrong.

## Chapter Two

For someone who had proceeded with slow caution for most of her twenty-six years, Anna Matlin felt as if she were speeding downhill on ice skates. For someone who had enjoyed invisibility for so long, she suddenly felt as if she were standing, quite naked, in the hot glare of a spotlight. And Anna wasn't altogether certain that she liked it.

Everything was happening so fast, so unexpectedly. First there had been Mr. Pinkerton and his astonishing request. Then, at the Edgewood Inn, where Anna habitually took her meals, when she quietly announced she would be gone for the next few weeks, everyone had seemed, well...disappointed. Even sad. Anna had been amazed, particularly when the cook, Miranda, after shaking Anna's hand, pulled her to her great, damp bosom and wailed how much she would miss her.

Right now, her landladies were behaving as if Anna were the center of the universe.

She had been a boarder in the big frame house on Adams Street for six years. She paid her rent on the first Saturday of every month and, when she wasn't working at the Pinkerton Agency, Anna spent most of her time in her third-floor room, reading. Her landladies, the Misses Richmond, had always treated her kindly while keeping their distance. Until tonight. Anna had asked to borrow a trunk. Along with the luggage, however, she was now receiving a good deal of unasked-for advice.

Little Miss Richmond—Verna—was perched on the footboard of Anna's bed at the moment, while big Miss Richmond—Dorothy—stood in the doorway, rather like a prison matron, jingling a set of keys.

"Your employer purchased a ticket for you, I presume," Miss Dorothy said now.

"Well, not exactly." Anna stuffed her hairbrush in the carpetbag, then took it out again and put it on the dresser. She'd be needing it in the morning. She reached into her handbag and produced a small but official-looking square of paper. "He gave me this, instead."

Miss Verna snatched it from her hand. "Oh, my. This is interesting. It seems to be a pass of some sort for the Chicago, Alton and St. Louis Railroad."

"I'd be more comfortable with a ticket, myself," Miss Dorothy said with disdain. "One never knows about these things."

"It looks quite official to me, sister." Miss Verna handed the paper back to Anna. "I'm sure it's all right."

"A lot you know," the larger sister snapped. "And just when did you last travel by train, Verna Richmond?"

"Actually, I've never..."

"Precisely." Miss Dorothy gave her keys an authoritative jingle. "I'd be much happier, too, if you weren't traveling alone, Mrs. Matlin. You did say that was the plan, didn't you?"

Anna merely nodded now, as she continued to take underwear from the dresser, fold it, then lay the garments carefully in the trunk. She had indeed told her landladies she was being sent to St. Louis alone, not knowing whether or not they would take exception or offense to the truth, unsure whether or not they would let her return after traveling with a member of the opposite sex. For, when this surprising assignment was over, Anna had every intention of returning—to this house and this room, to her quiet life.

A little ripple of excitement coursed through her, bringing goose bumps to her skin. She was going to St. Louis with *him*. With Johnathan Hazard. As his wife! Suddenly she wanted to pinch herself—again—to make certain this wasn't a dream. If it was, Miss Dorothy's voice broke into it.

"We'll want to know where you're staying, dear. I don't suppose your employer gave you a hotel pass, as well? You'll want to choose a simple establishment."

"Hotels can be dreadfully expensive," Miss Verna put in, but when her sister clucked her tongue, she quickly added, "Or so I've heard. I've never stayed in one personally."

Anna laid another chemise in the trunk. "Actually, I don't know where I'll be staying. Someone in the St. Louis agency is meeting me there. I'm sure he will have made all the proper arrangements."

Her landladies gasped in unison.

"He?"

"Who, dear?"

"Or she," Anna said quickly. "Come to think of it, the manager of the St. Louis agency is a woman."

It was a lie, of course, albeit a small, off-white one, but it allowed the Misses Richmond to let out their collective breath. After another few minutes of quizzing and advising, the two spinsters left Anna to her packing. Miss Verna came back a moment later to present her with a going-away gift—"A volume of verses by Mr. Browning, dear. I know how much you like to read. And do be careful with your spectacles. Traveling can often bring mishaps. Or so I've heard." The woman even kissed her on the cheek before retreating downstairs.

All things considered, it had been an amazing day, Anna thought when she had finished packing, then donned her cotton nightdress and finally slid beneath the covers of her bed. She laid her spectacles carefully on the nightstand, as was her habit, closed her eyes and crossed her hands over the counterpane, with every intention of falling asleep instantly, as she always did.

A second later, she was sitting up, staring wide-eyed into a moonlit corner of the room.

"Dear Lord, how did this happen? What in the world have I done?"

She knew precisely when it happened—that moment in Mr. Pinkerton's anteroom this morning when Johnathan Hazard's gaze met hers and sent her heart skittering up into her throat and her stomach plunging to the soles of her feet. It had been as if the man had hit her. She hadn't been able to catch her breath; she had even feared she might faint. Then he had walked out of the office, and for a second Anna had been tempted to run after him. She had stood there, her fingers clenched in the folds of her skirts, every muscle in her body about to explode with motion, every nerve screaming for speed.

Even now Anna wasn't sure what she might have done if Miss Quillan hadn't clapped her hands just then. "Ladies, it's time to get back to business," the secretary had proclaimed. Then, after conferring briefly with Mr. Pinkerton, Miss Quillan had added, "Oh, Mrs. Matlin. Would you be so kind as to remain here a moment, please? Mr. Pinkerton would like to have a word with you."

"Me?"

She had felt her face burning then, believing that somehow her employer had read her thoughts, that Allan Pinkerton, master detective, had detected her explosive heartbeat and was about to fire her for such inappropriate behavior.

But, instead, once Anna was in his office, the first words out of his mouth had been, "Mr. Hazard needs a wife."

After that, although he spoke at length, Anna had barely comprehended his meaning. She remembered nodding solemnly. She remembered saying yes and taking the railroad pass from Mr. Pinkerton's extended hand.

"Be at the depot at 8:30," he had told her. "Hazard will fill you in on the particulars."

The rest of the afternoon was a blur. Word had gotten out in the office, despite the fact that Anna hadn't breathed so much as a syllable. How could she have? She'd still been hard-pressed to catch her breath.

"Why did he pick you?" someone asked. Anna could only shake her head.

"Some people have all the luck," Mayetta had said with an indignant sniff.

Some people did, but Anna Matlin had never considered herself one of them.

And this wasn't lucky at all, she thought now as she stared at the packed trunk in the corner of her room. This was insane. Whatever had possessed her earlier, and made her agree to this preposterous adventure, suddenly and completely escaped her reckoning. And yet . . .

Anna lay back and closed her eyes. There had been that magical moment this morning, when Johnathan Hazard's eyes met hers. She couldn't even have said now just what color those eyes were. Gray, perhaps. Or a deep, disturbing blue. They were beautiful, though, like all the rest of him, and they had sent a shocking, nearly electric message all through her.

Even now, hours later, her heart began to beat erratically in her breast. *Come,* those eyes had said. *Risk it. Yes.*

"No." The word left her lips as little more than breath as Anna dug deeper into the familiar warmth of her bed.

The only risk she'd ever taken in her life had turned out badly. She'd come to Chicago with Billy Matlin, even when her father had warned her, "If you go, girl, don't bother coming back." She had married a young dreamer—sweet Billy—who had pursued his dreams beyond her and who had perished—somewhere in the mountains of Colorado in his quest for gold.

She'd never been a dreamer. It didn't make sense that now, at the age of twenty-six, she had suddenly allowed herself to be swept up in a dream. But she had been. In a single moment. At a single glance. *Come. Risk it.*

Not that she'd had much of a choice. Mr. Pinkerton had never said in so many words that there was

one, though his manner had been hesitant somehow, and there had been enough pauses in his speech
that Anna could have stopped him at any time. But
she hadn't. There she had been in Mr. Pinkerton's
office, not collecting papers before or after hours, or
dusting, as she occasionally did when he was out of
town, but having been invited in by the great Mr.
Pinkerton himself. And there he had been, looking
the way God might have looked sitting behind a
desk, asking her to act, if only for a while, as a
Pinkerton detective. She had been astonished beyond words and flattered beyond belief. It had never
occurred to Anna to say no.

Until now.

Still ... there was *him*. Johnathan Hazard. Mad
Jack as he was so often called. As a file clerk, Anna
was privy to a great deal of information about the
Pinkerton employees. It wasn't that she snooped,
exactly. It was just that it was difficult not to read
papers as she put them in their proper folders and
files. She knew, for example, that Nora Quillan was
thirty years old and divorced. And she knew that
Johnathan Hazard was the fourth son of an English
earl, and that he had come to America after being
asked to leave Oxford for "behavior unbecoming,"
whatever that meant.

He had begun working for Mr. Pinkerton ten years
ago, and by the time Anna started with the agency,
Johnathan Hazard had already been somewhat of a
legend in the Chicago office. Back then, of course,

in 1863, the war had been going on, and most of the agents, Mr. Pinkerton included, had been working as spies for President Lincoln and the Union army.

She remembered the day when word had come that Hazard and his partner, Samuel Scully, had been captured in Virginia and been condemned to hang as spies. A dark cloud had settled over the office, not to lift until the men received a stay of execution. Hazard had appealed to England, the country of his birth. It wasn't known just what Scully had done to escape the hangman's noose, but there had been talk of his giving information to his captors, especially when another Pinkerton spy was arrested and summarily hanged.

After four years, the gossip had died away. So had Samuel Scully, Anna thought. No one, it seemed, knew for certain what had happened in that Virginia prison. No one inquired anymore. Mr. Pinkerton stood staunchly behind agents, whether they were dead or alive, and he would have fired anyone who dared to suggest that Scully had been a traitor.

It had been after the war that Johnathan Hazard truly earned his nickname—Mad Jack. He had gone after and brought in the most daring of thieves and counterfeiters, all the while sending in the most outrageous expense reports Anna had ever seen. His file was thick with them, as well as with dozens of written reprimands from Mr. Pinkerton. They never seemed to hamper his career, however, or his dazzling reputation.

Still, in the past five or six months, Anna couldn't recall having filed a single paper in the Hazard file. A year ago he had been assigned to recover some jewels believed stolen by the Baroness Chloe Von Drosten. He had simply disappeared after that— from the office and from the files. There had been rumors. Rumors aplenty. That he had fallen into drink and dissipation. That he had retired. That he had been fired.

And then, suddenly—today—he was back. Dark and tall and elegant. Swaggering, even when he was standing still. Anna felt her lips curling up in a smile now as she pictured that. Johnathan Hazard's absence seemed to have made all the secretaries' hearts grow fonder. Maybe even her own.

She thought once more about her astonishing day. From the moment that man looked at her, it had been as if she were moving in some odd spotlight, being noticed by people who ordinarily ignored her. And not merely noticed, but cared for. She felt, well . . . quite special.

She had never wanted to be special, though. Quite the opposite. She had planned to live her life quietly, retiring from the Pinkerton Agency when her hair was gray and her bones were brittle, moving to the seaside, perhaps, where she would spend her remaining days taking quiet walks on the beach and reading all the books she didn't have enough time for now.

Of course, she still would. But now, when she retired, she would have one dazzling memory to savor. And that, Anna supposed, was worth a bit of risk.

In a month or so, she would be back in the file room, and invisible again. But no one would be able to take away the memory that for one bright and splendid month, she had been not only a Pinkerton spy, but Johnathan Hazard's wife, as well.

She was going to have an adventure. After that Anna thought as she drifted into sleep, she would return—to this room, to her filing, and to her comfortable oblivion.

It was well after midnight when Ada Campbell, the madam of the city's foremost house of pleasure, determined that all was well in the parlors downstairs and that she could at last retire to her personal quarters on the second floor, where Mad Jack Hazard was waiting for her.

Not that she was anticipating an evening of love, she thought as she climbed the ornate staircase, stopping once to peer at a nick in the oaken banister and then again to pick up a feather from the Oriental runner that led to her rooms.

Jack had been back for nearly a week. The handsome Pinkerton agent was one of the few men whom she permitted in her rose-brocaded sanctuary and to whom she gave her favors gratis. Only on this visit, Jack Hazard was behaving more like her guest than her lover. He hadn't touched her once. Damn it.

Ada frowned as she neared her door, questioning her own abilities at seduction. She'd never had to seduce this man before, though. Not Hazard. Not any other man, for that matter, but particularly not Hazard. He'd always been more than eager to join her in her bed, and more than creative once there. Masterful, in fact. The best. What the devil was wrong with him now? And how was she going to fix it? For, if she didn't, the madam decided, there was really no use in having him around.

She paused to adjust the frame of a French watercolor that had cost her a small fortune. If there was anything that Ada Campbell, the city's foremost madam, didn't need at this juncture in her career, it was a constant, live-in reminder that her personal charms were on the wane.

His head snapped up as soon as she stepped into the room, and he flashed her that cavalier grin she'd come to adore over the years. Good God, the man was handsome. It would be a pity to have to kick him out.

The bottle of sour mash—full as far as Ada could see—still rested on the draped and swagged table. Hazard's fist was still clenched around it.

"Hello, love," he said in a voice at once soft and sad and annoyingly sober. "All done downstairs?"

Ada sighed, fearing she was done upstairs, as well, unless she took some drastic action that would bring her former lover to his senses. She plucked her ear bobs off, tossed them in the direction of her jewel box and proceeded to take off her clothes.

With his fist tightening around the bottle, Jack swallowed a groan. Ada, it seemed, had reached the end of her tether, not to mention her patience. He had expected that. He was surprised it hadn't happened earlier—last night, for instance. Or the one before that, when he'd kissed her, then promptly turned his back and fallen asleep—or, more exactly, feigned sleep for both their benefits.

"What's the matter with you?" the madam had hissed into her pillow.

"Everything," he'd wanted to say. "Nothing. Dead men can't feel pain or passion. Aren't they both the same?"

He sat now and watched her undress—sinuously, seductively—sorry he had reduced the notorious madam to using tricks she hadn't had to resort to in years. Not that they did any good, he thought sourly.

She stood before the pier glass, having tilted it to give him a perfect and unobstructed view as she peeled away various layers of satin and lace. Down to her red corset now, she unhooked it slowly, held it closed a moment, then shed it the way a jeweled snake might rid itself of useless skin, letting it drop, forgotten to the floor. In the mirror, her breasts had a silvery sheen. Small, yet succulent. Not a feast, by any means, but a delectable dessert.

He ought to get up, Jack told himself. He ought to move toward her, to offer the palms of his hands like warm salvers, to take the delights the famous Ada Campbell was offering. A year ago, he would have, only it wasn't in him now. He couldn't move.

"I'll be leaving tomorrow," he said in response to the frown that was digging between her eyes and darkening her beautiful face.

"All right." Ada snatched up her corset and strode to the wardrobe, where she grabbed a silken dressing gown from a hook and shoved her arms through its sleeves. "You can sleep here tonight, but don't bother coming back," she said on her way to the door. "Ever."

She stood there a moment, shaking her head, her expression wavering between fury and dismay. "You were a lot more fun when you were drinking, Jack. In fact, I think I liked you better that way."

The ensuing slam reverberated through the room, probably throughout the house, but Jack didn't blink. His fingers merely tightened on the bottle.

It was a game he played every night. A test. He told himself he hadn't quit. He was in training—like an athlete preparing for a competition, like a Thoroughbred doing evening workouts around a track.

He was going to win, God damn it. And that sweet prospect was worth every insult and humiliation he'd had to endure, including begging Allan and suffering Ada's current disgust.

Nothing mattered except bringing the baroness down. Killing her would be too easy. Jack felt his lips sliding into a feral grin. He had imagined murdering her a thousand times, playing out a variety of scenarios in his head. But each time he pictured Chloe Von Drosten dead, it gave him no pleasure, because in death she looked so peaceful, so far beyond earthly pain.

The sad truth, he had to admit, was that he wasn't so certain he could do it. To murder the baroness, he'd have to be alone with her. It hadn't been so long since their last encounter that he couldn't imagine all his hard-won sobriety and all his rage shuddering and collapsing at the crook of a red-tipped finger or drowning in one of Chloe's wine-colored smiles. He was a damn drunk, but he wasn't a fool.

He needed a wife—a buffer. What a choice he'd made! A mouse to cower between him and the devil. Mrs. Matlin, the plain, bespectacled widow. The nonentity.

Ah, well. In a month, the little clerk would have served her purpose, and she could come back to the haven of the agency and fade into the woodwork. While he . . .

His fingers loosened on the bottle of sour mash now, moving slowly, caressing the warm, hand-heated glass. In a month, this would be his reward, and like little Mrs. Matlin, he could slip back into his own brand of oblivion.

His gaze swung to the door the madam had slammed with such disgust. "Ada, love, when I was drinking, I liked me better, too."

# Chapter Three

Anna was late getting to the train depot the next morning, first because she'd taken too much time brushing her hair and subduing it into a sleek bun at the nape of her neck, and second because the Misses Richmond had been intent upon giving her the benefit of some crucial, lengthy last-minute advice. In her efforts to disengage herself from her landladies and to escape from the house, Anna had nearly forgotten her spectacles and had to rush back up to her room on the third floor to retrieve them.

Up there, she had looked around the little room almost wistfully. "Don't be silly," she'd said to herself. "You'll be back in a few weeks, with memories. Memories galore."

The omnibus had gotten her to the depot with only a minute or two to spare. Then, after seeing that her borrowed trunk was properly stowed—"Keep a sharp eye on your luggage, dear," the Misses Richmond had cautioned—Anna herself had had a mere second to clamber aboard through a billowing cloud of cinders and steam. By the time she located a forward-facing seat—"Never ride backwards. It's bad for the digestion."—and settled into it, Anna's carefully tamed hair was wildly corkscrewed and her glasses were steamed up and sliding down her nose.

She extracted a hankie from her reticule, and was wiping the wet lenses when the train gave a long hoot and then, with a lurch, moved away from the depot. Anna planted her glasses back on and gazed over the rims in search of a familiar face among the passengers.

He wasn't there. Johnathan Hazard wasn't there!

Turning toward the window now, she scanned the wooden platform as the train moved slowly past it. She half expected to see the famed Pinkerton agent vaulting over a baggage cart, then sprinting alongside the train. A little smile touched Anna's lips as the image flourished in her brain.

Hazard would toss a valise through an open window, then time the rhythm of his stride perfectly as he reached for a metal handrail and levered his long, supple body onto the moving vehicle. He would stand in the doorway then, casually brushing the sleeves of his fine-fitting frock coat and straightening his waistcoat with a subtle tug. All the while, without even appearing to move those gray-blue eyes, he would be gathering information, and by the time the last car passed the depot, Johnathan Hazard would know just how many passengers were on board and their disposition in the various seats—and specifically, he would have found hers.

Easily, then, as if the train were standing still, he would move along the aisle to arrive at the vacant seat beside her. His breathing would be even, despite his race against the mighty locomotive. And, when he sat, there would be the faint aroma of bay rum and hearty exercise. He would cock his head in her direction, take her measure in a glance, and say...

"Ticket, madam?"

Anna's gaze jerked to the patent brim of the conductor's cap and then to the empty seat beside her.

"Conductor, you must stop this train. Immediately."

"Beg pardon, ma'am?"

"I said..." Anna was rummaging through her handbag now for the official pass Mr. Pinkerton had given her the day before. She hadn't lost it, had she? Or left it behind? Where the devil—? Her fingers gripped the cardboard pass, and she flashed it at the conductor. "I order you to stop this train."

The man smiled. "Ah. A Pinkerton, are you?" He looked at her more closely now. "I never would have guessed."

"My partner hasn't arrived," Anna told him, trying to subdue the plaintive note in her voice and the flutter of panic in her chest, attempting to sound more Pinkerton than pitiful. She was a representative of the world's foremost detective agency, after all. She had credentials.

"A lady, is she?" The conductor had to widen his stance as the train picked up speed. His gaze wandered around the car.

"No. A gentleman. A man by the name of Johnathan Hazard. He's..."

"Well, now, why didn't you say so before? Mad Jack's back in the smoking car." He angled his head toward the rear of the train. "Been there at least a couple of hours."

"Oh." The word broke from Anna's throat with pitiful relief. She smoothed her skirt then, adding a calmer, more authoritative, "Indeed."

"We'll be stopping in Coal City in about an hour to take on more fuel. I expect you can connect with him then."

"Yes. Thank you. I will."

"Have a pleasant trip, ma'am. My regards to Mr. Pinkerton." The man touched the brim of his cap and proceeded to make his way along the aisle.

Anna turned back to the window. The buildings dwindled in size as the train approached the city limits; the crowds of people thinned and eventually disappeared. She lowered her chin to consult the watch pinned to her bodice. It was 8:48. It occurred to her that she was eighteen minutes late for work. And then a wild little giggle roiled in her throat when she realized she *was* at work, right here, speeding south-southwest at thirty miles an hour.

Toward what? she wondered bleakly now. Anna sighed so hard, her breath clouded the window.

"Hazard will fill you in on the particulars," Mr. Pinkerton had told her. Suddenly, to Anna, those particulars loomed hugely, even vitally important.

In the smoking car, Jack bit off the tip of a thin cigar, lit it, and leaned back in his seat, smiling. He wondered now exactly what he would have done if he hadn't seen the little mouse scurrying toward the train at the very last moment. Stalked off, no doubt, and stormed into Allan's office, demanding a replacement for the missing Mrs. Matlin, giving his old friend another opportunity to call him obsessed, and possibly even to deny him not only a partner, but the assignment, as well.

Mrs. Matlin was on board, though, and Jack breathed a sigh of relief at the same time he cursed himself for needing her at all. He hadn't needed anyone in years. Not after Scully. Not professionally, anyway. As for needing anyone personally...well, there was his sister, Madelaine, of course. And then there had been Chloe, hadn't there? If one could call that sick and soulless dissipation need.

He blew a hard, thin stream of smoke toward the ceiling. Allan had been right, of course. He was obsessed. There was no other word for it. But he planned to use that obsession well—as the light at the end of his long, dark tunnel, as the fuel that would burn and sustain him until he did what he had to do.

Had Allan refused him, Jack thought now, he would have gone ahead anyway, merely paring down his plan to fit his own bankroll. It still would have worked. He wouldn't fail. Not at this. But with Pinkerton money behind him, his plan was a guaranteed success. It had "legs," as they said at the track. Especially now that the mouse was on board. "Bless you, Allan," Jack murmured under his breath.

He let his gaze travel aimlessly through the haze of smoke. Two women—one in acid-green satin, her cohort in royal blue—caught his attention. They sat flanking a scrawny, bald-pated fellow in a triple row of seats, leaning toward him and pouring their attention, as well as their sultry shapes, all over him. The little bald man was lapping it up. Poor sap had probably never been the focus of one female's ardent attention, let alone two, and Jack had been a Pinkerton agent too long not to recognize a bit of larceny in progress.

It was almost second nature for him to rise, clench his cigar in his teeth and move in on the bustling, hustling dollies.

When Anna got off the train in Coal City, a second blast of steam curled whatever hairs the first one had missed, in addition to nearly scalding the skin from her face. Good Lord, she'd be lucky to get to St. Louis alive. Right now, however, her immediate destination was elsewhere.

She approached the conductor, who was stretching his legs on the platform while winding his watch. Anna cleared her throat. "Excuse me, sir. Would you please direct me to the smoking car?"

The man dropped his watch. It draped over his belly by its thick gold chain as he peered down at Anna. "Sorry, madam. You startled me. I didn't notice you standing there."

"The smoking car," Anna repeated as her chin came up a determined notch. "Which one is it, if you please?"

"Oh, the Pinkerton lady. Looking for Mad Jack, are you?" He grasped her elbow firmly. "You just come along with me."

She hadn't really wanted an escort, Anna thought, or needed one. She had to trot to keep up with him, and when they reached the second-to-last car of the train, the conductor gave her a boost, which Anna wasn't quite prepared for. She stumbled headlong into the acrid, smoke-filled coach, stopping at a pair of high-glossed boots that shone even through the murk. Anna's eyes jerked up.

"Mr. Hazard?"

He sat, or rather reclined, with a female on each knee. He appeared to be wearing them, actually. Like trousers, one leg blue and the other a garish green. And he was also wearing a wide white grin that, under the circumstances, struck Anna as altogether brazen and shocking and, well . . . beautiful.

"Mr. Hazard," she said again, this time a little more breathlessly than before, and then she simply stood there, mute. What the devil did one say to a man with two women on his lap?

Suddenly the conductor was standing at her shoulder. "Well, I see you've found him. This little lady has been looking for you, Jack."

"And I've been looking for you," Hazard said to the conductor, ignoring Anna as he stood abruptly and the females went tumbling to the floor. "These women are pickpockets, Dooley." He bent and slid a lithe, long-fingered hand into a green bodice, coming up with an elaborately engraved pocket watch. "This is mine. There's more, if you'd care to search them. After that, I expect you'll want to turn them over to the local constable."

The women were struggling up from the floor now. "Bastard," the green one hissed at Jack, while the blue one gave out a blistering string of curses meant for anyone and everyone within hearing distance.

"Here, now." The conductor grabbed the women by their arms and hauled them to their feet. "You two have met your match with the Pinkertons, I'd say. With Mad Jack and his partner here."

Jack lifted an eyebrow. "Partner?"

The conductor blinked, then glanced from Jack to Anna and back again. "That's what she told me. She said she was your partner."

"More like my life partner, wouldn't you say, darling?" Jack purred as his arm reached out and reeled the unsuspecting Anna in. He grinned down at her—it was the same grin that only moments earlier had stolen her breath away—then angled his head toward the conductor. "She's my wife, Dooley. Although the knot's only been tied for... what, darling? Fifteen or sixteen hours?" He lowered his voice and closed one eye in a slow wink. "Haven't yet had an opportunity to make her truly mine, Dooley, if you take my meaning."

Anna caught it, and blushed. So did the woman in the green dress, who didn't blush at all, but rather shook her fist at Jack and bellowed, "Yeah, and here's hoping you never do, buddy! Her or anybody else, ever again."

"That will be enough out of you, ladies." The conductor tugged the two pickpockets toward the door. "Thanks, Jack," he called. "And my best wishes. To you and the little missus."

A moment passed—or crawled, it seemed to Anna—during which she cleaned her spectacles and stared at the floor while trying to recover enough breath and enough sense to speak coherently.

"Mrs. Matlin?"

His voice seemed to drift down and curl around her like warm woodsmoke. Anna didn't dare look up. Her face was on fire as she stood in the crook of Johnathan Hazard's arm, her hip quite plastered against his and the heat from his body seeping into her own. She couldn't breathe, and she feared it had nothing to do with the stagnant air in the smoking car. It was him. How in blazes was she going to work with this man if she went to pieces each time she looked at him? *Glue yourself together, girl.*

"Yes?" she managed to squeak, putting her glasses back on and raising her eyes as far as the middle button on his perfectly pressed white shirt.

"How do you do?" he said softly. His faint accent greeted her ears like elegant music. "I'm Jack Hazard."

"Yes. Yes, I know."

He chuckled now, a rich bass rumbling deep in his throat. "How can you be so certain, Mrs. Matlin, unless you look at me?" Warm, gentle fingertips found her chin then, and coaxed it upward. "There. Now that's better."

His eyes took her in then—fairly consumed her before coming to rest on her mouth. He made a tiny clucking sound with his tongue. What that meant, Anna didn't know. Nor could she fathom the meaning of his huskily breathed "Well, now."

She did know what "All aboard" meant, though, and when the cry suddenly sounded, Anna stiffened and stepped back.

"I ought to be returning to my seat."

"I'll come with you."

*Oh, don't.* Anna was thinking that if she could just get away from him for a moment or two, she would be able to pull herself together. But as she cast about in her brain for an excuse to go alone, Johnathan Hazard's warm hand folded over her elbow and he moved determinedly toward the door, and then, a moment later, those long, lithe fingers of his were fitting themselves to her rib cage as he lifted her down to the platform.

He held her then, just a fraction of a second too long, but long enough for Anna to recall how good it felt to be touched, to be in a man's possessive grasp. It had been years. Since Billy had left her, the most Anna had done was shaken hands. And now she was shaken to the very marrow of her bones.

She was hardly aware that she was being propelled along the platform now, her feet somehow managing two steps for each of Hazard's strides. Ahead, the big locomotive was building up a towering pillar of steam. On her right, the coaches were trembling and grinding at their couplings. Anna quickened her steps.

Nearly rushing now, she wasn't sure whether her haste was to get on board the departing train or to escape this unsettling, disconcerting man. Both perhaps.

"Where the devil are you going?" Hazard stopped, bringing her to halt.

"To my seat." Her words came out in a mortifying little wail.

"Up there?" He angled his head toward the second-class coach in which she had been riding earlier. The train gave a lurch as the wheels began turning. The couplings squealed, and the cars inched forward along the platform. Hazard's grip tightened on her arm.

"Yes! Of course!" Anna shrieked over the long blast of the whistle.

"I think not, Mrs. Matlin." He swung her around then, as if she were no more than a yarn doll, and propelled her toward the door she had just rushed past.

"But...but this is...this is first class, Mr. Hazard," she stammered.

"Indeed it is, Mrs. Matlin," he said as he lifted her up onto the moving train, then followed her in one long and graceful leap. "Indeed it is."

Anna immediately appreciated the additional padding in the seats in the first-class coach, though she wasn't one who required such luxury, and she meant to let her partner know that as soon as she found her voice.

Johnathan Hazard had deposited her in the luxurious chair, then settled in quietly beside her while Anna occupied herself in arranging and rearranging her skirts and experimenting with her handbag in various locations on her lap. Anything not to look at him. She adjusted the seams on her gloves. They wavered in a film of tears.

*You shouldn't have come. You aren't up to this. When Mr. Pinkerton singled you out, you should have run like the wind in the opposite direction. You aren't special, Anna Matlin. You're just a silly fool.*

"Comfortable?" That voice skimmed over her flesh like breeze-blown silk.

Anna glanced at Hazard's kneecap, not daring to look higher. "Quite." *No. I want to go home.*

A moment passed, and then that zephyr of a voice caressed her senses again. "Look at me, Mrs. Matlin."

She thought she might die if she did, or at the very least explode or self-combust, but Anna forced herself to raise her eyes to his. And then something quite inexplicable happened. It was as if she were seeing him for the very first time.

The eyes into which she was gazing were the same mixture of blue and gray she recalled, but rather than metallic, the hue was closer to that of a November sky on a day that wants to rain. Faint shadows lodged beneath his dark lower lashes, like remnants of nightmares and too little sleep. The creases at the corners were more plentiful, and far deeper, than she had realized.

The mouth that she had forever pictured in a dazzling grin seemed different now. Its natural bent, Anna noticed suddenly was downward, and its foremost expression seemed to be one of sadness rather than mirth. And the complexion she had always thought so dark and dashing was merely the result of whiskers, beneath which his skin was actually quite pale and somehow tender. Scarred, too, she saw quite clearly now, perhaps by hands that trembled when he shaved.

Johnathan Hazard was a human being! He wasn't a god, after all!

The notion struck her like a physical blow, a whack between the shoulder blades that put all her systems back into proper working order. The rough beating of her heart smoothed out. The pinch in her vocal cords let go, and her lungs expanded, filling with sweet air.

Johnathan Hazard was mortal! How incredible that she had never noticed that before!

"You look..." she whispered, barely aware that her thoughts had moved to her lips, "weary." Worn out, she might have said. Used up.

And then, as suddenly as she had glimpsed it, that vulnerability disappeared. It was as if she had never witnessed it at all, and once more Anna found herself gazing at Adonis, at the handsome Hazard mask.

"I am, Mrs. Matlin," he said as he snapped open the watch he had recovered from the pickpocket. "It's seven or eight hours to Alton, and I intend to sleep for the major part of them."

Anna blinked. He was going to sleep? Now? "But Mr. Pinkerton said you would inform me of the particulars in this case."

By now he was already settled deep in his seat, with his long legs stretched out, his arms crossed over his chest and his eyes closed. He opened one to a mere slit as he said, "You'll know everything you need to know."

"When will that be, Mr. Hazard?"

"When you need to know it, Mrs. Matlin."

"But..."

"Good night."

Anna bit down on her lower lip. She was tempted to tell Johnathan Hazard that she wasn't accustomed to being so curtly dismissed, but the truth was that she *was* accustomed to it. To being dismissed, if not outright ignored.

Funny, she thought as she turned her gaze toward the window. It had never bothered her before.

## Chapter Four

That evening, in Alton, on the high green bluffs above the Mississippi River, Jack Hazard was doing his damnedest to ignore the mouse. Just as he had been ever since that moment in the smoking car, when he'd lifted her face for a casual inspection and felt an immediate and far-from-casual response. His body had tightened like a bowstring.

That hadn't happened in months. Not since he'd quit drinking. His manhood, it seemed, greatly resented the loss of significant amounts of fuel. Either that, or his dissipations during the previous year had taken a final and rather fatal turn. It hadn't mattered to him much. It still didn't, although he had to admit the sensation had come with as much relief as sheer astonishment. And worry. He didn't want or need this kind of distraction. Not now.

The most astonishing part of it was that it had been Mrs. Matlin—Mrs. Matlin!—who made him hard as a shaft of granite, when, for all her wily and well-practiced endeavors, Ada Campbell had failed.

So had the two cool-handed pickpockets earlier on the train.

Jack was at a loss to understand it. All he had done was look at her there in the smoking car. At the blond curls that had escaped her neat chignon and ringed her head like a wild halo. At the flush of color on her cheeks. At her silly spectacles and then—dear Lord!—at her shockingly sensual mouth.

It must have been her mouth, he thought now as he sat safely alone in the dining room of the Riverton Hotel, and warned himself to avoid staring at her lush lips, the mere thought of which was once again having a significant effect upon his body. He shifted in his chair, glancing toward the door that opened onto the lobby. Where the devil was she? He had told her he'd wait for her downstairs while she freshened up. He glared at his watch. That had been nearly an hour ago.

The woman obviously wasn't accustomed to traveling, Jack thought with some irritation. Earlier, upon disembarking, he had left her with two quarters meant as a tip for the porter, and when he returned from securing them a carriage, Mrs. Matlin had handed him one of the coins.

"What's that?" he had asked, thoroughly confused.

"Half the gratuity," she had answered in that small, breathy voice of hers. "I helped with our baggage, Mr. Hazard. I'm sure Mr. Pinkerton will greatly appreciate our keeping an eye on expenses."

"Bloody hell!"

The mouse had flinched when he bellowed, but he hadn't been able to contain it. Spending—flagrantly, outrageously, blindly—was part of his damn plan. It was absolutely necessary. And now it seemed he'd picked a bloody accountant—worse, a skinflint—to help him accomplish it.

God Almighty, he hoped the woman wasn't upstairs pouting. She hadn't said two words on the carriage ride from the depot to the hotel, and hardly more than that once they'd been shown to their room. Then she'd seemed undisguisedly relieved when he announced he'd wait downstairs. Which he'd been doing now for fifty-eight minutes.

He cast a murderous glance at the water goblet before him, and his fists clenched under the tablecloth. Sweet Lord in heaven, how he needed a drink.

"You need to get downstairs," Anna urged her own reflection as she stood before the dresser, brushing her hair for the third—and last, she swore!—time. Not only was she famished, but she was also desperate to hear the details of this assignment.

In the mirror, the bed loomed up behind her with its two plump pillows. And though she kept looking—kept hoping, actually—the furniture refused to change, as did the mathematics. Two pillows. One bed.

She heard Mr. Pinkerton's voice again. "Mr. Hazard needs a wife." It wasn't that she had misunderstood him. Rather, it seemed that in all the excitement about the assignment, Anna hadn't quite thought through all the ramifications of Mr. Pinkerton's words.

As soon as they entered this hotel room, however, those ramifications had been obvious. Two pillows. One bed. She had felt the blood draining from her face. She was still a little pale, she thought, leaning closer to the mirror and examining her cheeks. Perhaps if she brushed her hair more vigorously it would bring some blood up to her scalp.

"Mr. Hazard needs a wife." That was what the man had told her. He hadn't said *partner,* although that was what Anna had deemed it. And she'd been so excited by the prospect of working with the legendary, glorious and godlike agent.

Now, though, after that brief glimpse of his humanity this morning, Anna realized all too well that Johnathan Hazard was a man. He was flesh and blood and all that those two qualities implied.

She swallowed hard. What in the world was she going to do? She had been so grateful when Hazard offered to wait downstairs, because she had needed time to think. But that had been an hour ago, and thinking about her situation hadn't improved it. It was time to take action.

It was also time for supper, her rumbling stomach reminded her. Anna exchanged her hairbrush for her handbag, then gave the bed a last glance before walking out of the room and descending the stairs to the lobby.

Though a small hotel in a small town, the Riverton seemed intent upon rivaling New York or Boston in brocades and crystal and glinting brass. It was quite elegant. Probably the finest hotel Anna would ever see, she thought, so she tried to take in each detail.

There was a uniformed gentleman near the front desk who bowed when she approached. "Allow me to show you to the dining room, Mrs. Hazard."

Anna nearly looked over her shoulder to see to whom he was speaking before she remembered that *she* was Mrs. Hazard. Oh, Lord.

"I'll find it myself if you'll just point the way," she told him, amazed and rather embarrassed by the attentions of this stranger.

He pointed a white-gloved hand toward a dining room that was far more elegant than any Anna had ever seen. She lingered a moment in the arched doorway, relieved to see that Johnathan Hazard sat alone in the room, and that his back was toward her, allowing her a little time to compose herself before confronting such a glamorous man in a setting that, while intimidating to her, seemed his natural habitat.

She drew in a wavering breath, found it laced with the fragrance from numerous bowls of roses on the candlelit tables, and steeled herself once more to demand to know the particulars of their assignment. Especially, and most critically, one particular room upstairs and one particular bed.

"Mr. Hazard. The particulars. I insist."

At the sound of that small but determined voice, Jack nearly shot out of his chair. He was not one used to being taken unawares, and now the mouse had crept up behind him and shocked the devil out of him. He wondered vaguely if liquor and opium had combined to strip his senses permanently. Then he decided it was merely the invisible, wraithlike qualities of the mouse. Allan should have made use of her years ago. The woman could come and go like smoke.

He seated her, and beckoned to the waiter who had been casting him anxious glances from the kitchen door for the past fifteen minutes. The fellow fairly flew across the room now, a plate in each hand.

Mrs. Matlin lifted her chin the moment he arrived. "I'd like something simple, but substantial, if you please," she said. "A chop would be fine."

The waiter cleared his throat and sent a wide-eyed signal of distress to Jack.

"I've taken the liberty of ordering for you, dear," *A chop, for God's sake.* He nodded to the waiter, who slid the plates onto the table and then quickly retreated.

"Oh, my," the mouse breathed as she gazed down at half a dozen succulent oysters, bedded in their shells upon shaved ice, and garnished with wedges of lemon and sprigs of parsley.

Good Lord, had the woman never seen an oyster, he wondered? She looked as if someone had just presented her with a dead cat for her supper. She nudged her silly spectacles up her nose and compressed her lips into a thin white line, contemplating the mollusks.

Of course, Jack thought suddenly, he wasn't all that sorry to see that lush mouth pinch into something less desirable and distracting.

"Enjoy," he told her coolly, proceeding to do just that with his own supper.

For a mouse, Jack thought as the meal progressed, her face had an infinite variety of expressions. First there was the near horror at the oysters, which she chewed doggedly after great deliberation over the trio of forks to the left of her plate. Then there was the consternation at the cream of celery soup, and the little twitch of delight when she picked up the soupspoon without hesitation. Next came what appeared to be relief at the sight of the trout and its accompaniment of spring potatoes. The woman was obviously hungry, and concerned, through the first two courses, that that was all the supper she was going to get.

The salad seemed to confuse her, and when the beef Wellington steamed her glasses, she began to look horror-stricken once again. The crème caramel pushed her over the edge.

"This is too much," she said.

Jack put on his most benign smile as he signaled the waiter for coffee. "Excess is part of the plan, Mrs. Matlin. It's one of the particulars." Having uttered the magic word, he watched her lean forward. Her eyes widened behind their perpetual windows of glass.

He kept her in suspense while the waiter poured their coffee. By the time Jack had gone through the ritual of lighting his cigar, she was nearly on the edge of her seat.

He aimed a stream of smoke toward the ceiling. "What do you know about the Baroness Von Drosten?"

Anna smiled, more to herself than at her companion. Well, at last! She'd felt like a fool all during supper, maintaining a grim silence while trying to contend with slippery lemon wedges, fish bones, and a whole drawer's worth of utensils. She might not be an experienced supper companion, she thought now, but she'd been an attentive file clerk for the past six years, and she knew more than a little about the infamous baroness.

"Chloe Von Drosten," she said with some authority, "is believed to be a jewel thief."

"She *is* a damn jewel thief," Hazard shot back.

"Ah, but no one has proven that yet. Even you, Mr. Hazard, were unsuccessful last year in your attempt to recover Mrs. Herrington Sloan's missing emerald necklace."

"It isn't missing," he said flatly. "I know exactly where it is."

Anna shook her head. That couldn't be right. If the necklace had been found, the case would have been closed and she would have moved the file to the Inactive drawer. She knew for a fact that she hadn't transferred the file. "The case is still active, Mr. Hazard," she insisted. "No one has recovered that necklace."

His fingers tightened on the handle of his cup. "No one ever will."

"I beg your pardon?"

"I didn't say the necklace had been recovered, Mrs. Matlin. I said I know where it is. And I also know why it will never be recovered now." His gaze drifted to Anna's full cup. "Would you care for a brandy with your coffee?"

He was lifting a hand to signal the waiter when Anna snapped, "No. I'd care for an explanation. I know what's in the files at the Pinkerton Agency. Mrs. Sloan's necklace is still missing. How can you claim to know its whereabouts?"

"Chloe told me."

Anna laughed. "Well, she may have confessed and disclosed its location, Mr. Hazard, but the necklace is still missing."

"Technically," he said very coolly, "it isn't even missing. The fact is, Mrs. Matlin, it's being worn by the queen of England." He leaned back in his chair and crossed his arms. "And worn quite frequently, as I understand."

Now Anna gave her glasses a little nudge up the bridge of her nose, as if that would help her see the situation more clearly. The man had lost her somewhere. If . . .

"She got away with it, you see."

Anna blinked. "Victoria?"

"Chloe. She presented the necklace to Her Majesty, not merely as a gift from herself, but as a token of esteem from the American government." His mouth twisted in a wry smile, and then he added, "Victoria was quite touched, I hear."

"But . . ." Suddenly Anna understood how something could be at once lost and found. She pictured the square-cut emeralds circling the little queen's neck. Her royal neck! "No one would dare demand them back," she breathed.

Hazard's smile twisted tighter. "Exactly." He leaned forward now, and when he spoke again, his voice was low and harsh. "Rather brilliant of the baroness, wouldn't you say? She earned not only the queen's favor, but her own guarantee of innocence, as well. Victoria cannot be wearing a stolen necklace, therefore there was no crime."

"More diabolical than brilliant," Anna muttered. She was thinking of her orderly files now, and she felt some irritation that one would be erroneously placed. Forever. When crimes were solved, the files moved from Active to Inactive. It was a part of her job that she enjoyed. Moving those files gave her a sense of participating in justice, somehow. But now...

Now she became doubly irritated as she realized that Johnathan Hazard had just spent a good ten or fifteen minutes talking about a past assignment, rather than their current one. Her voice was uncharacteristically brittle when she asked him, "Just what does the baroness have to do with anything?"

"Everything."

The word was simple enough, yet it had come from Hazard's lips like a curse. For a second, his face seemed less like an Apollo's than that of an avenging angel. Then, as quickly as it had appeared, the fury vanished. His smile turned affable. One dark eyebrow arched. "What do you know about horse racing, Mrs. Matlin?"

"Other than recognizing a horse when I see one, and knowing what a race is, Mr. Hazard, absolutely nothing," she snapped. "Does this have anything to do with our assignment?"

He didn't answer, but picked up his cup and drained it of coffee. Then he signaled the waiter for more. Anna's cup was still full. If she had even a drop of it, she thought, she'd be awake until dawn, lying in bed, staring at the— Suddenly she pictured that bed again, and her gaze flicked to the man across the table.

His dark hair had an almost sapphire luster now that the candles had burned down some. Their muted light carved the planes of his face with shadows and touched his cheekbones with gold. She allowed herself, for just a moment, to appreciate his legendary handsomeness. She let her heart skip just one beat.

After the waiter had refilled his cup and disappeared, Hazard took a sip and set the cup back with long-fingered grace. "Particulars, Mrs. Matlin," he said then. "We'll be posing as man and wife. But you already know that."

Yes, she did. Anna nodded, while trying to move that infernal bed out of her head. At last her partner had seen fit to apprise her of some facts, and now she could hardly take in his words. Not with that dratted bed taking up so much room in her brain.

"When I said that excess was part of the plan, I meant exactly that," he continued. "We're not only posing as a married couple, but as an extremely wealthy and free-spending couple." A small frown skimmed across his forehead now. "Since Chloe knows me, there's no reason to use an assumed name. And since she knows I'm not a fabulously wealthy man, the assumption will have to be that I married well."

Anna couldn't help it. A small giggle fought its way up her throat. "So I'm the rich one."

Hazard tilted his head. "Yes. Does that amuse you?"

"Well . . . yes, I suppose it does. I've never been rich. I've always been rather poor."

"Rich is better, Mrs. Matlin. Believe me."

"It probably is." She shrugged. "I've never given it any consideration."

"You've never dreamed of being rich?" His blue-gray eyes opened wider.

"I've never dreamed of anything," Anna answered, and then felt her cheeks flush because that wasn't exactly true. She had, in fact, dreamed of the man across the table from her now. And that bed, which was still looming like some square and monolithic granite monument in her head. "Well, nothing much," she added in a whisper. She cleared her throat, lifted her chin and forced a hopeful smile. "So, we're in pursuit of the baroness, then? Has she stolen more jewels?"

"Probably." Jack let out a bitter, almost brutal laugh. Its viciousness surprised even him. He wasn't used to disclosing his emotions that way. "It doesn't matter. Not even if she's made off with the crown jewels. What matters is Chloe's Gold."

"She stole gold?"

The mouse's blue eyes were huge behind her glasses, magnified by candlelight and curiosity. They were an intense blue. For a second, Jack felt as if he were swimming in their depths. Another little jolt of electricity shot through him. He sat up straighter in his chair.

He infused his voice with cool condescension that was in marked contrast with his body. "Chloe's Gold is the baroness's Thoroughbred stallion. A racehorse, Mrs. Matlin."

"Oh. I see." Her mouth tightened then—thank the Lord!—and she edged backward a bit, as if some of the air had gone out of her, while Jack watched a succession of emotions cross her face like banner headlines. Disappointment. Embarrassment. Chagrin at having expressed such unmouselike enthusiasm. Sadness at having that enthusiasm splashed with his curt cold water.

Damn! This wasn't about the mouse!

Even so, he tried to soften his tone. "They're opening a new racecourse in St. Louis next month, Mrs. Matlin, and running a race called the Carondelet Stakes, which promises a lucrative purse to the winner. Chloe's Gold is undefeated." He paused to let his tongue pass over his dry lips. "Naturally, the baroness will be there. And so, Mrs. Matlin, will we."

She sat quietly a moment, repositioning her lenses, contemplating the rim of her coffee cup, chewing her lower lip, before asking politely, "To what end, Mr. Hazard? You haven't explained—"

"To the baroness's end," he growled. Then he stood, so abruptly the water goblets sloshed over their rims onto the white linen tablecloth and, behind him, his chair tipped over. "Are you quite through, Mrs. Matlin?"

They were at the door of their room—Hazard having rushed her through the lobby, up the stairs and down the dimly lit corridor—when Anna remembered she hadn't addressed one extremely important particular.

The bed. It loomed up before her when Hazard pushed open the door. Its white linens shimmered in the lamplight.

"After you." He gestured with a fine, courtly hand.

She simply stood there, her feet numb, her mind a blank, her vision filled with plumped pillows and starched dustruffles and the counterpane that had been invitingly, almost lovingly, turned back.

"What—?" Johnathan Hazard's voice, so near her ear now, lowered to the depths of the chuckle in his throat. "The bed? Is that what you're worried about?"

Anna nodded. At least she thought she did. Her neck was stiff with tension. It took a monumental effort to turn and lift her gaze to the man standing so close behind her.

In the dim hallway, it was difficult to read the expression on his face, but her first impression was of sweetness. There was a softness to his features that she'd never seen before. And then he grinned. Not his usual devil-may-care and cavalier grin. But a sweet, almost shy tilt of his lips.

"Don't worry, little mouse," he said softly. "The bed's all yours. The pillows, too. Every fold and feather."

His hand was warm on her back as he gave her a little nudge across the threshold.

"But where will you—?"

"I don't sleep much, Mrs. Matlin." The tender warmth she had only just heard in his voice seemed to have dissipated, replaced by a thin chill as he strode past Anna toward his valise on the opposite side of the room. He opened it and, while Anna watched, lifted out something swaddled in cotton cloth that he proceeded to unwrap with meticulous care.

It was a bottle! A bottle of whiskey! So it was true, she thought suddenly. All the gossip in the hallways, and all those whispered hints about Johnathan Hazard's drinking, were true. She had worried about that earlier, but then had cast those niggling doubts about him aside. To her knowledge, the man hadn't had a drop of liquor all day—nothing on the train, and nothing more than coffee with his supper.

"What are you looking at, Mrs. Matlin?"

He was lowering himself into the chair beside the small writing table now, placing the bottle before him, keeping his hand on it, as if he feared she might snatch it away.

"Is that disapproval I read behind those windowpanes you're always wearing?" he added harshly. "What have you heard, Mrs. Matlin? That I'm a lush? That Jack Hazard prefers looking at the world through the green glass of a whiskey bottle, or perhaps up from the perspective of the gutter?"

Anna bit her lip and shook her head, even though that was precisely what she had heard. "There was gossip," she said. "I never gave it much credence."

His hand clenched more tightly around the bottle now. "Well, you should have. It's all true."

Her jaw slackened, and Anna could feel her breath passing in and out through her open lips. There were no words, though. She didn't know what to say. Johnathan Hazard sat there, glaring at her, silently demanding that she be shocked or affronted or even disgusted by his admission, when all she felt was an overwhelming sadness for him and a sudden, nearly desperate urge to help him, which made no sense to her at all, since she was the one—a woman alone in a hotel room with a man—who so obviously needed help.

"It's nothing you have to worry about," he said before she could speak. He smiled a little crookedly then, as if he had been imbibing from the bottle, rather than merely clutching it. "My tendency toward dissipation isn't contagious, Mrs. Matlin, if that's what you're thinking."

"It isn't."

"Good. And, as you've no doubt noticed, I am not, at the moment, drinking. I am merely caressing the bottle, which is what I will continue to do until our assignment is finished. After that..." His smile thinned to nothing, and his voice trailed off for a moment.

Still not knowing what to say, Anna perched on a corner of the bed and began to unlace her shoes. She sensed Hazard's blue-gray eyes on her. Even across the room, she could hear a ragged edge to his breathing. For a moment she thought she could almost feel his pain.

She glanced at him, but he was staring at the bottle in his fist now.

When he spoke, he didn't look at her, and his voice sounded faraway, almost ancient, infinitely weary. "Please feel comfortable with me, Mrs. Matlin, and feel free to do whatever it is you do when preparing to retire for the night. I've already seen everything there is to see, and I've done everything there is to do. I want nothing from you, little mouse. Believe me."

She did, and his words provoked a distinct surge of relief in Anna. But that relief came coupled with a sadness she didn't quite understand. A sadness she wasn't altogether certain she ever wanted to comprehend.

## Chapter Five

A flat-bottomed ferry carried them down and across the Mississippi River from Alton to St. Louis, and transported Anna out of Illinois for the first time in her life. She sat by the railing, contemplating the water, wondering how anything the color of mud could manage to glitter so brilliantly in the warm May sunlight. Ahead, on the river's western bank, the city of St. Louis was coming into view. Unlike Alton, which nestled upon high green bluffs, St. Louis marched right down to the riverbank in rows of red brick, granite, and twinkling window glass.

A little ripple of excitement ran down Anna's spine. Not that Missouri was California, or even Colorado, but it was farther west than she'd ever imagined she would go. She wondered now if she would have gone west with Billy Matlin if he had asked her. But he hadn't asked. He'd said he'd send for her. And then he never had.

She smoothed her skirt over her knees now. The poplin, not too different from the color of the river, was faring rather well, she thought, and didn't look at all wrinkled—which it should have, considering she had slept in it the night before.

For all Johnathan Hazard's reassurances, Anna had not felt comfortable in that hotel room. She had slipped her shoes off, then stopped, not once even considering removing her dress. Especially not with that whiskey bottle in evidence. By his own admission, Hazard was a drinker. If she was awakened by a roaring drunk, Anna had decided, she wanted to be dressed.

What awakened her, however, had been morning light, and the sight of Johnathan Hazard's chin dipping toward his chest and both his arms hanging limply over the sides of his chair. The bottle was where it had been the night before. On the table. Unopened.

Since she had been already dressed, Anna had waited downstairs while her companion shaved and added an additional nick to the collection on his face. She had been touched somehow by that bright spot of blood, just an inch or so above his strong jawline. She was thinking about it now on the ferry when the warm breeze suddenly carried the scent of bay rum.

"We'll be arriving shortly, Mrs. Matlin."

Anna tugged her gaze from the chimneys and church spires on the western river bank to the man who had just taken a seat beside her. By now, the new shaving injury had blended in with the rest.

Dark whiskers were already making a return appearance on his chin. The shadows beneath his eyes were darker. Grimmer, than yesterday. Or did they only appear so because she now knew just how Johnathan Hazard passed his long nights?

She smiled at him. In response, his mouth barely flickered at the corners.

"A husband normally addresses his wife by her Christian name, Mrs. Matlin," he said with a certain stiffness. "I'm afraid I don't even know yours."

"Anna," she whispered, and when he didn't respond, she said it more loudly, adding, with a hint of irritation, "Of course, if you don't care for it, you may call me anything you like, Mr. Hazard. False names are quite common in this business, as you well know."

"I didn't say I didn't like it. I was expecting—" he gave a small shrug "—something else. Ruth, perhaps, or Jane, or..."

"A plain name," Anna said. *For a plain woman.*

He didn't reply. Instead, he gazed at her, those blue-gray eyes drinking her in again and coming to rest, as they had the day before, on her mouth. "I like it," he said a bit huskily. "Your name, I mean. Anna. It's musical. And quite lovely." His gaze cut away abruptly.

"Thank you," she said quietly. "My husband..." Anna suddenly remembered Billy wooing her with a silly off-key song he'd made up about Anna in Havana. It seemed a thousand years ago.

"What are you thinking, Anna?" Johnathan Hazard's smoky voice intruded on her reverie. "What goes on behind those forbidding bits of glass?"

Her hand fluttered up to her spectacles, readjusting them. "Nothing, Mr. Hazard. Nothing interesting, I'm sure."

"Jack."

"I beg your pardon?"

"You'll have to call me Jack."

"I'll try, but . . ."

Hazard's eyes flicked toward a man who was fast approaching them along the ferry rail. He snagged Anna's hand and brought her fingers to his lips. "Do it, Anna. It's time to be my wife. Now."

His mouth caressed her fingertips, warmly, briefly. Then he let her go and rose to greet the bewhiskered man who had come to a stop by their chairs.

"Anna, this is Henry Gresham, on his way to St. Louis to oversee some last details at the new racecourse. Henry, may I present my bride?"

The man swept off his low-crowned hat and held it over a checkered lapel. "How do you, Mrs. Hazard? Your husband tells me you're from Michigan. Father's in lumber, eh?" He slanted a small wink toward Jack.

Anna felt dizzy for a second. So, it had begun. She was a Pinkerton spy now, and obliged to carry out this charade. Her father was not in lumber. When she last saw him, he'd been covered with coal dust, his pale eyes barely visible through a mask of grit. *If you go, girl, don't bother coming back.* That had been a thousand years ago. Now she was the daughter of a well-to-do lumberman, from... Where in blazes was she supposed to be from?

"Yes," she said. "Pine, for the most part." Her "husband" gave her a small smile of approval. Or was it relief?

Her reply seemed to satisfy the bewhiskered Gresham, as well. He nodded happily, then turned his full attention to Jack.

"Planning to enjoy all the prerace festivities, are you, Hazard? The city's fairly bursting at the seams already, I hear. People are coming from everywhere. New York State. Virginia. I understand the breeding business is picking up in Kentucky, too, after all the problems during the war. This will certainly be the biggest purse since then. Word has it that even the Baroness Von Drosten will be there with that horse of hers, Chloe's Gold."

"Really." A single eyebrow arched on Jack's forehead, while the rest of his face remained placid, disinterested. "I hadn't heard."

"She'll win the stakes, naturally. The baroness. Everybody expects it. That horse of hers hasn't lost a race in the two years he's been running. Seems—" Gresham stopped suddenly. He looked at Jack then, as if he were only just recognizing him. Color seeped through the whiskers on his cheeks. "Well, you'd know more about that than I, I suppose, considering your, er, relationship with..." Now the man's gaze fell on Anna, and his voice faltered. "Well, you know . . ."

No, she didn't, but Anna felt obliged to put the poor man out of his obvious and self-inflicted misery. "Where will you be staying in St. Louis, Mr. Gresham?"

"Oh, at the Southern Hotel, naturally. Is this your first visit, Mrs. Hazard?"

Anna nodded, thinking it was her first visit anywhere.

"Nice city," Gresham said. "We won't have to use these cumbersome ferries much longer, either." He angled his head toward a conglomeration of wagons and men on the western bank. "Just getting started with a bridge right there. In a few years you'll be able to cross the Mississippi in a matter of minutes." He shrugged then. "Well, we're nearly there. I'd best see to my baggage before some lackey dumps it into the murky waters, eh?"

He grabbed Jack's hand and pumped it enthusiastically, then tipped his hat to Anna. "A pleasure, Mrs. Hazard. Enjoy your honeymoon, eh? See you at the races, Hazard."

*Honeymoon.* The word took Anna by surprise. She had forgotten they were newlyweds. Freshly, thrillingly, in love. Her glance sprang up to Jack's face, but he wasn't looking at her. He didn't seem to be aware of her at all as he stood with his fists tightened on the railing and his eyes fastened on something, or someone, far away.

* * *

"That was a very credible performance," Jack whispered a while later as he held her elbow and guided her along the gangplank to the levee. "I think that blowhard Gresham really believes you're a lumber heiress."

"You might have informed me earlier, Mr. Haz—Jack," Anna said. "Is there anything else in my background I ought to be aware of?"

He came to a halt halfway down the gangplank and looked down at her. "Don't take this so seriously, mouse. All you have to do is hang on my arm and behave like a bride. Let me take care of the rest."

"Yes, but—"

Before she could argue, he was leading her along the narrow walkway again, and Anna focused her concentration on not plummeting into the river. Once her feet touched the paving stones on the wharf, however, she pulled her arm from her companion's grasp and took a step away from him.

"I'm your partner," she informed him, pointing her chin into his face.

That face darkened immediately. "You're my bloody wife. Your job is to confine yourself to that role. You are to share my accommodations and my meals, gaze up at me adoringly through those ridiculous lenses and look happy hanging on my arm." Jack's low voice slipped to a deeper, more menacing register. "Beyond that, Mrs. Hazard, you have no role. Do you understand?"

The look Jack gave her had sent more than a few men rushing for cover. But the mouse wasn't flinching. That lush mouth of hers was thin with ire now, and sunlight was snapping off her spectacles like sparks. The mouse was mad. For a second, Jack wanted to laugh at her surprising behavior. He might have, but out of a corner of his eye he saw Gresham cutting toward them through the crowd.

"Perhaps we ought to clarify one or two things," Anna was hissing, "before we proceed any further." Her fists were planted on her hips.

She looked more like a fishwife than a bedazzled bride, Jack thought. And Henry Gresham, who would carry any and all gossip with him along with his baggage, was bearing down on them fast.

"Did you hear me, Mr. Hazard?" she demanded now.

Gresham came to a standstill beside them. The man's smile was as murky as the river. "Lovers' spat, Hazard?"

Bloody hell. He had to keep the woman from ruining everything before it had even begun. Other than hurling her into the Mississippi, Jack could think of only one thing to silence her. He snagged her by the waist and clamped her hard against his chest, then stifled her furious mouth with a kiss.

He had expected to meet rigid, icy lips, but Jack knew immediately he'd been wrong. Maybe it was the sudden shock of it. Or maybe she hadn't been kissed in a long, long time. But, for whatever reason, Anna Matlin's mouth felt lush and luxurious beneath his. She received his kiss the way a pillow receives a weary head, while her body softened and warmed against his like silk sheets.

Without any volition on his part, his tongue tested the soft seam of her lips. They gave way. Instantly. Sweetly. It was heaven for a moment.

Bloody hell. Jack broke the kiss and cast Henry Gresham a victorious man-to-man look, while the mouse still clung to him like breeze-blown silk. "We'll be seeing you at the hotel, Gresham, no doubt. Sooner or later, eh?"

Jack's lascivious wink did exactly as he had intended. It sent the man off with an equally lascivious chuckle, and then Jack looked back at the woman in his arms. Even through her lenses, he could see a distinct glaze in her eyes. He wanted to kiss her again. Right then. He stepped back with an abruptness that unbalanced her.

He gripped her arm. "No more outbursts in public, Anna. You could ruin everything. Please, from now on, think before you speak."

"Yes. All right."

Anna was amazed that she could speak at all. And as for thinking... Well, just then she wasn't sure she'd ever again be able to rise to that monumental task. Jack Hazard's kiss had taken her by storm, the surprise of it sending streaks of lightning clear to her feet, the sensuality of it reverberating through every nerve and fiber.

He was ushering her along the levee now, and Anna was trying to make her feet move in concert with his. Not any easy undertaking at all, when her knees had turned to pudding a moment ago and were only now solidifying. This was no way for a Pinkerton agent to behave, she reminded herself as she rushed along.

It was no way for a self-respecting woman to behave, either. To be so flummoxed by a kiss. To have her legitimate and quite serious concerns turned into frilly bows and butterflies by a man's mouth on hers. And it wouldn't happen again.

Jack Hazard came to a halt. His dark face glowered down on her. "I apologize," he snarled. "It won't happen again, Mrs. Matlin. Mrs. Hazard. Whoever the hell you are." He let go of her arm to drag his fingers through his hair.

Had the kiss affected him, too? There was a definite flush to his face that Anna had never seen, and his fingers trembled as they threaded through that shiny black hair. Jack Hazard, master spy, seemed nearly as unsettled as she. Oddly enough, the notion, which should have perplexed her, calmed Anna instead. She could almost feel her features smoothing out.

When she spoke, her voice no longer bristled. "Apology accepted, Mr. Haz—Jack. In the future, you'll find a simple 'hush' will do if you require my silence. Or—" she demonstrated "—a finger placed just so upon the lips."

"Fine," he snapped, not even looking at her while he dug in his pocket. "Here's four bits for the porter." He slapped the coins in her hand. "All of it. Understand?"

"Yes."

"Good." He pivoted on his heel and stalked toward a line of waiting carriages, turning back just once to glare at her and growl, "And don't help."

There was a good deal of traffic, both vehicles and pedestrians, between the levee and the hotel, four blocks away. Jack sat in the carriage, his shoulders jammed into the corner, putting as much distance as he could manage between himself and the mouse, who was gazing out the window now, apparently enthralled by her new surroundings. Little murmurs of excitement kept riffling across her lips, and every so often she'd reach up to push her glasses up or tug them down a notch.

It was just St. Louis, damn it. Just a city. Not so different from Chicago. You'd have thought Anna Matlin was taking a carriage across the moon. Now Anna Hazard, Jack thought, correcting himself. His—God help him—wife.

Now that they'd arrived in St. Louis, all his energies and attentions should be directed toward his plan. Instead, his attention was focused on the woman beside him and his energies were concentrated below his beltline. Ever since that kiss.

That damnable kiss. He threw her profile a black glance, meant to be brief, then found his gaze once again drawn irresistibly to her lips.

He'd have thought she would struggle more when he silenced her so outrageously. But she had melted beneath his mouth. Not wilted, or given in like a cowering mouse, but warmed and softened like a woman. Of all possible reactions, that was the last one he had expected.

Or wanted, he told himself now as he wrenched his gaze away from her and stared out his own window. He wanted only one thing. Well, maybe two. He wanted to bring Chloe down, and then to celebrate his sweet victory with a toast that would go on indefinitely. And for all the warm luxuries of her mouth, Anna Matlin had nothing to do with that.

When the carriage came to a swaying halt in front of the arched main doorway of the Southern Hotel, he leaned toward her and whispered without warmth. "You're among the idle rich now, Anna. Your job is to conduct yourself accordingly."

# Chapter Six

The lobby was the grandest room Anna had ever seen. Its thick Persian carpets drank up the sounds of bootheels and the brass wheels of the baggage carts that whizzed by her, while it muted the dozens of conversations that were taking place all around her.

Jack had seated her smack in the middle of the room on a round velveteen banquette. "I'll be right back," he told her, adding a pointed "Mrs. Hazard," as if he felt the need to remind her of her role once more.

How could she forget? As Mrs. Johnathan Hazard, Anna had already received more attention in one day than in the rest of her life put together. Waiters, porters and cabbies looked *at* her now, rather than *through* her. It was an altogether new experience, and not one with which she was completely comfortable.

She peered through a maze of people and potted palms, letting her gaze rest on the tall, elegant man who was leaning against the marble registration desk. The polished stone mirrored his long legs and gave back the gloss on his boots. At this distance he seemed pure god again. She couldn't see the shadows that haunted his face, or the myriad little human nicks. He had an aristocratic air that perfectly suited this room. And then, she remembered, of course, he *was* an aristocrat by birth. The son of an earl, whether the first or the fourth, was all the same to the daughter of a hard-luck coal miner.

Her hands twisted in her lap. She couldn't do this. She hadn't the background to bring it off. Or, right now, the simple courage. Suddenly she wanted nothing more than to be in her little third-floor room in the big house on Adams Street, snuggled in her bed listening to the faint bickering of the Misses Richmond downstairs, reading a book, turning its pages and losing herself in distant places. Not here, where she was truly lost.

But it was too late. Jack's black boots were striding toward her now across the Persian carpets. He had a blue-uniformed bellman in tow.

"Baggage, madam?" he asked her.

Anna tilted her head toward her borrowed trunk. It had looked so fine when the Misses Richmond produced it for her from the attic. Now, here in the lobby of the Southern Hotel, the little camelback contraption looked pitiful.

"Just the one?" The young bellman seemed confused until Jack informed him, rather crisply, that the rest of their luggage had been shipped earlier.

The next thing Anna knew, she was wedged between the two of them in an elevator, going up.

"I've never been . . ." she whispered.

"Relax."

A warm hand spread across her back and, amazingly enough, Anna's heart slowed down and her stomach returned to its proper place inside. She was able to coax her wobbly knees along the hallway to an elaborately carved pair of doors at the far end.

"Your suite, sir," the bellman said, fitting a brass key into the ornate lock.

"Thank you," answered Jack, at the same time praying the mouse would keep her accountant's observations to herself when the boy finally opened the door.

She did, but just barely. A little gasp fluttered out of her. "Surely this can't be—"

Jack pressed a finger to his lips, then moved it to settle softly against hers. "Hush, darling. Naturally you've never seen a honeymoon suite before."

Before she could reply, he swept her up in his arms and strode across the threshold like an eager groom. He realized his mistake before he'd taken his second step. If Anna's mouth was beguiling, the feel of her body in his arms was pure temptation. She was as light as a little girl, but the curves of her body were warm against him, and indisputably a woman's.

Damn fool, he castigated himself. His bid to impress a simple—and hopefully talkative—bellman of their newlywed ardor had succeeded only in heating his own bloody bloodstream. The bellman was so busy drawing drapes, he didn't even notice.

He wanted to drop the mouse like a sack of grain then and there. He put her down with something like grim gallantry, then stepped back from her heat and her female fragrance.

"Send someone up to see to Mrs. Hazard's belongings, will you?" he said to the bellman, who was now opening a wardrobe to disclose an array of coats and trousers.

"Yours arrived last week, sir," the bellman said.

"Fine."

Anna glanced up from the seams she'd been straightening to see the display of elegant clothes. There were frock coats in shades from dove gray to rich ebony. All with trousers to match, she noted. There were white shirts, with and without ruffles, like drifts of pristine snow. On the wardrobe's door, silk neckcloths shimmered like gay ribbons. It was a haberdasher's dream.

The bellman had opened Jack's valise by now and was adding to the display. He unwrapped the whiskey bottle, gave it a knowing look and announced, "I'll have glasses sent up."

"No need," Jack snapped.

The uniformed man shrugged as he set the bottle on a table, then proceeded to take more items from the valise. While he moved silently from bag to wardrobe and back, Anna was watching Jack. He stood in the center of the room, seemingly ignorant of his surroundings, his whole attention focused on that bottle. A muscle jerked in his cheek. His hands drew up into white-knuckled fists. She could almost feel his craving sweeping through her own body, attempting to gain control, and she didn't wonder for a second why they called it "demon rum."

She didn't know what to do. Then her lips twitched up in a tiny, helpful smile. "Well, I believe I've some unpacking to do," she said, then turned toward her camelback trunk and felt in her handbag for the key.

It turned easily in the lock, and she tipped the lid back, then knelt there contemplating the contents, wondering where to put what and trying to recall how married people shared wardrobes and dressers. It had been a long time since she'd had to contend with that. And even then, she and Billy had had little space and few belongings to concern them.

She lifted the small silver frame in which she kept his tintype. Billy gazed back at her as he had for so many years—like a stranger whose wild hair had been slicked back for a few minutes before the camera, whose expressive face was uncharacteristically devoid of happiness and optimism. For a second, her heart squeezed tight, as she imagined her young husband's face if he walked into this room, more ornate than any he'd ever seen. A grin would split his face, and—

"What are you doing?"

Jack's sharp tone startled her. "What?" she squeaked as the tintype went clattering onto the polished oak floor. It was in his hand before she could even reach out.

The metal frame was warm from her hand. That was the first thing that registered on Jack. He had been standing there, staring at that damn bottle, feeling as if he were drowning, though he hadn't touched a drop. And he'd longed to drown. To go under and never come up again. To sink to the blessed bottom.

But all the while the wanting was ripping through him, he had been aware of another, bemusing desire. A wish to reach out and hold fast. To be saved. When he finally identified the source of that desire, he had wanted to laugh. Her. Anna. That she could stir his body wasn't surprising now, but that she could stir his hope...

Now, as he turned the tintype over in his hand, a bitter taste rose in the back of his throat, and he wanted to laugh again as he saw the image of the boy who more than likely had been Mr. Matlin. Of course the mouse had been married to a sapling. Innocents, both of them. Useless. There was no help. No hope. He'd been more than a fool to imagine it.

"Please. May I have it back?"

Her small voice drifted up to him.

He was beyond all that. Beyond redemption, even. There was just revenge. And that was enough.

"You're...you're crushing the frame, Jack. Please."

At the sound of her hushed plea, Jack's head cleared. The tintype's filigreed frame was bent in his clenched fingers. He gave it back abruptly and watched Anna slip it back among the folded garments.

"I'll put it away with my other things," she said.

"You'll do nothing of the kind." He grasped her arm and pulled her to her feet, hissing close to her ear, "Mrs. Hazard, someone will do that for you while you and I take lunch downstairs."

"But—"

"No buts." He ushered her to the door, stopping only to produce a small gold piece from his pocket and flick it across the room to the bellman.

Anna tried not to look at the prices on the menu, but her eyes were drawn again and again to the right side of the handwritten vellum sheet. "Oh, my!" escaped her lips before she could prevent it.

Across the table from her—across a field of silver and crystal, and above a bouquet of fresh flowers— a dark eyebrow lifted in a warning.

By her calculations, if they dined this way each day of their assignment, their expense report would send Mr. Pinkerton into an apoplectic fit.

"I believe I'll just have a clear soup and toast," she said, quietly but firmly. And quite obviously to no avail, for when the waiter appeared, Jack whispered something to him from behind his menu, and the white-jacketed man nodded solemnly, then quickly whisked away toward the kitchen.

Her partner was being high-handed again. Anna was framing another warning about expenses when Jack suddenly sent one of his Olympian grins across the table and said, "Tell me about yourself, Anna."

She blinked. What a silly thing to ask! "There's nothing to tell. Nothing of interest, anyway."

"Tell me about your life in Chicago." He leaned forward, arching one brow. "What do you do when you're not filing papers at the agency?"

"Nothing. Well, nothing special." She peered over her spectacles at him. "Why?"

Jack sighed. "I'm attempting to have a conversation, which isn't easy with a woman who seems to pride herself on being the world's most uninteresting person."

"I don't expect you to feign interest in my personal life," she said.

"I'm curious."

"Why?"

Jack took a long sip from his water goblet. Why, indeed? he wondered. Most people he knew were only too eager to talk about themselves, and they usually did so without even being asked. The mouse's reticence was as rare as it was commendable, but it was going to make for some deadly-boring meals if Jack had to do all the talking. His own life, despite its veneer of excitement, was dull at best, and damn lonely at worst. Anyway, he was truly curious about Anna Matlin.

"Tell me about your husband."

Her eyes opened nearly wider than her spectacles. "Billy?"

He nodded, thinking it wasn't surprising the cherub-faced fellow in the picture had a boy's name. His gaze lowered to Anna's mouth, and Jack found himself wondering if young Billy had taught her how to melt under a man's mouth the way she had under his. A little stitch pulled tight in his heart, which Jack immediately recognized as jealousy and which he quickly categorized as absurd. This was the mouse, after all, and her husband was...

"—dead," she was saying. "Six years ago."

"You were young to be a widow."

"Twenty."

He smiled. "Which makes you all of twenty-six now."

"Yes."

"Well, I'm thirty-six, Anna, so we do have something in common after all."

He loved the way she squinted through her lenses as if that would help her understand. "In common? What, exactly?" she asked.

"A six."

She laughed then. A sweet, melodious sound that escaped that lovely mouth almost without her being aware of it. It was the first time he'd heard her laughter, and he liked the music of it. Then it was gone, leaving him a little emptier than he'd been a moment before.

Serious again, she said, "I don't suppose we have much else in common. For instance, you've never been married. At least according to your files."

"Almost. Once. A long time ago," he murmured.

The surprise on her face was nearly as great as Jack's own surprise at his candor. Even greater was the shock of remembering the lovestruck boy he'd been at eighteen, when Gwenyth Sutherland was the center of his universe.

"Almost?" she asked. "What happened?"

Jack shrugged. "She married someone else." Someone richer, with better prospects. Someone with a freshly broken nose. "I came to America then."

Her head tilted slightly. "And do you love her still?"

Now it was Jack's turn to laugh. "No. No, I don't. I haven't even thought of her in years. What about you? Do you still love young Billy Matlin?"

He expected an affirmative reply, perhaps accompanied by tears. His tongue was poised to make a sympathetic little click.

"No," she said softly. "In all honestly, I'm not certain I ever did."

Jack's tongue suddenly felt like a lead weight. Honesty? He'd lived so many deceptive lives, and worked so long in this damn business, he wasn't sure he even recognized the concept anymore. And there was no question that he didn't know how to react to it. So, just then, when a plate of braised beef and roast potatoes appeared before him, he felt an enormous sense of relief. It didn't even bother him when, out of a corner of his eye, he saw Henry Gresham making his way toward them through the crowded room.

"Here comes our friend from the ferry," he warned Anna. "Remember who you are, Mrs. Hazard."

How could she forget? Anna wondered. And why would she ever want to? She smiled up—rather serenely, she thought, for a woman who had just confessed to a near stranger that she hadn't loved her late husband, an admission that she'd never even made to herself—at the big, bewhiskered man when he stopped beside their table.

"Glad I found you, Hazard," he said, barely acknowledging Anna. "Have you heard the news?"

Jack merely arched an eyebrow, which was all that was necessary to convince the eager man to continue.

"The Baroness Von Drosten has wired her official entry in the Carondelet Stakes. Chloe's Gold will definitely race." His mustache twitched. "Bad news for all the other entrants, I suppose."

"Why is that, Mr. Gresham?" Anna asked after a glance at Jack, whose face registered a quick but most definite "Good news."

"Chloe's Gold will win, of course," the man replied. "He hasn't lost a race yet. The baroness has probably won close to a hundred thousand in purses, wouldn't you say, Hazard?'' He didn't wait for a response before continuing. ''And the horse's value increases with each win. He must be worth close to a quarter of a million dollars by now. If not, he will be after the Carondelet Stakes.''

''Assuming he wins,'' Jack said.

Gresham laughed. ''Is there any other assumption? I know where my money will be on the afternoon of June first.''

He gave a little rap on the tabletop, then began to walk away, only to pause and turn back. ''By the way, Hazard, her wire also said the baroness would arrive early enough to participate in some of the prerace festivities. I, er... imagined you'd want to know.''

''Thanks.'' Jack fairly spat the word as Gresham made his departure. His expression was as dark as Anna had ever seen it as he pushed his barely touched plate away.

His sudden black mood disturbed her as much as the fact that he'd ordered an expensive meal and then chosen not to touch it. If they were going to be called on Mr. Pinkerton's carpet for their outrageous expenses, she thought as she sliced off a neat portion of her braised beef, they certainly ought to be careful that nothing went to waste.

When they returned to their suite after lunch, the first thing Jack saw was the bottle of Tennessee sour mash. It sat on a small gateleg table near the window, and sunshine was pouring through its contents, turning the whiskey to liquid amber. Immediately the back of his throat burned with anticipation and every nerve in his body tightened with need. As always, he battled down the urge for one soothing swallow, knowing that for him there was no such thing as a single swallow, when taste became torrent, when a first sip was merely a dangerous slide to the dregs.

So complete was his concentration on the whiskey, he wasn't even aware of Anna until she came to stand between him and the bottle, blocking it from his sight.

"Perhaps you should sit down, Jack," she said quietly. "You look pale." Her blue eyes darkened with concern behind their panes. Her hand fluttered upward, its fingers brushing his cheek for a fleeting instant before withdrawing. "Perhaps you need some sleep. Have we any plans for this afternoon?"

Plans. They rushed back into his brain, mercifully replacing his dizzying, nearly debilitating, need. Yes, he had plans, and they would culminate a month from now in the sweetest, longest, most victorious toast a man would ever drink. He most definitely had plans.

He strode to the wardrobe and pulled open its double doors, then stood there staring. "Didn't the maid unpack your trunk? Where the devil are your clothes?"

"Right there," she answered calmly, pointing to the right of his gray morning coat, where three wan frocks sagged from wooden hangers.

"Where are the bloody rest?"

"The rest?"

Jack rolled his eyes and gritted his teeth. He should have known, he told himself. What else would a mouse wear if not mouse clothes? Simple, service-able garments. He shoved them across the rod, one by one. Brown linen. Blue poplin. A dismal gray georgette.

He slammed the wardrobe doors. "These will never do."

"Pardon me?"

She had drawn herself up, stiff as a broom, her hands once again fisted on her hips, her glasses flashing in the sunlight.

"I said your clothes won't do, Anna."

"They've done quite nicely up until this minute, Jack. And besides, I—I don't have any others."

Jack smiled the smile that had always worked so well for him in the past. "You will."

# Chapter Seven

The gilded sign over the door said simply Madame Crillon—Modiste, but there was nothing simple about the dressmaker's establishment located two blocks from their hotel. The walls were papered in white and gold, and the black marble floor was polished to a mirror gloss.

*Modiste,* Jack explained as he ushered Anna through the etched-glass doors, was French for *dressmaker.* Anna filed that fact away, intending to tell Sally Mueller, who did her own fitting and cutting and sewing in a basement room on Washington Street, and who dreamed of moving up to street level. Madame Crillon, it seemed to Anna, had moved far beyond that.

''This is much too—''

Jack's finger pressed against her lips just as a tall, elegantly dressed woman appeared from behind a velvet curtain. She crossed the polished marble floor in a whisk of satin, her eyes sizing them up as she neared. She dismissed Anna with a brittle smile, then raised her most attentive, appreciative gaze to Jack.

"May I help you, *monsieur?*"

Anna recognized the symptoms immediately. Madame Crillon, for all her exquisite attire and her regal bearing, wasn't so different from the secretaries at the Pinkerton Agency when it came to Mad Jack Hazard. The man seemed to know it, too. A little glance up at his face revealed his utter confidence in the effect he brought to bear on the opposite sex. That knowledge seemed a part of him, as much as his blue-gray eyes or his finely shaped nose. And, like his handsome features, he seemed to accept that attraction as, well . . . natural, and of no great import.

He and Madame Crillon were deep in conversation now. Flustered, the woman had lapsed into French, and Jack had followed her, without missing a beat in their exchange.

Standing by his side, his arm linked with hers and his warmth seeping through her sleeve, Anna suddenly felt oddly possessive of him. And oddly antagonistic toward his new devotee. What did she know of him, apart from his astounding male beauty? When ogling his black lashes and blue-gray eyes, did she even see the shadows beneath them? When basking in the light of his smile, did she sense the darkness of his nights, and how those long hours were spent?

Anna did. Oh, she did! Her cool possessiveness caught fire as it turned to protectiveness. Jack Hazard needed her. She felt it in her soul. The knowledge nearly sent her reeling.

Jack's arm tightened imperceptibly on hers. Anna blinked and tried to attend to the conversation.

Madame Crillon had stopped speaking, however, and was surveying Anna from head to toe. She gave a small sniff then and reverted to English. "No. I am sorry, *monsieur.* I have a clientele, you understand, to whom I must be loyal." Her frosty gaze fell on Anna once more. "There is nothing I can do."

"Oh, good," Anna was tempted to murmur. Suddenly, in this woman's imperious shadow, she felt shabby and dreadfully mismatched with the man by her side. A part of her wanted desperately to run away and hide from this elegant pair, while another part of her longed to participate in that elegance, to stand on tiptoe and take in a great gulp of that rare air so far above her. Or any air, for that matter. Suddenly she wasn't breathing all that well.

The mouse's arm stiffened against his, and she made a soft little gasp—wounded, no doubt, by the Frenchwoman's barely veiled rejection. He wanted to reach out and twist Madame Crillon's upturned nose, but instead he reached into his pocket and withdrew a roll of bills.

"I appreciate your loyalty, *madame,*" he said as he riffled through the greenbacks as if they were a limp deck of cards. "Of course, there are always extenuating circumstances. And there are reasons for expanding one's clientele, wouldn't you say?"

Her gaze flicked from the money to his face. As much as women seemed to find his features appealing, he thought, most of them found cash infinitely more attractive. Madame Crillon was no exception.

"How soon would you require these garments, *monsieur?*" she cooed.

*Yesterday.* "As soon as possible, *madame.* My wife will take a ready-made for the gala tomorrow night. Early next week will do for the rest." He riffled the stack of bills again, allowing their soft green breeze to fan across the dressmaker's face. "I trust you'll be able to manage that."

*"Oui, monsieur."* The woman arranged her mouth in a smile and offered it to Anna while gesturing toward a fitting room. "Will you come with me, madame?"

Anna stood in the small fitting room, clad only in her chemise and pantelets, Madame Crillon having divested her of every other stitch with great speed and cool disdain. But Anna had been almost oblivious of the woman's brisk hands. She'd been thinking about Jack, and her sudden, shocking urge to protect him.

It seemed silly to her now, and more than a little misguided. He was the Pinkerton Agency's foremost operative, after all, and she was a file clerk. He had been in countless dangerous situations over the years and had managed to escape them all, while the most dangerous thing Anna had ever done was attempting to cross State Street in the path of a speeding fire wagon. She'd barely made it, and she'd lost a shoe in the process, too. Jack Hazard needed her protection the way a dog needed a vigilant flea.

Madame Crillon, measuring tape in hand, returned, and without a word began to push and pummel her, pausing only to make quick notations in a notebook. When she tugged the tape tight around Anna's waist, she was vaguely glad it wasn't her neck.

"Your *husband,*" the Frenchwoman hissed, "is a very determined man, no?" She snapped the tape away from Anna's hips and fitted it the length of her arm.

"Determined. Yes, he is," Anna replied, wondering why the woman was so out of sorts when she was making a small fortune for her efforts.

She took the measurement of Anna's wrist now, then held it between two fingers as if it were a dead fish, all the while shaking her head.

"Is there a problem, *madame?*"

"I dress the most prominent women in St. Louis society, *mademoiselle.* I have a reputation to consider." Her gaze dropped to Anna's hand. "I would not care for it to become common knowledge that I had dressed a whore. Please see that your *husband* provides you with a proper ring if he intends to continue this charade."

Anna drew back her hand and stared at the bare finger, less upset at being branded a whore than at the oversight. Why hadn't she thought of a wedding band. Or, better yet, why hadn't Jack, since he was the one who had all the experience? Married women wore rings. What was her excuse?

"I'll thank you not to call my bride a whore, *madame.*" The deep voice came from just beyond the velvet drape that served as a door. "As for the ring, it's a marquise-cut emerald that is still in my family vault in London. As for your opinions, *madame,* I believe I'm paying you to keep them to yourself. Is that clear?"

The velvet drapes parted to disclose Jack's towering figure and murderous glare. After stammering something half in English and half in French, the dressmaker whisked past him.

Anna was standing half turned away from him with her head bent, still contemplating her traitorous hand, wondering what else they had overlooked. Ordinarily, she paid attention to the most insignificant of details. And a wedding ring, in this case, was hardly insignificant.

"I'm sorry if that Gallic harpy hurt your feelings, mouse. I'd happily walk out of here this minute, but we haven't time."

Jack leaned against the drawn-back folds of velvet, letting his gaze drift over the scantily clad woman. He was usually good at predicting the size of females beneath all the yardage they wore. He'd been wrong about this one, though. The slim, almost scrawny hips he'd imagined were in actuality quite lush, flaring out from her tiny waist the way they did. He'd also been wrong about the lack of a derriere. There was plenty there. And the rest of her was just as rounded and luxurious in its appeal.

For all her curves, however, there was still something quite delicate about her. Something pale and fragile and breakable. Anger at the seamstress's snide remark surged through him again. In an effort to tamp down on it, he swallowed, and only then realized his mouth had gone dry.

She turned to him then, making no attempt to move her hands or arms in that annoying and usually hypocritical display of modesty so many women used. Like the rest of her, Anna Matlin's face was open and honest and . . . different. What was it?

"I should have thought of that," she said, her eyebrows drawing together in a frown.

He was trying so hard to decide what was different about her, Jack barely comprehended her words. Certainly her hair was less prim since her clothes had been wrenched over her head. But it wasn't that. "What?" he murmured, as much to himself as to her.

"The ring." She held her hand out toward him. "We ought to be more careful. I'm sure we can find something inexpensive. A simple band, or a mounted bit of glass . . ."

"That's it! The glasses!" It was the first time he had seen her without her silly spectacles. It was the first time he'd been able to see the true color of her eyes, which turned out to be a blue to put the most perfect sapphire to shame. Extraordinary.

"I beg your pardon?" she exclaimed.

"You aren't wearing your glasses." He felt as if he were pointing out the obvious, but even so, her hand flitted up to the bridge of her nose. "How well do you see without them, Anna? How many fingers am I holding up? Here." He raised his hand, tucking his thumb into his palm.

"Four," she snapped, turning now to rummage through a pile of crinolines.

"And now?"

She glanced over her shoulder, told him, "Three," and then returned to her rather frantic quest.

"What are you looking for?"

"My spectacles." Her answer was muffled by the yards of muslin she was poking through.

Jack was tempted to join her, to find the damn windowpanes first and hide them in his pocket. He wasn't quite sure why, though. What difference did it make to him whether she wore them or not? Whether or not he could clearly see the jewel-like color of her eyes or the perfect, unobstructed oval of her face?

He remained where he was, crossing his arms now and surveying her pretty curves, enjoying the rush they provoked in his bloodstream. It felt damn good to feel like a man again. Not that he intended to do anything with those feelings. And even if he did, it surely wouldn't be with the mouse.

* * *

"Perhaps we'll find an affordable jewelry store before we reach the hotel," Anna said. She resettled her spectacles on her nose and peered over their metal rims to read the signs on the buildings on both sides of Walnut Street, along which she and Jack were walking at her insistence. Carriage fares added up and, as she had informed Jack, "even rich people need exercise."

It was a lovely late-spring afternoon, and a warm breeze blew at their backs as they continued along the sidewalk. Anna gave her glasses another reassuring touch. She supposed she could have replaced them if they had been lost at the dressmaker's. The prospect of that additional expense didn't please her. Nor did the idea of spending days or even weeks without being able to read, although she would be able to see in the distance well enough. She focused on a sign up ahead, just to test herself.

"Oh, look at that!" She pointed to a brass plaque where the name of the Pinkerton National Detective Agency shone forth in the afternoon sun. Quickly, then, she consulted her watch. "It's only 4:30. We really ought to check in."

"Why the devil would we want to do that?" Jack muttered just behind her.

He grasped her elbow then to continue toward the hotel, but Anna didn't budge.

"I've read the handbook," she said. "All operatives are required to report to local offices whenever and wherever possible. It's on page seven, I believe."

Jack sighed. It was on page eight, actually, but it wasn't something he ever did, unless he needed cash he couldn't otherwise obtain. He never checked in because he communicated directly with Allan and he worked alone. Until now. He glared down into the mouse's bespectacled, eager face, then nodded his grudging assent and followed her into the building and up one flight of stairs.

"Bloody hell," he muttered when he read the name of the agent in charge, stenciled on the glass of the door. He'd hoped never to see the name Frederick Broome again, much less the actual man. Broome was as by-the-book as they came. Young, eager, relatively capable—in a dithering way. "You and Mr. Broome ought to get on quite well," he snarled as he followed Anna into the office and slammed the door behind him hard enough to rattle the glass.

The thirty-year-old blond agent shot out of his inner office as if a bomb had gone off in the anteroom. His center-parted, slicked-back hair was nearly standing on end. Jack felt a devilish grin tickling his lips.

"Hello, Broome," he said.

The younger man composed himself by giving a firm yank to each shirt cuff and clearing his throat. "Hazard. No one told me you were coming."

"Obviously." With some reluctance, Jack shook Broome's extended hand, angling his head toward Anna. "I'd like to introduce my wife."

Now the agent's eyes nearly pinwheeled. "Your—"

"My wife," Jack repeated, slowly and distinctly, as if he were addressing someone with impaired hearing and limited powers of comprehension.

"Yes, I heard you, but..." Broome blinked down at Anna. "How do you do, Mrs., er..."

"Matlin," Anna announced. "Mrs. Anna Matlin. From the Chicago office, Mr. Broome. The marriage is a professional subterfuge. I'm sure you understand."

"Oh, yes. Quite."

Broome took her hand now and shook it enthusiastically. Jack wasn't quite sure whether the expression on the agent's face was the remnants of his astonishment or a sign of relief that the woman at whom he was so fondly gazing was unattached.

Either way, Jack had had enough of it. "Well, we just stopped in to say hello. Hello and goodbye, Broome." He took the mouse's elbow, but she politely shrugged away.

"I don't suppose there are any messages for us, are there, Mr. Broome? From Chicago?" she asked.

"No. I had no idea you were coming." He ripped his adoring gaze from the mouse and narrowed it on Jack. "For what purpose, if you don't mind my asking?"

Jack minded a lot, but before he could answer, the mouse squeaked enthusiastically. "The Baroness Von Drosten. We're going to get her this time."

"I see." The young agent raised what Jack considered a haughty brow. "*This* time," he repeated as his lips sidled into a sneer. "Had some bad luck last time, I understand, Hazard."

Resisting the fierce urge to break the agent's nose, with the muscles bunching in his shoulders and his jaw clenched, Jack said, "Don't believe everything you hear, Freddy. Maybe you'll learn that after you've been in this business a bit longer."

He turned on his heel then and walked to the door, where he paused only long enough to growl, "Coming, Anna?" before he slammed the door on his way out. This time the glass not only rattled, it cracked down the center, leaving Frederick Broome's name suddenly and oddly disjointed.

"Oh, dear," Anna breathed. "I suppose I ought to go."

"Must you?" Frederick Broome said. "I wouldn't want to be anywhere near that foul temper. I'm surprised he didn't strike me, to tell you the truth. He's done it before."

"Really?"

"Well, not to me. I've heard stories."

She'd heard more than her share of gossip about Jack Hazard, Anna thought. She preferred the truth. "I really must go," she said, on her way to the damaged door.

Broome walked with her, reaching for the knob, pausing before he turned it. "You're new, Mrs. Matlin. And rather inexperienced, I gather. Are you sure you know what you're getting into?"

It would have been easy to take offense, but the look on the man's face was so earnest that it made Anna smile and respond quite honestly. "Probably not, Mr. Broome. But I'll be careful, I assure you."

"Please do." He opened the door a few inches, then added, "And please know that I'm here and available at any time, should you find you need me. Any time. For anything."

"Thank you." Anna nudged the door open farther and got a shoulder out. She half expected to see Jack Hazard glowering at her from the top of the stairwell, but the hallway was empty. She pushed the door all the way open and stepped out. "I'll remember that. Thank you so much, Mr. Broome."

"Good day, Mrs. Matlin," the agent called as Anna rushed down the hall. "I hope to see you very soon."

Jack was halfway down the block before he stopped and looked over his shoulder. When he didn't see the mouse scurrying after him, he sighed, withdrew a cigar from his coat pocket, lit it and leaned against a lamppost.

Freddy Broome! Damn the man. And while he was damning Broome for needling him that way, Jack also damned himself for letting those needles get under his skin. He used to be better at holding his temper. Before Chloe. Before Anna Matlin.

He envisioned again the besotted expression on Freddy's face when he was looking at the mouse. At the mouse, for God's sake! A woman who was all but invisible, except for an occasional glint from her silly spectacles.

Then he pictured her as she had been earlier, in the fitting room at Madame Crillon's, in her thin chemise and simple drawers. Natural and open and alluring. Strikingly beautiful, somehow. Had Freddy seen instantly what it had taken him days to discern? Had he become partially blind to such sweet, simple qualities?

He took a long pull of his cigar, and watched the breeze thin the smoke he blew out. He wasn't blind, thank God, but it surprised him—even shocked him—that after his time with Chloe he could still appreciate simplicity and innocence. He would have bet the baroness had robbed him of that ability. If he'd ever had it at all.

Well, once... In England. A thousand years ago. Gwenyth Sutherland had been simple and innocent, too. Simple enough to listen to her overbearing bulldog of a father and innocent enough to believe the man when he told her it was best she marry someone else. Someone rich and malleable and not subject to violent fits of temper. Jack had proved the old man partially correct when he bashed in the face of Gwennie's intended.

The way he'd wanted to break Freddy Broome's nose a moment ago. Damn him.

He dashed his cigar to the pavement and ground it to shreds with the toe of his boot, reminding himself that there was really only one person of his acquaintance worthy of damnation, and that if he didn't focus on her and her alone, he might not be up to the task. Not only was Chloe a formidable foe, but she was capable of defeating him, as no one else was, by making him defeat himself. She'd done it before, God knew, and so, apparently, did Broome and everybody else at the agency.

Anna, too? His gaze was drawn by a quick glint of light, and he raised his head to see the mouse approaching, her shoulders squared and her pretty mouth crimped in disapproval as she hurried toward him.

But when she stopped just a few inches shy of his lamppost and raised her face to his, Jack saw that it wasn't disapproval at all, but worry, that drew her mouth into a thin pink line. And somehow, knowing she was worried about him made him want to smile. At the moment, he thought, that concern wasn't entirely misdirected.

"Mrs. Hazard, I presume," he said softly, then cupped his hand at her elbow and led her back to the hotel.

## Chapter Eight

Early the next evening, Anna stood looking out one of the windows in their suite. She wasn't wearing her watch, so she could only estimate the time. From the way the sun was dipping into the trees to the west, it was probably five-thirty.

Her brow creased with irritation. She hated not wearing her watch, but there was no place to pin it on her low-cut ball gown. Not unless she stabbed it directly into her bosom, which she had tried earlier, when Madame Crillon's assistant delivered the ready-made gown and then helped Anna into it.

"Oh, no, *madame*. Not the watch. That will never do." The girl had frowned then. "Have you no jewels?"

No, she had no jewels, Anna thought irritably now. More importantly, she still had no ring on her left hand. And, furthermore, she barely had a husband. Jack had made himself absent most of the day.

From the moment he awakened in his chair, he'd been distant to the point of rudeness. When he informed her he was going out for a while, Anna had almost been glad. She was nervous enough about the prerace ball they were to attend this evening, without having to contend with a sullen, storm-dark face all afternoon.

He'd been that way—dark and distant—ever since their visit to Frederick Broome's office yesterday afternoon. The St. Louis agent had been rude, without a doubt, but she didn't think Jack Hazard was the sort of man to let a little professional jealousy get under his skin. Or goad him into breaking a door.

It was lack of proper sleep, she'd concluded. Anna turned from the window and regarded the large four-poster bed with its brocade coverlet. There was room enough for two, she decided. Ample room. With a pillow between them . . .

She imagined the heat of his body warming the down of the pillow and that warmth extending to her side of the bed. She imagined the sound of his breathing—even and deep and relaxed—as their heads lay side by side near the carved walnut headboard. She imagined inching her foot, just so, under the soft linens and finding his strong calf. Anna smiled. She walked to the bed and let her fingers drift over the coverlet.

"Silly," she said, shaking her head, just as the door to their suite opened. She jerked back her hand as if it had been on a hot stove. As if it had been on the imagined body of the man now standing in the doorway.

"You're ready, I see." He closed the door behind him. "It will only take me a moment."

"Yes. All right." Anna sauntered toward the window, away from the bed.

"Did you have a pleasant day?" he asked in a pleasant, but rather offhand, tone.

Not so different, Anna thought, from a real husband. At her back now she could hear the sound of a man undressing. There was the whisk of sleeve against coat lining, the faint click of buttons, the light clink of a metal belt buckle. She felt the color rising in her face, nearly matching that of the setting sun.

"A very pleasant day," she said, attempting to achieve his casual air. "Quiet. At least it was quiet until the dressmaker's assistant arrived."

He didn't respond immediately. Anna could hear the swish of fabric and the thunk of a wooden hanger against the wardrobe. She turned, finally, to see him angling an arm through the sleeve of a black frock coat. He looked down, straightened the lapels, then glanced up. "The dressmaker did a fine job," he said. "You look quite beautiful, Anna."

Her hand rose automatically to her spectacles, then faltered halfway there. He was the one who was beautiful. Especially now, in his evening wear. "You needn't flatter me, Jack. I have a good idea how I look, and I assure you I'll do my very best to live up to this extravagant gown and to play Mrs. Hazard properly."

"Speaking of which . . ." He chuckled softly as he reached into the pocket of his discarded coat. "I have something for you, Mrs. Hazard."

"What?"

"One of those particulars you're always so concerned about," he said. He walked to the window and stood mere inches from her. "A *particular* particular. Give me your hand, little mouse."

He caught her fingers as they were flitting up to her glasses, and held her hand in his a moment. It was warm and trembling just like a tiny, captured mouse. His immediate reaction to even such a small touch reminded him precisely why he'd avoided her most of the day. Jack slipped the gold band on her finger. It was a perfect fit. Somehow he'd known it would be, he thought as he let her go.

"There," he said coolly. "That should take care of anyone's suspicions."

He walked back to the wardrobe, whisked a silk neckcloth from a hook on the door and proceeded to put it on. Ordinarily he succeeded on the first try. Even when he was drunk. The damn tie wouldn't cooperate, though, and he was reluctant to admit it was because his own hands were trembling. It wasn't the woman, he swore. It wasn't the sight of those sweet curves, or the sweep of her blond hair, or the sudden desire to place a kiss on her pale, tender neck. It wasn't the feel of her warm hand in his.

It was, Jack told himself, because he needed a damn drink. He aimed a glance over his shoulder toward the bottle on the table, only to find that Anna had moved from the window and positioned herself to block his view.

She knew! What the devil did the woman do—read his mind? What was she, a blond witch lurking behind supernatural and all-seeing shards of glass? With a muted curse, he turned back to the mirror and resumed his battle with his tie.

"I'd like to help you," she said softly.

"Thanks. I've almost got it."

"No. I mean with...with your problem, Jack. Tell me what I can do."

Giving the silk noose a final yank, he wheeled around. "What can you do?" He put as much frost as possible into his tone. "You can play your part to perfection, Mrs. Hazard. And you can keep in mind, at all times, that it is merely that. A part. Beyond that, I don't need your help. Or want it."

"But I—"

He took her arm, a bit more roughly than he'd intended. "Shall we go? I believe we're already more than fashionably late."

When Anna stepped out of the carriage in front of the stately home of Senator and Mrs. Adolphus Kerr, she took one look at the other fashionably late couples standing at the door, thought she recognized another senator, a general and even Mrs. Ulysses S. Grant, and immediately knew she had gotten in way over her head. She was a file clerk, not a spy! She was Anna Matlin, from the bleak coal-mining hills of southern Illinois, not—

"Mrs. Hazard," Jack murmured conspiratorially as his warm hand settled against the small of her back and urged her forward.

She took in as much air as her French corset would allow. You can do this, she told herself, just before Jack whispered the same encouraging words, adding, "Stay close to me, mouse. Smile and say as little as possible."

That wouldn't be so very difficult. Her vocal cords were in knots, anyhow. Anna felt her lips ratchet up into something she hoped resembled a smile as they stepped into the brightly lit foyer.

The next hour went by in a blur of introductions, during which she clung to Jack's arm like the shy, adoring wife she was supposed to be, all the while feeling more like a woman drowning in a sea of watered silk and perfume, hanging on to Jack for her very life.

He moved through the crowd with practiced ease, greeting gentlemen affably and bestowing kisses on ladies' hands as if born to do only that. Their conversations centered mostly on horses—sires, dams, past races, jockeys—so it wasn't difficult for Anna to remain silent.

And into that silence, as they weaved through the room, came a single name. Whispered or hissed, but always at their backs. Behind them, like an ill wind. The name of the Baroness Chloe Von Drosten. Anna didn't doubt for a moment that Jack heard it, too, but his mask of social affability never slipped an inch.

Anna's mask, unreliable as it was, slipped badly when they were called into the dining room and she discovered she was to be seated at least a mile away from Jack at the great table, which was laid for forty guests.

He seated her, then bent to place a warm kiss in the hollow of her neck. Anna barely felt it. She was counting forks—four—and plates, of which there appeared to be three, and the neat array of goblets—four!—at her place. She started to get up, but Jack took that opportunity to shove her chair more closely to the table.

"You'll be fine," he whispered at her ear. "Just do what everyone else does."

And pray you're not sitting between two louts who don't know their salad forks from their elbows, Jack thought bleakly as he moved to take his own seat between the giggling Miss Eliza Bourke and the already overstuffed Mrs. Porter Patterson.

He was grateful the two ladies seemed to find him unapproachable and therefore confined their conversations to the gentlemen on their opposite shoulders. It gave him time to think. Well, as much as he could, while peering through the floral centerpeice at the mouse.

Damned if she wasn't the most desirable woman at the table, a fact that her neighbors noticed instantly. If the fools didn't stop leaning toward her in order to get a glimpse down her low-cut bodice, Jack thought, he might just have to slap his napkin on the table, rise and announce his God-given right to sit next to his bride.

She was doing rather well without him, he had to admit, although he'd never seen a more cautious diner. She wasn't being overly cautious with the wine, however, and as the meal progressed, he watched her sample the soft Rhine wine, the deeper chardonnay, the full-bodied burgundy—all while he guzzled glass after glass of tepid water. With each course, the mouse's smile increased, the flush on her face ripened, and her interest in her neighbors intensified.

Jack couldn't get out of his chair fast enough when their hostess announced that the dancing would take place in the ballroom on the third floor.

"Jack!"

He was propelling her into the foyer as if the house were on fire, or as if she had made some terrible mistake. But, for the life of her, Anna couldn't imagine what that might have been. Unless it had been when she dropped her dessert spoon. She had leaned down to retrieve it, only to be stopped by that sweet Mr. Holmes, who had placed a hand on her arm and had said, "Let the footman do that, dear Mrs. Hazard."

"What did I do wrong?"

"Nothing," Jack growled. "We'll go upstairs, have one obligatory waltz, and then we're gone."

She jerked up her skirts as he fairly pushed her up the marble staircase. Lord, her head was swimming, and now Jack was shoving her along as if he couldn't get away from this affair quickly enough. And what had he said about waltzing?

The ballroom was awash in the light of hundreds of candles, and music was already playing when they entered.

"There you are, dear Mrs. Hazard. Remember, you promised me the first waltz."

Anna nudged her spectacles down a notch, peeked over the rims to see the pudgy face of Mr. Holmes, her companion from dinner. No sooner had she recognized him than he was begging Jack's pardon and taking Anna's hand to lead her onto the dance floor.

The dance floor! No, she couldn't possibly have promised a waltz, first or last, to Mr. Holmes. She didn't know how to waltz. At the moment, she barely knew how to walk.

Then, suddenly, she found herself being tugged against a solid wall of white shirt and black frock coat and she heard Jack's deep voice. "My wife's first waltz is mine. Sorry."

"This is terrible," she said into a shirt stud.

"Hush. We'll have one waltz, and then we'll leave."

"I can't." Her voice was a strangled wail now.

"You can't what?"

"Waltz."

"Bloody hell."

Anna felt his chest expand and contract in a mighty sigh, and she heard the curse he grumbled, but she didn't quite understand the next thing he said.

"I beg your pardon?"

"Swoon, damn it."

"Oh." Actually, at the moment, there was nothing she felt like doing more, what with her head swimming the way it was and her breasts crushed against Jack's solid form. Anna let her eyes close and her knees slacken and her brain simply drift away.

The mouse was on the bed, right where he'd dumped her, and Jack was in his customary chair. He had tossed away his cravat and his coat and unbuttoned his shirt, but he hadn't bothered to light a lamp, so the bottle of sour mash was now merely a dark shadow on the table before him. Even so, it drew his gaze the way a flame played siren to a moth.

God in heaven! With his own problems with drink, did he now have to contend with Anna's? He stretched out his legs and tipped his head onto the back of the chair, knowing he was exaggerating the situation, willing to take at least some of the blame for what had happened this evening. It was his fault for failing to warn her about the wines. His fault, too, for leaving her virtually alone and at the mercy of those two idiots who'd flanked her at dinner.

He wouldn't do it again. In fact, what he ought to do was send her back to Chicago tomorrow, headache and all. Only...

The soft sound of her breathing came to him across the room, and he angled his head to see her small form atop the coverlet. When he carried her up to the suite, her arms had linked around his neck and she'd nestled her face into his neck, murmuring, "This is nice." Jack had wondered at that moment if she imagined she was in the arms of young Billy Matlin, but then he recalled her statement about not having loved him. Why not? he wondered now.

If she hadn't loved Billy Matlin, could she ever love Jack Hazard? As quickly as the thought occurred to him, Jack banished it. The answer, of course, was no—for a wealth of reasons, not the least of which was the lack of innocence that he knew damn well made him unworthy of love.

His sister loved him, but then, Madelaine had known him since he was an uncomplicated child. He wasn't a child anymore, and as for complications—God knew his soul was as tangled as a spider's web. Chloe knew, too. And she knew just which strands to vibrate, and exactly which filament to undo in order to bring the whole web down. But not this time. He wouldn't allow himself to be alone with her. He was, after all, a married man.

So much for sending the mouse back to where she belonged. He needed her—desperately—but not the way her innocent and helpful heart imagined.

The bedsprings squeaked.

"Jack?" Her shadowy form sat bolt upright on the bed. "Jack?"

"I'm right here."

She sighed. "Thank heavens. I didn't know where I was for a minute."

"Wine has a tendency to do that, especially to novices."

Now she sagged back down. "Oh. I remember. I hope I didn't do anything to disgrace you."

His voice was quiet, distant. "I've been in worse fixes."

Yes. Anna supposed he had. How ironic, she thought, that she had been so concerned about Jack's drinking and then had been the one who succumbed. A fine Pinkerton agent she'd been this evening. Anna levered herself up on her elbows now. Without her spectacles, it was difficult to distinguish Jack from the darkness on the other side of the room.

"I'm wide awake," she said, and received only a murmured "Hmm" in reply. "Jack, will you do me a favor? Will you teach me how to waltz?"

"If you like."

"Oh, good." Anna was off the bed and across the room instantly. She grasped his hand. "Come on."

"Now?"

"Well, why not?"

He sighed. "For one reason, it's well past midnight."

"Are you sleepy?" she asked.

"No."

"You'll have to come up with a better excuse, then." She tugged his hand, to no avail.

"All right, then. How about this? If I hold you in my arms for a waltz, it's more than likely I'll want to kiss you."

Her heart did a quick little handspring in her chest. "Really?"

"Really."

His thumb was tracing across the back of her hand now, sending a tingling warmth the length of her arm. Suddenly there was nothing in the world Anna wanted more than for Jack Hazard to kiss her.

"Then please do," she whispered.

It wasn't what Jack had expected. His candor, he had assumed, would send the mouse scuttling back to her side of the room, leaving him to contend with the darkness and the desire just touching her hand had engendered in him. But her quiet invitation had him up and out of his chair before he was even aware of it. He didn't have to reach for her. She was simply there, entering his embrace as if she'd done it a million times before, fitting into his arms as if that were where she'd always belonged.

He took her lush mouth gently at first, in a tentative kiss, one he thought he could control. But the minute her lips parted in a soft little moan, he was utterly lost. Or found. He didn't know which. Desire ripped through him like fire along a fuse. He deepened the kiss. She tasted like wine, and he wanted to drink her, consume her, get drunker on her than he already was.

His hands curved around her rib cage and rose to the heat of her breasts. He dipped his head and let his tongue trace the soft skin just above the lace edge of her corset.

He was burning for her. He hadn't felt such searing heat since...

Chloe. And suddenly it was as if she were there in the room. Jack thought he could smell her. Like a civet cat. Like a bitch in heat. He could hear the slither of silk, the sharp crack of a whip. Damn her. Damn her to hell and back. He jerked his head up, trying to see through the dark.

"Jack?"

Anna's whisper brought him back.

"Are you all right?" she asked as her arms tightened around him. "You're shaking."

"Ah, God..." he breathed. He rested his chin on her head and closed his eyes. The fire that had been raging through him had turned ice-cold. "No, little mouse. I'm not all right. But I will be. Soon."

## Chapter Nine

When she awoke the next morning, Anna didn't open her eyes immediately. Rather, she lay there, in her private darkness, thinking about the night before, preparing herself for the sight of Jack, slung out in his chair, as beautiful in his sleep as he was when awake, perhaps even more.

The sight of him could only be a distraction now, and Anna needed to think, to come to some conclusion about their relationship. And what in heaven's name was that? she asked herself, digging her shoulders a bit more deeply into the mattress, feeling a frown begin to pull her features down. Theirs could hardly be called a strictly professional alliance anymore. They had, in fact, behaved quite unprofessionally last night.

*You ought to be ashamed of yourself, Anna Matlin.* But she wasn't. Quite the opposite, in fact. She was eager to kiss Jack again. It hadn't been she who stopped last night. She wasn't so sure she would have, either. Not just because his kiss had set her aflame, but also because she had been responding to the raw hunger she perceived in him. A need that went beyond mere sex. A need for all the warmth and love she possessed.

Needing to see him, suddenly—if only to reassure herself that she hadn't been dreaming the night before—Anna opened her eyes and lifted her head. He wasn't there. The chair was empty. Her hand shot out to snatch up her spectacles and came into contact with a note.

She recognized Jack's handwriting from the files. Strong, bold, as finely shaped as the man himself.

Anna,
    I've gone to Louisville for several days. Please continue in my absence. Accept all invitations. Decline all wine.

                       Regards,
                         J.

At the bottom of the sheet, he had added a postscript. "Don't forget your fitting at Mme. Crillon's this afternoon."

After half a dozen readings, Anna was still unable to find a hint of affection, the merest suggestion of anything personal. The note struck her as strictly professional, and she chided herself for ever having imagined anything otherwise in her relationship with Jack Hazard.

It wasn't like her at all to get so carried away, although she knew from recent experience that she wasn't the first female to forget her purpose in Jack's presence. But she had a job to do. That was why she was here, after all. She would simply have to behave more professionally, and put all personal considerations aside.

Feeling better for the renewal of her determination, Anna decided she would begin by skipping breakfast. It would be her own contribution to cutting down their expenses. And anyway, she wasn't very hungry after all.

She would become a consummate professional, and by the time Jack returned, she would be quite capable of playing his wife. Playing, she reminded herself firmly. Not being.

Later that afternoon, Anna's rekindled determination had had more than a little cold water thrown in it. Mrs. Elihu Stover, the wife of one of the racetrack officials, had invited her for lunch. Anna had gracefully accepted the invitation, but the meal had been a succession of small disasters, not the least of which had been the snails. *Escargots,* Anna had wanted to snort. She knew a snail when she saw one. Rich people, she had concluded dismally, ate worse than the poor.

They did dress better, however, and Madame Crillon had made that abundantly clear when she gathered up Anna's gray georgette, gazed at it for a moment and then inquired, "How would you like me to dispose of this?"

Well, the georgette *had* seen better days, Anna admitted to herself now, as she walked back to the hotel in her brand-new afternoon ensemble of peach satin with green cording to match the covered buttons. Madame Crillon had made off with her underwear, too, and supplied her with a variety of ruffled lawns and lacy silks.

She caught a glimpse of herself in a window, and smiled. She certainly looked the part of Mrs. Johnathan Hazard, wife of the fourth son of a British earl. Now if only she could acquire social skills as easily as she had acquired a new wardrobe.

Well, she thought as her gaze lit on the brass plaque of the Pinkerton National Detective Agency, Frederick Broome had said to call on him for assistance at any time, for any reason.

"I wonder if Mr. Broome knows how to waltz?" she said out loud as she turned into the building and headed up the stairs.

"Indeed I do, Mrs. Matlin, and I'd be more than happy to instruct you," the blond agent had said when Anna posed the question.

Frederick Broome had seemed so happy to see her walk into his office that Anna felt instantly comfortable with him. Once again, the agent had struck her as courteous—to her, anyway—and competent. Hardly the buffoon that Jack had made him out to be. He was even handsome, in a pale sort of way. More importantly, the man knew how to waltz, and was more than willing to pass along his expertise. After discovering that Jack had left for Louisville, Frederick Broome had eagerly suggested dinner and dancing at a German beer garden that very night.

As she sat in the hotel lobby now, waiting for him, her feet began to move in three-quarter time beneath her skirts. It shouldn't take her long to master the basic steps, she thought. And Jack would be so surprised and pleased. Well, surprised. She cautioned herself to stop thinking about pleasing him. It wasn't professional.

"Anna, you look lovely."

Somehow Frederick Broome had crossed the lobby without her having detected him. She realigned her spectacles with a quick touch of her fingertips, thinking that for a Pinkerton agent, she still had a great deal to learn. For instance, was it typical of the profession, she wondered, for agents to use each other's Christian names so early on?

"Thank you, Mr. Broome."

"Freddy," he murmured, smiling down at her as he took her hand. For a moment, he looked as if he were going to kiss it. "Shall we go?"

The evening was, well…unspectacular, and Anna found herself wondering if several days with Jack Hazard had ruined her ability to enjoy the company of any other man. And since when had an unspectacular evening left her feeling vaguely discontented? And in just a matter of weeks, they would resume.

"You look pensive, Anna. What are you thinking?" Freddy leaned across the table, shoving a mug of beer out of his way. His fifth or sixth, by Anna's calculations. Remembering Jack's advice about wine, she had declined the dark German ale and confined herself to water.

"I was thinking about Jack," she said, realizing it was the first time she had spoken his name all evening, though hardly the first time it had crossed her mind.

"Don't," Freddy said. "I'd much rather you thought about me." He reached across the table now, to enclose her hand in his.

Anna pulled away. "That's extremely unprofessional, Freddy."

"Sorry. I just couldn't help myself."

In spite of his apology, however, his smile remained unabashed. "I asked for your assistance," she said as sternly as she could. "Not your affection."

"Well, perhaps you shall have both." After a quick sip of ale, he pushed his chair back and stood. "Shall we have another go at a waltz?"

With a distinct twinge of reluctance, Anna let him lead her onto the dance floor then—and on the next three nights as well, after meeting him outside the hotel to avoid any hint of impropriety.

Soon, to her delight, she had mastered not only the waltz, but also the intricacies of silverware. Each time Freddy reached for her hand, Anna had reminded him that it was unprofessional. Once, when he refused to let her go, she'd blurted out, "Please, Freddy. I'm married."

"I've never seen an agent take her job to heart the way you do," he'd replied.

Although Anna had countered that she was a serious person, she wasn't completely certain it was the job she had taken to heart, and not the man.

Jack lifted a boot onto the bottom slat of a white fence and leaned his forearms on the top rail. He took in a deep breath of warm Kentucky air, then let it out slowly, directing a soft whistle toward the mahogany bay stallion just a few feet away.

"Come on, fella. Come on, North Star. You're not too proud to eat a lowly carrot, are you, old man?"

The horse pricked his ears forward, tamped the tall grass beneath him with a hoof, then snorted and wheeled around. Jack chewed contentedly on the spurned carrot while he watched the stallion run toward the deep green shade of a hackberry tree on the opposite side of the pasture.

"He's still beautiful, isn't he?" His sister's wistful voice sounded at Jack's back, and he turned to see a feminine version of his own face. A happier version, and for that he was enormously glad and grateful.

She'd had her sorrows, heaven knew, the majority of which were her elder brother's fault. She'd be in England now, if it hadn't been for Jack's capture by the Rebs. They'd sentenced him to death, along with his partner, Samuel Scully, and it had been Madelaine—British consul in tow—who saw to Jack's stay of execution as a British subject. It had been during those visits to the desolate Castle Thunder that she had fallen in love with Samuel. And it had probably been Samuel's desperate love for Madelaine that made him tell the Rebs everything he knew to avoid his own execution.

Poor Madelaine. Samuel had turned traitor out of love for her, and out of love for her—and what was left of his honor—he had killed himself, mere days after their release from prison, never knowing that she was carrying his child.

Jack smiled down at her pretty face, which was framed by two neat twists of hair as dark as his. Her blue-gray eyes were like looking at his own. He looped an arm around her delicate shoulders. ''That old stallion was probably the smartest thing either one of us ever did, Maddie.''

He remembered the day, not long after his release from Castle Thunder, not long after Samuel's death, when he and his sister had pooled their money and bought the champion Thoroughbred at auction. For a horse who had proved himself a dismal failure at stud, North Star had still cost a small fortune. They'd brought him to Kentucky, where Madelaine intended to raise her child while she raised and trained Thoroughbreds, and where the climate apparently agreed with North Star. Indeed, it seemed absolutely to inspire him, for in the past four years the old boy had sired three fleet-footed daughters and four fast sons.

Four fast sons—two of which were identical, despite the fact that they had different dams. They'd been born mere days apart—Polaris out of Belladonna, and Southern Cross out of Lady Zephyr, the fastest damn mare Jack had ever seen.

Madelaine tilted her head to rest it on his shoulder. "I wish I could say that what we're doing now is smart. It's foolish, Jack, not to mention illegal. And the fact that it will put you near that—that woman—again makes it appallingly dangerous."

He chuckled softly. "For the baroness, perhaps."

"No. For you," she insisted. "Why can't you see that?"

"I told you. I have a little wife to keep me at arm's length from Chloe's dubious charms."

Madelaine sniffed. "At quirt's length, don't you mean?" Then she sighed. "I won't even pretend to know all that took place between you and that vixen last year, Jack. You said some things when you were ill, but I tried not to listen. To tell you the truth, I don't ever want to know. But how you can believe an inexperienced—what was it you called her?—mouse can provide any security is just beyond me. Does she know, this little mouse of yours? Does she know how ill you were? Does she have any idea of the dreadful hold that woman had on you? Still has on you?''

"Enough.'' Jack pushed off the fence and turned his back on his sister. "That's enough, Maddie,'' he added, attempting to soften his voice somewhat for the woman who had seen him through the darkest days and nights of his life, the sister who loved him in spite of everything. In spite of himself.

"I don't understand why you can't simply leave Chloe Von Drosten alone,'' Madelaine said now. "Let someone else—''

"There is no one else,'' he hissed, cutting her off. Then, seeing his sister wince, he put his hands on her shoulders. "This is for you, too, Maddie. Can't you see that? After Southern Cross wins the Carondelet Stakes, you'll be in constant demand as a breeder and trainer. The racing world will stop ignoring you just because you're a woman. You know they will. Your future, and little Sam's, will be secure.''

She shook her heard. "It isn't worth the risk.''

"Yes, it is.'' He slid his arms around her and rested his chin on the crown of her head. "You deserve this victory, sweet sister. And I—'' His voice faltered for a moment. "I need it.''

# Chapter Ten

The levee was bustling with activity at three o'clock in the afternoon. Shoeshine boys darted from one customer to another, elbowing their small competitors aside in their eagerness to make a few more cents before the crowd, gathered for the arrival of the *Artemis K. Swain,* had dissipated.

Anna edged her skirts around the wheeled cart of a fruit vendor and moved closer to the river's edge in order to scan the deck of the steamboat. When she didn't see Jack, she reached into her handbag for his telegram to confirm that this was indeed the correct boat and time. As if she hadn't read it a thousand times already, she thought, reseating her spectacles on the bridge of her nose. If words wore out from being read, the telegram would be a blank sheet of paper by now.

Scanning the deck once more, she tried to compose her face into a calm, professional mask. But she wasn't calm, and she wasn't feeling all that professional. He'd been away four days, and she had missed him. Dreadfully. Longing just to be with him, she'd even gone so far as to smooth her hands over the clothes he'd left in the wardrobe, to drape one of his ties around her neck and to revel in the scent of it and its silken drift against her skin. The mere recollection of her behavior brought a flush to her cheeks now.

Silly.

And then she saw him.

Her heart gave an odd little lurch before it went plunging to the pit of her stomach. Anna pushed her glasses down in order to peer over the rims. He seemed taller. More dashing. More darkly handsome than before. He was absolutely beautiful. And he wasn't alone. The woman by his side appeared equally beautiful.

Anna had been about to wave, but now she dropped her hand to her side. If Jack had seen her, he gave no indication. He seemed completely enthralled by his companion, bending his head to catch a whispered phrase, curving an arm around her minuscule waist and drawing her closer to his side, smiling at her the way Apollo might smile down upon a lovely mortal.

Mr. Hazard was carrying on as if Mrs. Hazard didn't exist, she thought suddenly and sourly, only to immediately remind herself that Mrs. Hazard did not, in fact, exist. It was Anna Matlin who was jealous. Not only was it unprofessional, it was petty, and it should have been beneath her. She forced the emotion down, as grimly as she could, while raising her hand in a wave of greeting.

"I don't see anyone down there who remotely resembles a mouse, Jack." Madelaine leaned over the rail as she surveyed the crowded levee. "Perhaps your wire didn't arrive."

"Damn," Jack swore, then added cavalierly, "Well, it doesn't really matter whether she's here or not." Except it did, somehow. It mattered very much.

He had left for Louisville several days before he'd planned to, leaving Anna a note so cool it might have been written in ice water. His motives had been clear to him then, and his need to leave had been crucial. He wanted the mouse, therefore he had fled.

But during his stay at Madelaine's, it hadn't made sense to Jack at all. And now, standing on the steamboat's deck, it seemed a cowardly retreat.

And suddenly, with his sister by his side, with one fast horse below decks and another to arrive this evening, with his plan falling perfectly into place, Jack wasn't afraid of being distracted anymore. Quite the opposite. He welcomed it. Damn! He longed to see Anna's serious little face, and her lush figure, swathed in mouse-colored clothes.

"You did say that Mrs. Matlin is fair-haired, didn't you, Jack?" Madelaine inquired at his shoulder.

He nodded, and nodded once again when his sister asked if Anna was small of stature.

"And you told me she wears spectacles, correct?"

"That's right," Jack answered absently, his eyes scanning the crowd.

Madelaine sighed. "Well, the only woman I see who comes anywhere near fitting that description could hardly be called a mouse."

Jack looked in the direction his sister was pointing. "No. That couldn't be—"

Just then, the sunlight glanced off one of her lenses, and she raised a hand to adjust the silly things.

"Anna."

He hardly realized he'd said her name aloud until Madelaine responded, "Lovely name. A lovely woman, too. I'm surprised you'd leave her, Jack. You didn't have to. I could have managed to get the horses here without your help."

More than lovely, Jack was thinking, in her pale green satin, with insets and sweeps of lace. Her plain hair was done up in ringlets of pure gold. For all her surliness, Madame Crillon had done her job to perfection. The mouse was a miracle.

She lifted her hand to wave, and for a moment Jack felt as if he were coming home, which made no sense because St. Louis wasn't home. It was merely the last stop on his way to perdition.

But a pleasant stop, all the same.

"Can you manage without me now?" he asked his sister.

She gave him a knowing look and squeezed his arm. "Of course. But don't get so enthralled by your mouse, dear brother, that you forget to collect Polaris later this evening, will you?"

There was a spring in his step when he came toward her down the gangway. Jack Hazard seemed younger, happier, handsomer—if that were possible. Anna was wondering if the changes were attributable to the mysterious woman who had vanished from the deck just moments ago. And she was reminding herself once more that jealousy was most definitely not a Pinkerton trait when Jack swept her up in his arms.

"Hello, mouse," he whispered against her ear. "I missed you."

"Oh! Did you? I missed you, too. Terribly." The words flew out of her mouth before she realized it. "Well, what I mean is—"

"Shh..." Jack pressed a finger against her lips. "Don't take it back," he murmured as he lowered her to the paving stones. "Now, let me take a look at you. I hardly recognized you, Anna."

When he took her hands and held them away from her body to permit his warm gaze to rove over every inch of her, Anna hardly recognized the succession of emotions that leapfrogged through her mind and body. Pleasure. Pride. Delight. And something close enough to wild abandon that it shocked her to the tips of her shoes. A Pinkerton agent wasn't supposed to abandon herself to a wild current of desire. She was supposed to be calm and in control. Anna struggled to maintain what little control she still possessed.

And she was still trying hard to keep her composure in the elevator as they rose to their floor. Jack had missed her! To her knowledge, she'd never been missed before. It made her feel quite special. Beautiful, even. The butterflies congregating in her stomach fluttered wildly when the elevator came to a halt.

"Home sweet home," he murmured when they entered the suite, astonished to realize that he meant it.

"We probably ought to hurry," Anna said as she tossed her handbag onto the bed, then crooked her arms behind her back to begin unfastening her dress.

What the devil? Jack had been uncomfortably aware of his own desirous condition ever since he'd seen Anna on the levee. And she'd seemed uncommonly glad to have him back. But surely not so glad she was ready to wrench off her clothes the second they were alone.

"What the devil are you doing?" His voice was closer to a croak than he would have liked. And closer to a sixteen-year-old boy's than that of a thirty-six-year-old man who had decided long ago that life in general—and women in particular—held no more surprises for him.

"I'm trying," she uttered through clenched teeth, "to undo these infernally small buttons."

"I can see that for myself. I suppose I meant to ask why." Had he ever, he wondered dismally, asked a woman why she was undressing? And had his heart ever held so absolutely still at the prospect?

"Why?" She laughed, as if it were a silly question. Then her gaze met his—his own gaze, which was probably smoldering, as far as Jack could tell—and he actually saw Anna's breath catch in her throat, just before her cheeks turned to flame. "Oh, you didn't think... I mean, you couldn't have... Oh, dear."

His heart gave an absurd and disappointed little lurch, then began beating properly again. "No, I didn't think that for a moment, mouse," he lied. "But I haven't a clue as to the true reason."

"The gala, Jack." She dismissed her buttons with a sigh and let her hands fall helplessly to her sides. "Oh, but of course you couldn't know. The invitation only arrived this morning."

"A gala? This evening? I had, er... other plans."

The look of almost childish disappointment that crumpled her pretty face astonished him, and perplexed him, as well. After their last foray into St. Louis society, he would have assumed she'd be relieved, even overjoyed, to have an excuse to avoid such affairs. Her teeth were worrying the very devil out of her lush lower lip now.

"I'm disappointed," she said softly, as if she needed to explain the emotion etched so vividly on her countenance.

Jack did some quick calculations. He didn't have to meet the next steamboat from Louisville—the one that would be transporting Polaris—until close to midnight. Depending on where this gala was being held, there ought to be plenty of time. And just now he felt a ridiculous urge to do anything, including moving heaven and earth, to make this woman smile.

He moved closer to her, then turned her by the shoulders and began to make short work of her buttons. "Never let it be said that Jack Hazard disappointed a lovely lady. Now, tell me about this party, while we get you out of one dress and into another."

Her little cry of happiness was all the reward he needed, but he had to admit that serving as her dresser offered more than a few additional ones.

The party, given by the newly formed Carondelet Racing Club, was held at the Sedgewick Hotel. Hundreds of guests dined in the gilded indoor dining room, and hundreds more, Jack and Anna among them, ate less formally in the hotel's torchlit English garden.

It hadn't been Anna's choice. Jack had suggested it, no doubt believing she'd be more at ease, or less liable to embarrass him. She'd been looking forward to showing off her newly acquired table manners, but she consoled herself with the thought that at least she'd be able to demonstrate her skill on the dance floor. Her conversational skills, on the other hand, were still deficient. Basically, she hung on Jack's arm and smiled pleasantly while everyone, men and women both, talked about horses.

"You're such a lovely couple," the top-heavy Mrs. John Stevens Bissell was saying to them now. "I do hope, when your honeymoon is over, you'll consider remaining in St. Louis."

"We're already considering it, aren't we, darling?" Jack pulled Anna a little closer against his side.

He was such a charming and consummate liar that she often found herself believing him herself. "It is a lovely city," she agreed, quite truthfully.

Mrs. Bissell smiled and clapped her heavily ringed hands. "That's marvelous. I even know a house that would be perfect for you. My nephew built it for his wife, but the poor dear expired before they could move in. He's rather anxious to part with it. Won't live there himself. Says it makes him too sad. You really must take a look at it."

"We'd love to," Jack said, then added, to Anna's astonishment. "Would tomorrow be convenient?"

Mrs. Bissell looked a bit astonished herself. "Well...well, yes," she stammered. "I should think so. Tomorrow would probably be fine. I'll speak with my nephew this evening. He's here somewhere."

After the woman wandered off in search of her nephew, Anna whispered, "That was unkind, Jack. The poor man will be so disappointed when we don't show up to view his house."

"But we will show up."

"Why?"

He hugged her more closely to his side. "It's what newlyweds do, Anna. Search for the perfect nest. It might be an amusing way to spend an afternoon. And, if nothing else, it will further convince people of our story."

"I see," she murmured. "It just strikes me as more deceitful than anything we've done so far."

He laughed. "Well, it probably is." He tipped her chin up. "We're in the business of deception, or have you forgotten, mouse?"

Just then, in the blue-gray light of his eyes and the rare warmth of his smile, Anna did forget. She found herself lifting on tiptoe, aching for his kiss. And, wonder of wonders, he was going to kiss her. Anna could see the flicker of desire in his eyes as he began to lower his head.

"There you are, Hazard. I've been looking all over for you."

Whatever spell had gotten hold of them was immediately and thoroughly dispelled by the sound of Henry Gresham's booming voice and the thud when one of his hands clapped Jack's shoulder.

"What's this I hear about you paying a staggering late fee to enter a horse in the stakes?"

Jack straightened. "I'm considering it." He plucked his watch from his vest pocket. "The animal's due to arrive tonight, as a matter of fact. Why don't you accompany me to the levee and get a good first look, Henry? You might even want to put some money on Polaris."

"Against Chloe's Gold?" Gresham snorted. "Surely you jest. Why, your horse would have to be a saddled lightning bolt to beat the baroness's mount. I think you must be suffering from honeymoon fever, man. What do you think, Mrs. Hazard?"

Anna didn't know what to think. The woman in her was still reacting to a kiss that hadn't taken place, while the Pinkerton portion of her brain was wondering just what "staggering" meant when it came to a fee, and whether or not it was refundable, and why in blue blazes Jack hadn't mentioned this particular part of his plan to her.

"We need to talk," she said stiffly, ignoring Gresham and staring what she hoped were daggers—double-edged and lethal—at Jack.

"Oh. Sorry." The big man cleared his throat and took a step back, as if to get out of range. "Hope I haven't let the old cat out of the bag. Perhaps I'll pass on that levee business this evening, Hazard. Evening, madam."

Anna didn't know whether she was angry or hurt. Both, no doubt. She was angry that Jack continued to exclude her from the details of their assignment.

She was hurt that he apparently felt he couldn't confide in her. It was difficult, but she forced a note of professional Pinkerton calm into her voice.

"As your partner, Jack, I demand to know what's going on. Preferably in advance." And stop using that Olympian smile on me, she added inwardly. I'm thoroughly immune.

He was smiling at his watch now, and Anna was faintly surprised the timepiece didn't melt in the palm of his hand. After snapping the watch closed, he took her arm.

"It's time to go, Anna. I'll dazzle you with all those particulars you crave on the way to the levee."

Leave? "Oh, but..."

Although she'd hardly been aware of it before, the orchestra in the ballroom seemed to increase its volume, and the strains of a waltz filled the garden air. Anna could feel her disappointment tugging the edges of her mouth down, when she ought to be smiling, because her partner had just promised to apprise her of his plan.

"The music is so lovely," she said wistfully. "Perhaps we could have just one waltz?"

Agreeing to stay for a single dance had been his first mistake. And he'd agreed to her wistful plea in spite of his better judgment, believing that they'd once again encounter disaster in three-quarter time and the mouse would have to swoon once more to save herself. As a consequence, he'd taken her in his arms and held her tightly against him, in the hope that he'd be able to guide her properly through at least a few steps. Taking Anna's warm body into his arms and holding her so close had surely been his second mistake, for his body had responded immediately and electrically. In all his jaded years, Jack couldn't remember when or if a mere dance had ever undone him so.

Or a mere glance. As they began to move in concert with the music, Anna had gazed up over the rims of her spectacles with a kind of delicious expectation in her eyes. He'd held her tighter then, hoping to absorb her awkwardness. But there hadn't been any. She'd moved with him, against him, *in* him, as if they'd been partners for years.

Bloody hell. He wasn't sure whether he'd exclaimed it out loud or not, but he felt her delicate rib cage shift as she took in a gulp of air.

Her worried face lifted to his. "Is it... Am I waltzing properly?" she asked. "It was a surprise, Jack. To please you. Have I succeeded?"

They were gliding around the dance floor now— effortlessly, as far as Jack could tell. His brain, at least, had absolutely nothing to do with his feet, and he had no control over the smile he could feel tugging the corners of his mouth upward.

"In surprising me or pleasing me?" he asked.

"Either one."

"Both." He was beginning to think she was about the most surprising woman he'd ever encountered. "I'd say you've succeeded in both. Admirably."

She giggled. "Oh, good."

Jack drew his head back and narrowed his eyes. "How the devil did you become a prima ballerina virtually overnight?"

Her lashes fluttered up and, instead of answering, she smiled in a distinctly unmouselike manner. Mysterious and knowing and seductive all at once. Ancient. Feminine. Feline. Jack could feel his heart pick up speed, and his blood burn accordingly. He had a vague notion who had tutored her in his absence—Broome—and he felt capable of killing the man just then, for nothing more than having cast a glance Anna's way.

He wanted her that moment with a fierceness he had never felt before. The intensity wasn't the astounding part, but rather the sheer, overwhelming, and nearly painful sweetness of it. It was like drowning in warm honey. For a second he thought he could forget everything—everyone—but the woman in his arms. For a stunning heartbeat, she made him feel whole and good and—yes, even innocent. Dear God, he was falling in love with her. Headlong, heedless, horribly.

His feet came to a leaden halt, and he let her go. "We need to leave."

"But..."

"Now." He swore roughly. "We've already wasted too much bloody time with this silliness while there's business to get done."

Anna waited in the carriage while Jack attended to the unloading of the horse. She watched him now, giving instructions to the groom who had apparently accompanied the animal from Kentucky and would tend him in St. Louis. Since Jack had imposed a dark wall of silence between them as they rode from the hotel to the levee, Anna still hadn't the least idea what was going on.

Nor did she know, when she leaned out of the carriage, the better to attend their conversation, who the "she" was to whom they kept referring. It wasn't the baroness, Anna was sure. Jack had a tendency to hiss when he spoke her name, and he wasn't hissing now. And the "she" in question wasn't the horse. Not that Anna knew much about the beasts, but she knew enough about anatomy to discern that Polaris was most definitely not a mare. The stallion was a beautiful animal, she thought. Sleekly muscled and shimmering in the moonlight. Not so very different from the man who stood beside him.

The man who had summarily chastised her not so long ago for her unprofessional behavior. Anna leaned back against the buggy's tufted leather seat and lifted a hand to chew thoughtfully on a nail. Jack had been right, of course, to reprimand her. Still, there had been that moment just before his display of temper, when she sensed a bond between them that had nothing to do with the fact that she'd been waltzing in his arms.

Silly, she told herself. Why she had ever believed that her ability to waltz would bring the legendary Mad Jack Hazard to his knees was beyond her now. And that she allowed herself to be jealous of the mysterious "she" in his current whispered conversation with the young groom was simply more of the same silliness. She would apologize to Jack for her unseemly and unprofessional behavior, and she vowed that, from this evening on, she wouldn't think of him in any way other than her partner. Her business partner.

It wasn't until they were back in their suite at the hotel that he seemed willing to listen to her at all. Then it was Jack who apologized first.

"I was rude, Anna, on the dance floor. I'm sorry. It won't happen again."

"It was my fault. You were perfectly correct in reminding me of the business at hand." As she spoke, Anna was sitting on the edge of the bed, nudging off the heel of one slipper with the toe of the other. Her feet hurt, despite the fact that she'd barely had a chance to dance.

She massaged her instep absently as she said, "You promised to tell me the details of your plan, Jack. I believe it's time I knew more of the particulars, don't you?"

He settled into his customary chair—tableside, bottleside. Anna saw his hand move toward it, and then draw back in a fist, which he let fall on his leg.

When he sighed, she couldn't tell if it was out of frustration with her or over the whiskey.

"The plan," he said then, "is very simple. You saw Polaris. He's going to win the Carondelet Stakes."

"And?"

"And nothing."

Anna stopped rubbing her foot. "That's it?"

"That's it. Polaris wins. Chloe's Gold loses. End of race. End of story."

"And my part in it is what?" She frowned. "You know I haven't a clue about horse racing."

"You've done your part already. By posing as my lumber-heiress wife, you've convinced everyone that Jack Hazard can afford to own and train Polaris."

"That's it?" she said again.

He smiled at her now, with more warmth than she had witnessed in the past hour or so. When he spoke, his voice was warmed by amusement. "What did you expect, little mouse? Did you have visions of badges flashing and guns blazing? Of hot pursuits down dark and dangerous alleys?"

Perhaps she had. Anna felt her face flaming with embarrassment and her heart deflating. "Then I'm finished? I've done my part?" She swallowed the absurd need to wail, "Don't send me away! Oh, please!"

"You've done your part quite well, but you're not finished." He laughed softly. "It wouldn't do much for my reputation if my bride left me in the middle of our honeymoon, would it?"

Anna nodded her head in agreement and stifled a whoop of glee, while inside she was breathing a great sigh of relief, the total effect of which seemed to translate into something resembling a yawn, for Jack commented that she looked tired and probably ought to get some sleep.

He patted his knee then. "Come over here, mouse, and I'll make short work of that dazzling array of buttons down your back." When she hesitated, he murmured, "Come on. I'm harmless. Surely you know that by now."

She knew nothing of the kind, Anna thought as she perched tentatively on his knee and felt the warmth of his hands as they worked her buttons with a finesse that made her wonder just how many buttons this man had dispatched in his long career as a spy and, yes, as an accomplished rake, too.

When he was done, however, instead of a rakish caress, he jounced her playfully on his knee. "Off to bed with you now, little mouse."

She stood, and before she even realized she was doing it, Anna was bending to place a soft kiss on the top of his head. He didn't say a word, though, and she couldn't be certain he had even felt it, for he merely sat there, already staring at the bottle that would occupy his vision and most probably his every thought until he sagged into sleep.

Later, long after she had trimmed the lamp and snuggled beneath the covers, Anna whispered, "God bless you and help you through the night, Jack Hazard." She didn't know whether Jack heard her, but she decided it didn't make any difference. Her prayer hadn't really been meant for his ears, anyway.

## Chapter Eleven

The next morning, Jack slipped into a fresh shirt and out of the suite before dawn. He rode west, looking over his shoulder to make sure he wasn't being followed, trying to keep his sleep-deprived senses trained on what he had to do, banishing every thought of Anna that managed to work its way into his brain, refusing to listen to the whispered prayer that kept echoing through his head. Let her say her useless prayers. For all the good they'd do.

The sun was well up, warming his back, when he reached the small farm he'd rented for Madelaine and her four-year-old son. The two-story frame house needed painting, he noticed now as he approached. The shutters, too. A pair of those were missing from an upstairs window, giving the place a hopelessly cockeyed look. The impression of squalor was hardly alleviated by the half-dozen scrawny pullets that were pecking around the front porch.

It was temporary, he reminded himself, and utterly necessary. When his plan succeeded, he'd see

that his sister had a decent farm and an income be-
fitting the daughter of an earl.

He had hardly dismounted before Madelaine was
rushing out of the front door to greet him. Chickens
squawked and fluttered in the wake of her skirts.

She raced into his arms, hugging him tight. "I'm
so glad you're here, Jack. I always worry so."

"You worry too much," he murmured. "Where's
little Samuel? Still asleep?"

Madelaine laughed. "Your nephew spent hours in
pursuit of these chickens yesterday after we arrived.
The poor things were actually fat yesterday."

Still holding her close, Jack gazed around the
woebegone weed patch that served as a front yard.
"This place is a shambles, love," he whispered. "I'm
sorry. You deserve better."

"Nonsense." His sister shrugged out of his embrace and gestured toward the rear of the house.
"Look there. All that matters are those twenty acres
of lovely green meadow for Southern Cross to consume."

He nodded glumly.

"There's nothing wrong, is there, Jack? Did Polaris arrive without mishap?"

"Fine. Everything went fine."

"Not fine enough for you to sleep, though."
Madelaine's worried gaze swept over his face. "You
can't continue this way, Jack. You'll—"

"I'll sleep next month," he said, cutting her off,
as he linked his arm through hers and began walk-

ing in the direction of the barn and telling her about Polaris's arrival and subsequent stabling near the racecourse.

"Give him a day or two to adjust to his new surroundings before you start his workouts," Madelaine advised. "He's likely to be just as touchy as his half brother."

As they stepped into the dim interior of the muggy barn, Southern Cross's big, sleek head bobbed up over the stall door. He gave a snort, shook his head imperiously, and then proceeded to ignore his visitors. At the sight of the magnificent stallion, Jack found that his breath had hitched in his chest.

"He's glorious, isn't he?" Madelaine murmured, as if reading her brother's thoughts. "Not that Polaris isn't, mind you. But even though there's no telling the two of them apart, there's a fire in those eyes that Polaris doesn't have. He'll be ready for the race. He'll win for you, Jack."

"He has to, Maddie."

She tightened her arm on his and smiled sunnily. His own smile, Jack thought. The one he used to cajole and deceive and achieve his own devious ends. But on Madelaine that smile was beautiful—because it was genuine.

"Come on," she said, tugging him toward the door. "You've ridden a long way, and I won't allow you to leave until you've eaten some breakfast with Samuel and me. And while you're eating," she added with a laugh, "you can tell me all about that lovely creature you've so erroneously nicknamed the mouse.''

Jack returned his borrowed mare to the stable, a discreet quarter mile from the hotel, then walked the rest of the way under a warm noon sun, amazed that he wasn't thinking about a drink to wash the dust out of his throat, but only about a bath and a change of clothes. Those small pleasures. And Anna. Her name drifted through his head like music. As soon as he entered the hotel lobby, however, a lace-gloved hand with an iron grip snagged his sleeve.

"There you are, Mr. Hazard. We had just about given up hope."

He found himself blinking stupidly into a determined, matronly face, not comprehending either who the devil she was or what in blazes she wanted from him. A kind of panic raced through him, coupled with a wild urge to shove the woman out of his way as he made straight for the bar. He'd been wrong to think that sobering up would be beneficial, for his brain felt dull now, and unresponsive. He needed a drink to sharpen his senses. Now.

Seeing Jack's bewilderment—it was hardly surprising, since the man hadn't slept more than a minute the night before, and then had disappeared before the sun was up—Anna stepped between him and Mrs. Bissell, politely but firmly loosening the woman's hand from his arm and replacing it with her own. She could feel the tension there, tightening every muscle, snapping through his every nerve.

"Mrs. Bissell has arranged for us to inspect her nephew's home, Jack," she said calmly. "I told her I thought you had more important engagements this afternoon and that I'd be happy to accompany her myself."

A fine sheen of perspiration had broken out on his forehead. He blinked at Anna now. "I need . . ."

"Sleep, darling," she finished for him. "And that's precisely what you're going to have. Mrs. Bissell, I'm afraid we'll have to postpone viewing the house for a day or so, until my husband's refreshed. I hope you don't mind terribly."

Mrs. Bissell lifted her numerous chins and sucked in a good deal of breath. "I must say I do mind, my dear. It's been arranged. My nephew is waiting. Of course, if you're no longer interested—"

"We're interested." Jack's adamant voice cut through her windy indignation. He looped an arm around Anna's waist and brought her close against his side. "Aren't we, love?"

A quick glance at his face was enough for Anna to know that her partner was in control again. That mystified expression had given way to one of his glorious smiles. As she felt him relax, she dared a small smile of her own.

"Whatever you say, dearest."

* * *

Grand Avenue, Anna decided, had been aptly named. The wide boulevard was lined with young oak trees and a succession of fine new homes, and with scores more under construction. As they rode along in her barouche, Mrs. Bissell seemed to take inordinate pleasure in pointing out just which fine family resided in which fine home.

"The Spencers are building there." She waved her hand toward a massive stack of lumber, and enough limestone blocks to construct a fort. "You'll find that most of the racing crowd lives in the vicinity."

Anna nodded politely, made what she hoped were the proper murmurs of interest, craned her neck in every direction, and all the while worried about Jack.

Whatever had come over him earlier in the lobby of the hotel, whatever had made him look frightened and lost, was decidedly absent now as he chatted affably with their hostess and tour guide, gifting her again and again with smiles that ran the gamut from the merely amused to the absolutely enchanted.

And when they arrived at their destination—a red sandstone edifice with arches and turrets and a porte cochere—Mrs. Bissell handed Anna over to her nephew while she personally conducted Jack through room after empty room.

The nephew, Mr. Lawrence Bissell, still wore a black mourning band on his sleeve, and he gave Anna the impression that he'd rather be anywhere else in the world than in the house he had had built for his late wife.

"I'm sorry for your loss," she told him, after which he merely sighed wetly and announced that he would wait outside, if she didn't mind, and that she and her husband should feel free to take all the time they liked in looking around.

Anna wandered around the empty parlor and its adjacent bare-shelved library, wondering if she'd ever be comfortable with deception, the way Jack seemed to be. Probably not, she decided as she peered out a window to see poor Mr. Bissell standing on the lawn, his head bowed and his hands clasped behind his back, patiently waiting for Mr. and Mrs. Hazard to reach a decision about his home.

The decision, of course, would be no, and poor Mr. Bissell would have to stand out in his yard again, in hopes that another couple would choose to live in the house he had meant for his wife.

The Pinkerton business—this business of being a spy, of assuming a name and a role in pursuit of crime—left a lot to be desired, she decided. Jack had been doing this so long it was a wonder he even remembered who he really was. And then it suddenly occurred to her that that might be part of his problem, that he was forced so often and for so long to play parts that he might not be able to simply live as himself anymore. Assuming there was still a self beneath all that handsome and deceptive exterior.

Poor Jack. She wondered if inside he was as empty as poor Mr. Bissell's house. Perhaps that was one of the appeals of whiskey. Perhaps it filled that hollow space, that empty cup inside.

"Lawrence? Where are you, dear?" Mrs. Bissell's question reverberated off the paneled walls and the bare oak floors.

"He's waiting outside," Anna told her when the woman turned the corner into the parlor.

"Ah. Well, perhaps I should join him, and let you and your husband have the house to yourselves. Take your time, my dear."

For such a large woman, Mrs. Bissell moved fast, and she was nearly out the door before Anna could reply that it wasn't necessary. This was a foolish business, this house-hunting, no matter its purpose. Anna gave a little shrug and then climbed the oak staircase, with every intention of finding Jack and putting an end to this charade.

She found him in a back bedroom—a small one meant, no doubt, to be a nursery. It wouldn't be now, at least not for Lawrence Bissell's children. Anna sighed softly as she looked at Jack, who was sitting on a cushionless window seat with his head tilted back against the frame and his eyes closed.

"It's a lovely house," she said as she crossed the room to look out at the carriage house in the rear. "But sad, somehow. And empty."

"Shall we buy it, love?" Jack spoke without opening his eyes. He reached out to catch Anna's hand, as if he knew exactly where it would be.

His question made her laugh in sudden surprise. It was almost as if he were speaking to someone else. As if he had reached for another woman's hand. Then she frowned and gave his hand a tug. "Let's go, Jack. You're much better at this game than I am."

A little smile curved his lips. It was not, Anna thought, one of his characteristic expressions, put on like a costume to help him play a part. This smile was real, and quite wistful.

It was a game—a bloody awful game—and Jack had been thinking exactly that when the mouse tiptoed into the room. He'd also been thinking that for once he wished it was real—that he and Anna were what they claimed to be, a newly married couple seeking a house, a pair of turtledoves in search of a sweet nest.

When she tugged at his hand, instead of getting up, he pulled her onto his lap.

"Hush," he said when she let out a little cry of protest. "It is a game, so why not enjoy it? Play it with me, little mouse. Let's pretend."

"Pretend?" She echoed the word as if she had never heard it before, as if its meaning were incomprehensible. Her soft body was as rigid as a rifle in his arms. Primed not to shoot, but to run.

"Pretend, Anna," he crooned, "the way you did when you were a child."

He tightened his arms around her, intensely aware of his need to hold her, suddenly cognizant of a fierce urge to possess her, if only for a moment, if only through fantasy.

"What did you pretend when you were a little girl?" he whispered.

"I . . . I never did."

That wasn't a surprise. She was real, after all. Solid, for all her softness. Inherently serious and sober. Her instinctive honesty had probably come early, preventing play.

He shifted beneath her, forcing her a bit more off balance. "Lean your head back against my shoulder."

She did, but she felt like a watch spring working against itself.

"Close your eyes," he commanded softly.

A nervous sigh whispered from her lips. "Jack, we . . ."

"Close your eyes."

She did, relaxing another notch. His arms slipped farther around her, enfolding her now.

"Imagine this is our house," he said, pressing his cheek to the warmth of her hair.

"I can't!" she wailed.

"Yes, you can. What color is the carpet in the parlor?"

"There is no carpet."

"But if there were . . ."

Her hands fluttered in frustration on her lap. Funny, he thought. He could almost hear the cogs working inside her head as reality rubbed against fantasy. Her uncommon common sense was grasping at make-believe and discovering only wisps of smoke, ropes of water. Try, love, he wanted to say. Make it real. Live here with me. Just for now.

"What color is the carpet in the parlor, Anna?"

She sighed mightily. "Oh. Blue, I suppose."

"Good." He smiled. "What shade?"

She gave a little shrug.

"Azure? Robin's-egg? Or a royal blue, to match the crest on our best set of Haviland?"

Anna laughed now at the notion that she'd ever possess a set of expensive Haviland china, let alone one with a royal-blue crest. "Jack, this is silly." She made an effort to sit up, but her movements merely allowed his arms to move more tightly around her.

"All right, then," he said with mock solemnity. "Silly blue it shall be. That will go rather well with the giddy green of the drapes, don't you think?"

"Oh, definitely." It was silly, most definitely, and yet Anna was beginning to feel a giddiness that had nothing to do with the color of imaginary drapes. Jack's solid chest felt so good against her back, and his warm breath was tickling her ear.

"And the ridiculous red of the leather sofa in the library, too. What color shall we paint the walls in the kitchen?"

"Ludicrous lemon?" Anna laughed at her own suggestion, and the sound of that laughter amazed her. She had never considered herself an unhappy person, despite the fact that she rarely, if ever, laughed. A smile was normally as far as she went in expressing pleasure. But Jack made her laugh. And it felt good. Almost as good as the warmth of his arms surrounding her. Not nearly as good as the touch of his hand, which had somehow shaped itself to her breast and was now caressing her, gently, idly.

Lost in his daydreams, he probably wasn't even aware he was doing it. Well, perhaps not completely unaware, for not all of the man was totally languid and daydreamy. Not the part of him that was pressing hard against her lower back.

Anna was so aware of her own body's reaction to his touch that she didn't hear anyone coming up the stairs until a polite cough sounded from the door. If Jack hadn't sat her up briskly then and pulled her to her feet, she doubted she'd have been able to move.

"Well, Mr. Hazard," Lawrence Bissell said. "Have you reached a decision?"

"We have," Jack answered, all business now as he gave his cuffs a quick yank and straightened his cravat. "Unfortunately, Bissell, my wife doesn't care for the color of the carpet in the parlor. Sorry. We've decided to continue our search for the perfect nest."

Anna looked over the rims of her glasses in time to see one of those Mad Jack grins. He crooked his arm and drew hers through it, murmuring, "Come along, darling."

The downcast Mr. Bissell stepped aside to let them pass, then followed them down the stairs. Before they all exited the house, Anna was certain she saw the poor widower cast a rueful glance toward the parlor and mutter, in some confusion, "There is no carpet. Surely he must have meant to say floor."

"That was cruel, Jack," Anna said after Mrs. Bissell's barouche had dropped them off in front of the hotel. The woman had been out of sorts—and rightly so—at first, but it had taken Jack a mere four blocks to win her back.

They were standing on the sidewalk now, Anna's wide skirts and Jack's broad shoulders forming an obstacle for passersby.

"Terribly cruel," Anna said again. "You're toying with people's hopes and dreams." Not to mention her own, she thought.

"Yes, I am," he replied with utter calm. "It's my job."

"Then it's a shameful occupation." Anna poked her spectacles farther up the bridge of her nose.

He didn't say a word. He merely stood there, gazing solemnly down at her, as if in complete agreement. The shadows beneath his eyes seemed to deepen. The edges of his mouth dragged down. He looked like a man who never had and never would know how to smile.

"Nevertheless, little mouse," he said softly, "it's all I know to do to survive." He took a step away from her then, and his features hardened. "I'll be back late. Don't wait for me to dine. Or to retire."

He was striding down the sidewalk, away from her, before Anna could protest. She longed to call after him that perhaps it was he who needed to retire. And this time she didn't necessarily mean sleep.

## Chapter Twelve

During the next few days, Anna's concerns increased, for the only thing predictable about Jack's behavior was its unpredictability. He was warm and charming in public, only to become cool and remote the minute they were alone. Professionally, she couldn't reach him, all her questions receiving vague answers at best. Worse, she didn't seem to be able to touch him personally. The dratted chair remained his bed, and the demon bottle his bedmate. Often, without a word, he left in the middle of the night.

The shadows under his eyes deepened. His smiles, still beautiful, were brief and appeared merely pasted on his face. Each day, when he wasn't disappearing at odd hours, he seemed to be a bit more on edge, a little less in control—like a rockslide about to happen. He needed help.

*She* needed help! And there was only one place Anna knew to seek it—the local Pinkerton agency, where Frederick Broome appeared delighted to see her as he took her hand and led her into his private office.

The company symbol—an eye that never sleeps—gazed calmly down at her from the wall, momentarily reassuring her that, yes, everything would be all right. This wasn't emotional chaos she was involved in; it was business.

A very busy business, judging from the amount of paperwork that littered Freddy's desk.

"I've wanted to see you again, Anna," he told her as he took a seat. "But I've been buried under all these reports." He stared at them glumly. "A necessary evil, I suppose."

For some, she was thinking. She hadn't seen Jack make a single notation or record a single expense. And his lax attitude seemed to be rubbing off on her, because only this morning she'd almost forgotten to make a note of the additional and thoroughly outrageous cost of the imported Canary Island oranges at breakfast.

Freddy was gazing across his desk now, his eyes a warm hazel until Anna cleared her throat and announced, as professionally as she could manage, "I'm worried about Jack."

His eyes frosted immediately as he leaned back in his chair and steepled his fingers. "Aren't we all?" he said with a smirk. "What's Mad Jack up to now?"

"That's the problem, actually. I'm not quite sure. He, well…he…" Anna had intended to be open and explicit, but suddenly she didn't want to disclose any of the more painful, personal particulars about Jack. Although they were what was distressing her the most, somehow she didn't feel comfortable sharing those problems with anyone, especially someone who seemed to hold Jack in such low esteem.

"He keeps disappearing," she finally said. "For hours. When I ask him where he's been, he merely says out. It's all very mysterious." She sighed, feeling foolish now, and thinking that perhaps it wasn't so mysterious after all. Jack's disappearing act had begun immediately after she called him cruel and his profession a shameful one. The man didn't have the skin of a rhinoceros, after all. Naturally, he didn't want to spend more time than necessity required with a woman who had insulted him. What she ought to be doing, instead of appealing to Freddy, was apologizing to Jack.

Her hands had been fidgeting with the strings of her reticule, but now Anna clutched it tight and stood up. "This is silly. I'm sorry I bothered you, Freddy. I'll handle the problem—whatever it is—myself."

"Obviously it's a woman."

Anna had turned to leave, but she turned back now to stare blankly at the agent behind the desk. "I beg your pardon?"

"Is he boozing again?"

"No." She gave an indignant sniff and made a quick jab at the bridge of her spectacles. "Certainly not."

Freddy arched a wheat-colored brow and leaned forward on his elbows. "Are you sure?"

"Of course I'm sure."

"Opium?" That pale brow climbed higher. "Word is he added that to his repertoire in the recent past."

"Absolutely not," Anna snapped.

"Then it's a woman." His tone was decisive, and cool with disapproval. "Probably has a mistress stashed away somewhere. Seems to me that's Hazard's style. What I can't understand is why Mr. Pinkerton ever paired him with you. Or, for that matter, Anna, why you'd ever consent to be partnered with such a reprobate."

Anna stood there, barely comprehending Freddy's words. Her brain seemed to have stalled permanently on his earlier remark. *A mistress stashed away somewhere. Hazard's style.* It *was* his style. She knew that only too well, from years of office gossip. Yet she felt stunned and painfully wounded, rather like a wife upon first hearing news of her husband's philandering.

"A sweet and serious young woman like you shouldn't have to be subjected to such vices, even if you are a Pinkerton," he droned on. "I, for one, will be happy when Hazard and his likes are drummed out of the organization. Or when they finally drink and dope and—well, er, carouse themselves into early and well-deserved graves.''

Freddy seemed to blur before her, and his complaints were only a faint buzzing in her ears. You're not Jack's wife, Anna was telling herself. You have no legitimate reason to feel wounded. No cause to be jealous. None.

Realizing Freddy had fallen silent, Anna blinked him into focus. He sat there with his arms clamped over his chest and a sour slant to his mouth. All she could think of was Jack's beautiful grin. Her heart squeezed tight.

So did her throat. ''I believe you've answered all my questions,'' she managed to say. ''I won't take up any more of your time.''

He rose, smiling warmly once more. ''I hope you know how glad I am that you came, Anna. I'd see you back to your hotel, but—'' he gestured toward the littered desktop ''—I'm swamped with paperwork just now.''

''Yes, I understand.'' Her glance fell to the piles of paper now, and Anna recognized the forms—the expense tallies, the investigators' initial report forms, the suggestion memos that Mr. Pinkerton encouraged and that she'd surely be filing next month in Chicago, when she resumed her regular job and her life resumed its former shape and pace. Its former quiet and invisibility.

Without Jack. Dear God. She felt the blood draining from her face, and the next thing she knew,

Freddy had rushed from behind his desk to hover over her.

He urged her to sit, but all Anna wanted to do was leave. At the door, he kept his hand firmly cupped to her elbow.

"Are you sure you're all right?" he asked.

No. She wasn't sure at all. All she was sure of was that she needed to get away before tears exploded from her eyes. "I'm quite all right. Goodbye, Freddy."

She pulled away, and was making a dash down the hallway when he called out.

"About Hazard. If his carryings-on are interfering with his performance, you can always get the specifics and file a report with the home office. I'd be happy to do it for you, only I've got all this confounded paperwork."

Anna came to a halt at the top of the stairs. "The specifics? What—what do you mean? How?"

"You're a detective, aren't you Anna?" Freddy winked. "Detect. Follow him."

Jack turned a bend in the road and pressed a bit more speed out of his rented horse. A minute later, he was easing back on the reins. That was how it had been all the way from the city as he made his way to Madelaine's farm, with Anna Matlin following him like some daft bird dog. He'd ride faster, having decided to ditch her, but then he'd worry and pull back. He'd spur his horse, needing to get away from the woman who was playing havoc with his brain and his body and his heart. He'd swear and slow down to a walk, all the while hearing her buggy wheels squeal and her flea-bitten gelding snort in protest at the constant changes in speed.

Did she think he didn't know? Did she believe a mere veil would suffice as a disguise? Did she imagine he hadn't memorised every curve of her body, and each tilt of her chin as she made adjustments for her silly spectacles? Did she think he couldn't have distinguished her from every other woman in the world, even if he was blindfolded?

Bloody hell. He'd been trying to escape her for days, both mentally and physically, ever since the afternoon he'd found himself wanting to play house. What a childish, addlebrained, lovestruck thing to do. He'd even been on the verge, the very brink, of begging her to run away with him...anywhere. It hadn't mattered. Just away. Somewhere. Somewhere safe.

He might have, too, if she hadn't brought him back to his senses by reminding him that he was a cruel man in a shameful occupation. Her words had cut him like a knife at the same time they punctured his boyishly romantic notion that loving her could salvage whatever goodness might be left in him.

There was none. Or, if there was, he was dredging up the last of that goodness and bestowing it on his family—on Madelaine and Samuel—in the hope that they would remember him with a little warmth after he abandoned them forever.

He raised his eyes to the heavens, intending to mutter a curse, but instead he smiled as he noticed the storm clouds boiling up in the west. He'd make it to Madelaine's with only moments to spare, he calculated, before the weather broke. The mouse, in her dramatic veil and her low-rent buggy, might not be so lucky. Teaching her she wasn't ready to perform a solo as a Pinkerton spy, he decided, might be the best gift he could give her.

He stabled his horse, and he was still grinning when Madelaine met him at the door. She hugged him, then tipped her head back and narrowed her gaze. Too polite, or perhaps too frightened, to ask flat out if he'd been drinking, she merely said, "You're looking awfully bright in the eye, Jack."

"Bright-eyed and sober as young Samuel here," he said as he scooped his nephew up into his arms, then carried him to a chair, where he bounced him on his knee. The child wasn't altogether comfortable with his uncle, having seen him at his worst last winter. Jack was determined to remedy that, too, and have the boy remember him fondly, rather than fearfully.

"This is the way the lady rides...." he began, jouncing the boy on his knee.

Still at the door, Madelaine said, "There's someone out there, Jack. I can just make out a horse and buggy through the trees."

"Trotty, trot, trot, trot, trot..." he continued as Samuel began to chuckle with delight and anticipation. "That would be Mrs. Matlin," he told his sister offhandedly, "out practicing her Pinkerton skills."

Then he took up the game with Samuel once more. "And this is the way the gentleman rides...."

"Jack, it's beginning to rain," Madelaine called.

"Is it?" He bounced his nephew higher on his knees. "Canter, canter, canter...."

"She'll get soaked."

"Undoubtedly," Jack answered with a sigh. Then he grinned at Samuel. "Ready?"

The child nodded enthusiastically and held on tighter, his tiny knuckles white on Jack's dark sleeves.

"And this is the way the cowboy rides...." Jack growled. "Gallop. Gallop. Gallop."

Samuel was squealing now, trying to cling to the galloping knee, as his mother cried out from the door. "Oh, look! There she goes, the poor thing, racing for the barn. She's quite soaked."

Madelaine stalked across the room and plucked the giggling Samuel off his uncle's lap. "Do something, Jack," she snapped. "The woman's liable to catch her death."

More liable to catch the very devil from him, Jack thought as he sprinted across the weedy yard to the barn. Anna Matlin was a file clerk, damn it, not a bloody agent. She had no business following him—and badly, at that—or anybody else. He intended to drive that point home like a nail, for her own future safety.

The barn was dim and muggy, its mingled fragrances of horse and hay accentuated by the rain. Jack didn't see her at first, but as his eyes became accustomed to the dark, he managed to pick her out—a soggy shadow poised in front of Southern Cross's stall.

"I shouldn't have come," she said softly, staring down at the floor. "I'm sorry. I'll leave as soon as the rain stops."

When he heard her wet sniff, whatever intentions Jack had entertained of lecturing her dissolved like salt in warm water. She was already castigating herself quite effectively, he decided as he came to stand behind her.

"Enough tears now," he murmured as he lifted a few drenched tresses from her collar. "You'll spook the horses, mouse. And, anyway, Pinkertons never cry."

He crooked a finger under her chin and nudged her face upward, smiling when he noticed the big raindrops on her lenses. "Let's dry these off, love, and the world will look much better to you." He eased them gently from behind her ears, trying not to take note of the huge, shimmering eyes he was uncovering.

"Why the devil were you following me?" he muttered as he proceeded to rub the glasses with his handkerchief.

She shrugged, biting her lower lip.

"Anna?"

Once more she lifted her shoulders, and then she let out a tremulous sigh and launched into a long list of her worries about their assignment in general and him in particular. Jack was barely listening. As he continued to dry her spectacles, he was battening down the urge to toss them away, then take Anna by the hand and lead her to the pile of clean hay in a nearby stall. Her wet dress would fall heavily to the floor. Not like her underclothes, which would come skimming away under his fingertips. Her skin would be cool until his hands warmed her.

So easy. It would be so easy to seduce her and take all the sweet pleasures he craved here and now. So easy and so good.

And so very wrong. For a thousand reasons. He gave the lenses a final rub, shoved his handkerchief back in his pocket, then slid the metal earpieces through her damp hair and brought the lenses gently down—less to assist her vision than to shield himself from that shimmering gaze that was giving him all the wrong ideas.

"So that's what I plan to do," she said firmly. "I think you ought to go back in the house now. I'll wait here until the rain stops, and then I'll head back to the city. I never meant to disturb you and your mistress.''

''My what?'' Jack's wayward attention snapped back now. ''What did you say?''

Anna let her breath out in what she hoped would sound like an indulgent, worldly sigh, while she corrected the seat of her spectacles over her ears. She peered over the rims at him then, trying to suffuse her voice with cool, if not chilly, sophistication. ''Your mistress. The woman in the house.'' She sighed again. ''It's all right, Jack. Really. I understand.''

She did understand, Anna told herself. A man like Jack, well— Not that she'd meant it when she said it was all right, however. The fact that he wanted someone else wasn't all right at all. But that was her problem, and not Jack's. She wasn't his wife, after all. She wasn't anything to him. Obviously.

Then why, she wondered, was he looking down at her with such an odd grin right now? What did he think was so damn funny? ''What?'' she demanded.

''My mistress, did you say?'' He crossed his arms and leaned a shoulder against the horse stall, that insolent grin still prying up the edges of his mouth. ''Did I hear that correctly, Mrs. Hazard?''

''You did.'' She crossed her arms, too, thinking he needn't be so smug about another in a long list of feminine conquests. Herself, unfortunately, included. At the bottom of his list, though, and in small nearly illegible letters. *Anna Matlin, file clerk and fool.*

He nodded thoughtfully a moment, then levered himself off the wall. "Come on," he said, gripping her by the shoulders and pointing her toward the door. "Since you're both so enormously curious about each other, I think it's high time the two of you met."

As quickly as it had begun, the rain had stopped, leaving the sky tattered with clouds and leaving a swamp in place of the lawn. Anna balked in the doorway as she stared out at the chocolate-colored weed-clotted muck that lay between them and the front door.

She didn't want to meet Jack's mistress in the first place, and she wanted even less to ruin her clothes in the process. When Jack nudged her to the brink of the wood barn floor, she clasped the door frame.

"This is a hundred-dollar dress," she hissed. "And it's not even mine, you know. It's Mr. Pinkerton's."

His eyes gleamed with sudden mirth. "It's much more becoming on you, mouse." He was standing so close, Anna could feel the warmth of his low chuckle on her cheek. It was followed by a sigh, after which he slipped one arm beneath her knees and swung her up against his chest.

"God forbid we should destroy company property, Mrs. Matlin," he told her gruffly. "Let's just ruin my eighty-dollar boots instead, shall we?"

Then, with Anna clinging to him, he stepped out into the swampy yard and strode toward the house.

About to protest vehemently, Anna decided against it. She was, after all, right where she had longed to be. In Jack Hazard's arms. Pressed against his solid chest. Her heart was beating against his, and her whole body was absorbing each of his long, smooth strides. She closed her eyes and tightened her arms about his neck in order to savor the moment— perhaps the last before she encountered the mistress whose company he preferred to hers, whose kisses he preferred to hers, whose body he held dearer.

She inclined her head a bit, just enough to feather her lips along a hard-carved inch or two of jawline, to breathe in his fragrance of shaving soap and wet wool and sheer maleness. When he mounted the porch steps, Anna clung a bit more tightly. And when he set her down, she sighed a kind of farewell, just before the door opened on the tall, rain-soaked form of Frederick Broome.

# Chapter Thirteen

"Freddy!"

"Hello, Anna." He smiled warmly, but then his expression cooled, when he looked over her shoulder at Jack. "Hello, Hazard. Your sister was kind enough to let me in out of the rain."

Jack snorted. "I'm surprised it even occurred to you, Broome." *Idiot. Meddling dolt.* The agent had obviously followed Anna, who'd been following him. They'd been like a bloody parade! The last thing Jack needed was Mr. By-the-Book Broome discovering Southern Cross. He had to get the man away from here. Now.

He needed a plan. No. To trap a bureaucrat like Broome, what he needed was a form. A bloody piece of paperwork. Only Jack wasn't at all sure his liquor-logged, opium-riddled brain could come up with one.

And then there was the mouse to be reckoned with. She had whirled around to face him, her pretty mouth battened down with indignation and her fiery eyes nearly melting those silly lenses of hers.

"Your sister!" she hissed. "But you said—"

"No, mouse." Jack's voice was a model of calm, considering the frantic activity taking place in his head. "It was you who said she was my mistress. Rather insistently, too."

"You might have corrected me, Jack."

"I would have, but you seemed to be relishing the mystery so much that I didn't want to disappoint you." He swore he could hear her teeth grinding then, and it was all he could do not to laugh when her glasses suddenly steamed up.

She seemed on the verge of either kicking him or slapping him when Madelaine stepped between them.

"How do you do, Mrs. Matlin? I'm Jack's sister, Madelaine Scully. I've offered Mr. Broome some tea. Would you care to join us?"

"No tea, Maddie," Jack said. "There's no time. Anna needs to return to the city immediately, to send a wire to our office in Chicago."

Anna blinked up at him now through her foggy lenses. "What wire?"

"What wire?" *Oh, God. What wire?* Jack widened his eyes and let his jaw drop a fraction. "Why, the bimonthly status report." He crinkled his forehead in a frown. "This is the fifteenth, isn't it? Broome? You've already telegraphed yours, I'd imagine."

The agent, bless his zealous and bureaucratic heart, did precisely what Jack had anticipated. He straightened his shoulders, firmed his jaw, looked Jack squarely in the eye and said, "Absolutely. Yesterday, as a matter of fact."

Anna, bless her own dutiful heart, cast Broome a quick, quizzical look.

"This *is* the fifteenth," the agent said calmly, sympathetically, despite the little beads of sweat that were beginning to dampen his forehead.

And now—Lord love her—it was Anna's turn to frown, as well as to gnaw at her lower lip. Jack smiled to himself, ticking off the seconds.

There were exactly five before she announced, "Well, then, we must return immediately."

Broome promptly clasped her arm. "I'll drive you. I insist."

*Snap.*

Jack's smile increased. He had a mouse in his trap, as well as one officious fool. And perhaps, just perhaps, his brain wasn't quite as addled as he had feared.

Broome was sprinting for the buggy. Well, as much as anyone could sprint through the weeds and muck in the yard. To Jack, the tall, lanky agent looked more like an inebriated crane picking its way along a jagged shoreline.

"There goes another man ruining his boots on your behalf," he said softly as he came up behind

Anna on the porch. After a quick hello and good-bye to Madelaine, she had walked outside, where she stood now with her arms wrapped tightly around her.

The rain had done a kind of miracle with her hair, Jack noticed now. Its customary sleekness was gone, replaced by wild, golden curls. He expected they'd be curling even tighter once she discovered his deception.

"I wouldn't worry too much about that report," he said now, in an effort to reassure her. When she didn't reply, he put his hands on her shoulders. They were trembling.

"Are you cold, mouse?"

"I'm angry." She shrugged out of his grasp. "You're my partner, Jack. I wish you wouldn't lie to me."

"About my sister, you mean? I'd hardly call that a lie."

"About everything," she said with a sigh. "It seems to come so naturally to you. Lying."

He was about to defend himself, but realized it would only be another lie, so he said nothing as he watched Broome maneuver the rented buggy toward the house, then kept watching as the two of them drove away.

Madelaine's footsteps sounded behind him as she came out onto the porch. "Have they gone?"

Jack nodded.

"He didn't see Southern Cross, Jack. I'm certain." She smoothed her hand back and forth across his shoulders, as she often did with Samuel. "Just two more weeks until the race. Southern Cross will win, and then everything will be fine."

He didn't answer. Dear God, he was so tired of lying.

Freddy held the reins in one hand. With the other, he kept checking his watch.

"I wouldn't worry, Anna. There's plenty of time for a wire to reach Chicago." He clicked his watch closed. "That form is easy to forget." He flicked her a worried glance now. "Considering it's so new, I mean."

"Yes. I know." Anna stared ahead. Brand-new, as a matter of fact. Invented in a flash of inspiration by that master spy and consummate liar, Jack Hazard. If there was anything a file clerk knew, it was forms. And there was no such thing as a bimonthly status report. Even if there was, she thought, Jack wouldn't know one if it jumped up and bit him on the—

"As soon as we get to the city, Anna, I'm afraid I'll have to drop you off at your hotel. I just remembered a bit of pressing business at the office."

I'll bet you did, Anna thought. Was she the only competent and honest person in the agency?

"Damn," Freddy muttered almost to himself. "And I've already wired Mr. Pinkerton once today."

She raised an eyebrow. "Did you? Concerning what?"

"Your partner, as a matter of fact. When you informed me that Hazard was behaving oddly, I thought the boss ought to be apprised of the situation. Considering the stakes, you know."

"What stakes?"

"Well, the baroness, of course. Hazard made a mess of his last assignment. Never did recover those jewels."

"That's true, although there may have been extenuating circumstances." The queen of England being one, Anna thought, recalling her conversation with Jack.

His reply followed an indignant cluck of his tongue. "I don't consider drunken debauchery an extenuating circumstance, Anna."

No. Neither did she. "What exactly happened during Jack's last assignment, Freddy?"

He took out his watch once more, glowered down at it, then snapped it closed. "I'd rather not say. You're much better off not knowing. And you'd be much better off in Chicago, too, which is what I also advised Mr. Pinkerton. I'm sure he'll agree."

Jack had made certain no one was snooping around his sister's house or her barn before he took the long way back to the city, riding ten miles north before turning east, cursing that idiot Broome every quarter mile. Not that he actually believed anyone would have been interested enough in dear old

Freddy to follow the St. Louis agent out to Madelaine's, but there was no point in taking chances.

His only consolation was in conjuring up images of the man, first as he took apart his office in search of the nonexistent bimonthly status forms, and then when he attempted to compose a telegram explaining his unfortunate oversight.

And those images were only amusing until Jack began to picture the mouse scurrying along in concert with Broome, equally intent on locating the elusive forms—if not more so. Damn. He could almost imagine her earnest expressions and her encouraging words. For dear old Freddy. Poor old Jack, on the other hand, was a laggard, a liar, and a cruel man in a shameful occupation.

Hard as he tried, Jack couldn't shake those images from his brain. Anna and Broome sharing an ink pot, making precise notations on page after page as they composed an apologetic wire. Their blond heads tilting toward each other. Lifting their heads now and again to offer encouraging smiles. Perhaps, when done, Broome would suggest a simple meal, "something light," and after that a promenade.

It was dark now, and Jack glanced up at the sky. No moon, thank God, over which dear Freddy could wax poetic. No moon to add glints of silver to Anna's golden curls. No light at all to prevent Broome from pausing somewhere along the sidewalk and drawing Anna into his rangy embrace and whispering some damn drivel about wanting to kiss her.

Let him. Let the bungling stickler kiss her. They were a perfect match. Let them marry and produce a dozen little sticklers like themselves. What difference did it make? After two more weeks, not only would Jack not be around, he wouldn't be in any condition to care or remember how his heart was squeezing like a fist now and his teeth were clenching and his heels were urging his horse faster and faster toward the city.

It didn't make a difference—damn it—but once he arrived at the hotel, Jack found himself stalking silently down the corridor and turning the key soundlessly in the lock, then thrusting open the door and lunging into the room like some beet-faced boor of a husband, only to discover his "wife" quite alone, propped up in bed, absorbed in a book.

"Jack!" She gave her spectacles a punch. "You nearly frightened me to death."

"I'm sorry." He could feel his lips contorting in a strange, unfamiliar way, then realized it was what could only be called a sheepish grin. An odd mixture of relief and happiness seeped through him, yet those visions of Anna in Broome's embrace wouldn't quite disappear. At the very least, they would have dined together after their paper chase.

"Have you had your supper yet?" he asked, trying to sound casual, if not completely unconcerned with her reply, and beginning to undo his cravat as if that were his sole focus.

"No. I waited for you." She laughed softly. "Freddy was in such a rush to pursue your phantom paperwork that he nearly pushed me out of the buggy in front of the hotel." Anna wagged a finger at him now. "Shame on you, Jack."

"You knew." The loosened tie slipped through his fingers.

"Well, of course I knew. I may not be the best of detectives, but I daresay I'm an excellent file clerk. I file forms. You know—those pesky rectangular things? And in six years I've never filed anything called a bimonthly status report." She tossed her book aside, then curled her arms around her knees. "Now I'm waiting for my partner to tell me—truth-fully—why he wanted Freddy out of his sister's house so fast." Her eyebrows lofted over the rims of her glasses. "Take your time."

Now the relief Jack felt was complete and his sense of happiness almost idiotic, which was also the way he was smiling as he bent to pick up the fallen cra-vat. After looping it carelessly around his neck, he winked and said, "I'll be right back."

"Oh, no, you don't, Jack Hazard. Where the devil do you think you're going?"

"To the kitchen, mouse, to secure you a bit of cheese."

It wasn't cheese he returned with, but strawberries—fat ones—two oranges, and a bottle of champagne that Jack claimed to have found, "open and fairly crying to be consumed," in an ice bucket in the deserted kitchen.

He seemed so pleased, almost boyishly so, with his treasures that Anna stifled the urge to ask if he'd left a few coins behind to pay for this decadent feast.

"It's a decent enough vintage," he said as he poured the pale liquid into a fluted crystal goblet that also had apparently been abandoned downstairs. "*Salud*, mouse."

He handed her the glass, and as Anna prepared to take a sip, she crinkled up her nose.

"Is it supposed to be this, well...energetic? Perhaps it was off, Jack, and that was why it was returned to the kitchen."

He chuckled as he and the bowl of strawberries took up residence beside her on the bed. "It's fine. I promise. Drink it."

Anna took a tiny sip. The liquid seemed to evaporate on her tongue even before she could swallow it, so she took another, larger sip. "I think I like it."

"Dom Perignon will be relieved to hear it."

"Don who?" she asked between sips.

"Hush." He plucked the stem from a berry and held it before her mouth. "Eat this before you take the next sip."

She did, somewhat suspiciously. The champagne made the berry almost explode in sweetness on her tongue. He fed her another, then another.

"Aren't you going to have some?" she asked after licking berry juice from a corner of her mouth.

"I'd rather watch you eat them." His voice was unusually thick.

"Well, champagne, then." She offered him the goblet. "I can't possibly drink all this. Surely one glass of this liquid candy wouldn't hurt you." Oh, but it would. Anna saw that instantly, in the darkening of his eyes and the compression of his mouth. "Oh, Jack. I'm so sorry."

He closed his eyes a moment, dredging up whatever strength he had left for the battle. But this time the battle was over almost as quickly as it had begun, because he realized at that particular moment that he wanted the taste of Anna more than the blaze of alcohol down his throat. He wanted her wet, berry-stained lips, and the sweet warm succor of her breasts. He wanted to lose himself inside her. And the sad truth was that he couldn't have either one— the liquor or the woman—without risking everything. He let his breath out in a long sigh.

"You wanted the truth," he said quietly. "The truth about Jack Hazard is that he really is what everybody says. A drunk." When she started to protest, he held up a hand to silence her. "You wanted the truth, so just listen. And believe me. Drinking isn't what I do, Anna. It's what I am. I have no control over it. I used to. For a long time. But not anymore. Not since..." His voice faltered for a moment. "Well, let's just say that when and if I take that next drink, it will be a never-ending one."

Without a word, Anna unfolded her legs, rose and carried the goblet to the washstand, where she upended it into the porcelain basin. "My apologies to Don Whatever-His-Name-Is," she said as she filled the glass with water from the pitcher and brought it back to him. "Thank you for telling me the truth."

Jack took the goblet and raised it in a toast. *"In aqua veritas,"* he said. He grinned then and proceeded to drain it dry. As he had suspected, there wasn't enough water in the world to snuff out the flames this woman continually lit inside him.

"Now tell me more." She sat back down and began peeling an orange. "Why did you want to get rid of Freddy this afternoon?" After a little giggle, she added, "Inventing that form was brilliant, by the way. He's such a stickler."

He laughed. "And you're not?"

"No." She frowned at the orange a moment, wedging a nail beneath the peel. "Is that what you think I am? Just a silly stickler?"

"Anna." Jack tucked a finger under her chin to raise her face to his. He'd been about to tell her he thought she was clever and competent, but it came out otherwise—hushed and strangely wistful. "I think you're quite beautiful."

"Do you?" Her big eyes blinked behind their lenses.

"Yes," he whispered. "Yes, I do."

Color flooded her cheeks. She looked away. "You were saying . . . about Freddy?"

For a second, the name didn't even register on Jack. He'd never met a woman who didn't pursue a compliment like a bloodhound. But then, he'd never met a woman who surprised him at every turn, the way Anna persisted in doing.

"Freddy," he said, when the idiot's name finally sank in. "I didn't want him to discover Southern Cross."

"Who?"

"Southern Cross. The horse in my sister's barn."

"I thought that was Polaris." She lifted the half-peeled orange to give her specs a nudge. "Wasn't it? He looked just like Polaris."

"Yes, he does. And that, my dear mouse, is exactly what I'm counting on." Smiling, Jack leaned back on an elbow and proceeded to outline his plan for winning the Carondelet Stakes.

As he spoke, he watched her expression change from curiosity to concern, her blue eyes narrowing and the creases in her forehead deepening until they were veritable grooves. The mark of the stickler, he thought as he tried to guess what the first words out of her mouth would be when he finished, and finally settled on a string of adjectives that included *dishonest, illegal* and *highly unethical*.

"Well, that's the sum of it," he said, then waited for her to explode into a million appalled and indignant pieces. Waited for her to shoot off the bed, fired by the wrath of the Almighty and her own honest, law-abiding soul. And waited while she traced a finger along a fold of the bed linens, jabbed at her glasses with the other hand, and finally lifted her gaze to his. She searched his eyes as if she thought she'd find a bloody pilfered diamond there.

Jack couldn't stand it a second longer. "Well? Damn it, what do you think?" *Go on. Fly apart. And while you're doing that, rip me to shreds with your opinion of me and my shameful occupation. God knows your friend Freddy would never stoop to such horrible deception.*

"I think your plan is brilliant."

Jack felt his jaw come unhinged. "You what?"

"I said, I think your plan is brilliant."

Bloody hell. He raked his fingers through his hair and simply stared at her as, quite casually, she popped a segment of orange in her mouth and chewed it methodically.

"Of course you realize it's altogether illegal," she said then, following her pronouncement with a quick pass of her pink tongue over her lips to catch a bead of juice. "But brilliant, nevertheless. I say the law be damned for once, in the pursuit of justice. Let's do it."

All he could do was laugh. Inanely. Convulsively. Like a dim-witted schoolboy. He dropped back onto the mattress and laughed, laughed as he hadn't laughed in years, until tears leaked from the corners of his eyes.

Anyone would have thought she'd just repeated a risqué or ribald limerick, Anna thought, the way Jack was carrying on. "I don't know what I said that was so blasted funny." She drew herself up and squared her shoulders, then fussed with the ruffle at the neck of her nightgown.

"Oh, mouse." He dabbed a knuckle at one eye. "You are an infinite delight."

"Am I?"

"An infinite delight and a continual surprise." He sighed. "If I were a different sort of man, I'd be head over heels in love with you now. Absolutely dizzy with it."

"Would you?" Her question was barely more than a soft, indrawn breath.

"Yes."

After a moment, she asked, "What sort of a different sort of man?"

"Hmm?" His eyes were closed now, and his entire body seemed more relaxed than Anna had ever seen it. All the tension had drained from his face, leaving his forehead smooth and his mouth a perfectly carved line that tipped up slightly at the edges in a peaceful smile.

"You're so tired," she whispered, letting her hand come to rest on his arm. "Sleep."

He jerked slightly, as if he meant to get up, but Anna said again, "Just sleep."

"Busy tomorrow," he murmured. "Have to start Polaris's workouts."

"Oh, dear."

"Hmm."

"I promised our great friend Mrs. Bissell we'd look at another house. The woman was so adamant. I suppose we could always..."

"Morning or afternoon?" he asked sleepily.

"Afternoon."

"No problem. Polaris. Morning..." His words were engulfed in a yawn as he pushed his head deeper into the pillow. "Mouse," he said then, softly. "Dear one."

Careful not to jar the mattress, Anna cleared the orange peels and the berry dish from the bed. She took off her glasses and placed them carefully on the nightstand, then dimmed the light and settled her head on the pillow.

Her mother had never sung her a lullaby, she thought, but if she had, it couldn't have been more comforting than the sound of Jack's deep and even and oh-so-peaceful breathing as he lay so close beside her.

If he were a different sort of man, he had said, he would love her. Love her! If he were a different sort of man. She fell asleep wondering if he would love her if she were a different sort of woman. But different how? Like the baroness, perhaps?

## Chapter Fourteen

"Will you be breakfasting alone this morning, Mrs. Hazard?" the waiter asked.

"Yes, I will." Quite alone, Anna thought as she watched him clearing the unnecessary silver from the table. The man who had slept so peacefully by her side all through the night had been gone when she awakened. She had hoped...

"What may I bring you, madam? We have some excellent trout this morning, and I might also suggest—"

"A bowl of oatmeal, please."

"Yes, madam. And after that?"

Anna snapped the leather-bound menu closed. "The oatmeal will do."

"Very good," he said, although from the slope of his mouth and the height of his brows, Anna could tell he didn't think her choice was very good at all.

Nor did it look very good when he placed it before her in a gold-rimmed porcelain bowl. It looked, well...plain. Uninspired. Probably, she thought, not so different from the way she herself had looked a mere two weeks ago, before Mad Jack Hazard inspired her.

Get used to it, she admonished herself while spooning the gluey cereal into her mouth. In a mere two weeks, your inconspicuous and uninspired life will resume, Anna Matlin. That was, after all, what she had planned. Before Jack.

*If I were a different sort of man.* His words echoed in her head.

If she were a different sort of woman...

She *was* different from the woman she had been two weeks ago, though. And it wasn't just the expensive clothes and elegant surroundings to which she'd become somewhat accustomed. She wouldn't mind one bit when the time came to give those things up. Anna glanced at the gold band on her left hand, vaguely wondering if she'd have to give that back, too. Probably. No, certainly. It was company property, after all. Another agent could use it on another assignment. When the time came, Anna would close her eyes and twist the ring off her finger and deposit it in a newly labeled file—Accessories: Wife. She wouldn't mind so much.

Not so much. She might, she thought, if she were a different sort of woman, but...

"There you are. I've been looking all over for you, Anna." Freddy Broome's voice broke into her reverie. "That oatmeal looks wonderful. Mind if I join you?"

Without giving her a chance to reply, Freddy took a seat across the table from her. Anna couldn't help but notice the faint swatches of purple beneath his hazel eyes, or the fact that his normally slick-combed hair was rumpled, as if his fingers had been ripping through it. No doubt from his frantic and unsuccessful search for the phantom bimonthly forms. The poor stickler.

"How was your evening, Freddy?" She bit down on a grin. "Restful?"

His wheat-colored brows edged together a moment, before he began, "Well, actually—" only to be interrupted by the waiter's request for his order, and another glowing recommendation of the trout. "I'll have oatmeal," Freddy told the man. "The same as Mrs. Matlin."

"Hazard," Anna said quickly.

"Pardon?"

She waved her ring as discreetly as possible, under Freddy's nose, repeating, "Mrs. Hazard."

The agent scowled. "Oh. Right." He looked to the waiter again. "I'll have oatmeal. Not too hot. Cream on the side. And I'll be needing a copy of the bill."

Now it was Anna who felt her eyebrows creeping together. Was she as much of a stickler as Freddy? Did she pounce on every detail, no matter how minute? Did she pick every nit? No wonder it irritated Jack.

Once the waiter was gone, Freddy angled back in his chair, crossed his arms and smiled adoringly across the table. Much too adoringly for such a public place, it seemed to Anna.

"Now, where were we?" he murmured, brushing a bit of lint from a sleeve, then realigning his starched cuff.

"You were telling me about your evening."

"Ah. I went back to the office, actually, and— Oh, damnation, I nearly forgot." He patted his pockets, then pulled an envelope from one inside his coat. "This letter came for you in care of the office. From Chicago. I, er...couldn't help but notice."

"Chicago?" Anna took the letter hesitantly and held it by one corner, as if the cream-colored vellum might go up in flames any second. Though she had spent the past six years diligently filing hundreds, perhaps even thousands, of pieces of business correspondence, she herself had only received a single letter in her life—the one from the U.S. marshal in Colorado informing her that Billy Matlin was dead. Pressing her spectacles more firmly against the bridge of her nose, she narrowed her gaze on the flowery script of the return address.

"It's from Miss Richmond! My landlady. Whatever could the problem be?" She turned the envelope over and stared at the flap.

"Open it," Freddy suggested.

"What?"

"Open it." He leaned back to allow the waiter room to set his place with the Southern Hotel's heavy silver. "Go on, Anna. Open it."

"Now?" Anna glanced at the waiter, who didn't appear to be taking an inordinate interest in her mail. Nor did anyone else in the dining room, as far as she could tell. But one could never be sure. "Here?"

After a little sigh, Freddy took the envelope from her, picked up the knife the waiter had just slid into place and slipped it beneath the vellum flap.

Anna eased the paper out and began to read. A moment later, she glanced up. "They miss me," she said. "Oh, how very dear. Miss Richmond writes that both she and her sister have been terribly worried about me."

"That's nice," Freddy murmured.

"It is, isn't it?" Anna smiled. "She goes on to say that they have grave misgivings about the postal people. That they surmise my correspondence has either been lost or stolen. They can't imagine that I haven't written, and..." Anna turned the page over, reading aloud now. "'And in consequence, my dear, or unless we hear otherwise, Sister and I are considering a trip to Missouri to reassure ourselves of your well-being.'" Anna's voice dwindled to a whisper. "'With warmest regards and deepest concern, Dorothy Richmond.'"

"That's quite nice," Freddy said.

No, that was terrible, Anna thought. Where had her head been? She should have written her prim and proper landladies immediately upon her arrival in St. Louis, to tell them she was safe and sound, to inform them of her return in several weeks. But, of course, her head had been in the clouds—or forever turned toward Jack. She hadn't given the Misses Richmond so much as a passing thought. What if they came? What if they discovered what she was up to—and, worse, who she was with while she was up to it? Why, they'd return to Chicago aghast, in a fit of such monumental proportions that they would promptly pitch all Anna's belongings out their third-story window onto Adams Street.

Unless they heard from her immediately. But what if this letter had been written so long ago that they were already on their way? She flipped the paper, looking back at the beginning. "There's no date." She snatched up the envelope, squinting at the upper right-hand corner. "Well, this is no help. The postmark is blurred."

Across the table, Freddy was no help, either. He lifted his shoulders in a shrug and kept gazing at her like a moony boy who obviously had no inkling that the object of his silly affection was about to be thrown out on her ear.

When the waiter placed Freddy's breakfast on the table, Anna stood abruptly, the letter clutched in her hand. "I must be going, Freddy. Enjoy your oatmeal." *I hope it will keep you well occupied while I try to figure out how to salvage what used to be my life.*

Calm down, she told herself while crumpling another half-composed message, then tossing it across the suite. Just write that you're well, but terribly busy. Apologize for not having communicated sooner. Tell them—firmly—not to come. But why?

Why? She reached for a fresh sheet of hotel stationery and picked up the pen to tap it thoughtfully against her teeth. She could tell the Misses Richmond that St. Louis was currently closed to visitors. Just closed. Quarantined even. Because of disease. Severe disease. Rampant. A pestilence. Cholera would be good. Bubonic plague might even be better.

Anna could feel an impish little grin pulling at the corners of her mouth, and she tried to subdue it as she dipped the pen in the inkwell. She was lying again. She was becoming quite proficient in her ability to conjure up a deception—even a plague—to suit her purpose.

Good Lord! She was becoming just as bad as Jack! Or, she decided as she felt her lips crook upward, escaping her control entirely now, she was becoming just as good.

Twenty minutes later, Anna was blotting her signature when the door to the suite opened and Jack walked in, smiling one of *those* smiles. The ones that always made her breath catch in her throat.

"Good morning, Mrs. Hazard. Or perhaps I should say good-afternoon." He crossed the room to drop a kiss on the crown of her head. "You're looking rather pleased with yourself, I must say."

"You're looking..." Beautiful, Anna thought. More than ever, in tall boots and gray riding breeches that clung to his muscular thighs. If he were a different sort of man... She dropped her gaze back to the letter that was so crucial to her future, finishing softly, "Well rested."

"That I am, mouse." Jack sat on the edge of the bed to take his boots off. "That I am." And thanks to you, he thought. He'd returned from the race-course, curious to see Anna's sweet, expressive face, wondering about the exact shade of the flush he'd witness there when she insisted on discussing the particulars of the night before, when she tried her damnedest to make some professional sense out of the fact that they had shared a bed.

This bed. Boots off now, he leaned back on both elbows, regarding her. All her attention was focused on a piece of blotting paper. Where were the recriminations? Where were her professional concerns and grave reservations? Why wasn't she stabbing at her silly glasses and babbling chapter and verse from the agency handbook, instead of taking last night in surprising stride?

Her behavior not only confused Jack, but irritated him, as well. Predicting behavior was part of his job, and he'd always been rather good at it. He had had to be good, since, more often than not, his bloody life depended on it. But now the mouse was nothing if not a puzzle.

He'd anticipated her argument, and he'd returned with every intention of reassuring her that their proximity the night before meant nothing and that it wouldn't happen again. He'd planned to tell her there would be no further distractions, pleasant or restful or otherwise, from the business at hand.

Distractions such as now—the way her blond head was bent so seriously over the writing table, the way her tongue darted out to wet her lips, the way her right foot jiggled under the folds of her gown and the way the fabric curved over the bewitching shape of her left breast. Distractions such as the way need flickered in the pit of his stomach and desire flashed along his every nerve and his brain was emptying of everything but her. Damnation!

He shoved himself upward and cleared his throat, at the same time trying to clear his brain of everything but business. "What time is our engagement with that bulwark of society and preeminent hawker of real estate?"

"Three o'clock this afternoon."

Her casual tone and continued indifference to him irritated him all the more. He wrenched his arms out of his jacket. "Then I suppose I ought to wash off some of this racecourse dust. I'm surprised you agreed to another house-hunting expedition, Anna. I thought you were above such deception." He raised an eyebrow now, half quizzical, half aggrieved. "Or have you decided that our little charade is necessary, and perhaps not so shameful after all?"

He'd meant to mock her, but suddenly visions of that day in Mrs. Bissell's nephew's house swirled through his brain. Visions of Anna leaning back, resting her pretty head on his shoulder while he tried, rather desperately, to draw her into his pitiful, and perhaps even perverse, domestic fantasy. Visions of Anna chastising him later for tampering with people's hopes and dreams, berating him for his shameful occupation. "Well?" he demanded.

"Perhaps." She fiddled with that bloody blotting paper, then pushed back from the table and stood. "Mostly, though, I decided that a drive in the country would be rather nice. This house is several miles away, and Mrs. Bissell said it's been uninhabited for months, so there won't be any owner on the premises to disappoint."

Jack unbuttoned his shirt and grumbled, "God forbid we disappoint anyone. And, while I'm at it, I probably ought to pray that my face doesn't crack down the middle like a damn walnut from smiling at that woman for all bloody afternoon." He wrenched his arms out of the shirt and glared across the room.

"You won't have to." Anna offered her own smile. "Mrs. Bissell won't be accompanying us this time. She is otherwise engaged, so we have the use of her carriage and driver for the entire afternoon."

"Alone?"

The mouse's smile turned curiously catlike, and her gaze—Jack couldn't help but notice—kept returning to his bare chest, before skittering off again.

And only now did her cheeks begin to flush with the color he had expected earlier.

"Quite alone," she said, with a touch more huskiness than usual, after which she gave her spectacles a firm tap and plucked the envelope from the table. "I'll wait for you downstairs, Jack. You needn't rush. There's plenty of time."

God Almighty, Jack thought as he watched the last bit of her hem whisk through the doorway. Alone? In a cozy carriage on a lovely summer afternoon? Destined for an empty country house? Alone with this desirable creature, the way his blood was running now after merely looking at her across the room?

Suddenly, the prospect of feeling his face split in half by false-hearted smiles aimed at Mrs. Bissell— real estate magnate and chaperone extraordinaire— seemed preferable to feeling his body on the verge of explosion all afternoon and his brain so besotted with Anna that he would be hard-pressed to remember anything else but the fact that he wanted her. Her sweetness, and the constant surprise of her. Her sober little visage, and those sapphire eyes behind her silly spectacles. Wanted her as he had never wanted anyone before in his life. More than anyone or anything. More than air or food or—

His eyes flashed to the bottle Anna had pushed to the side of the writing table. Sweet Jesus! Need coiled in the pit of his stomach like a snake, and his hands cramped into fists. One taste. One swallow to slake the flames. One searing gulp to burn Anna out of his brain so that he could concentrate. A single endless, bottomless drink to blur his conscience, to drown his exhausted soul.

Not yet!

He stood there a long time, stock-still, staring, not even daring to blink, for fear the slightest movement would send him over the brink. The beautiful, beckoning brink.

Jack's sister inched up the dark veil that covered her face, the better to see the blonde who had just entered the lobby alone. Thank heavens. Why Jack persisted in calling such a stunning woman a mouse was beyond her comprehension, really. Unless, of course, a lifetime of pain and a year of utter dissipation had finally destroyed her brother's eyesight, in addition to his soul.

Madelaine watched from beneath her veil while Anna Matlin tapped the shoulder of a bellboy and handed him an envelope. Then she appeared to be delivering a lecture, pointing to the envelope again and again while the boy nodded and shrugged and shifted impatiently from foot to foot. Good Lord, for all the woman's seriousness, anyone would presume the letter contained news of the imminent end of the world. As Madelaine had surmised from their brief meeting the day before, Mrs. Matlin was a most serious young woman.

It went without saying that the woman was in love with her brother. Madelaine had yet to see a female go unsmitten by those Hazard charms. But unlike Jack's habitual beauties, Anna Matlin seemed to possess some depth and strength of character beneath that pretty face and behind those spectacles. Good. Because after hearing what Madelaine had come here to tell her, Jack's mouse was going to need a spine of steel, as well as the sharp claws of a tigress.

*If* Madelaine told her.

Her shoulders sagged back onto the cushions of the settee as she felt her courage wither a bit and her determination wane. Family secrets ought to be just that. Secrets. Soiled laundry, stuffed out of sight. She'd never told a soul.

Who would believe it? Who could possibly believe such a sordid tale of a father who was a demon and a darling at once? A man so handsome and engaging that his children craved his attention, no matter the form that that attention took. How could she possibly explain that Charles Ian Hazard, earl of Bridgewater, highly regarded peer of the realm, a thoroughly charming and devilishly handsome man, had derived horrible and unholy pleasure from inflicting pain on the objects of his affection? How could she explain it, when she could barely comprehend it herself?

How did you tell someone in hushed tones and veiled terms that your mother had taken her own life because the woman could no longer endure the pain and shame her husband inflicted upon her behind closed doors? How to explain in euphemisms, in sugarcoated words fit for a busy hotel lobby and Anna's innocent ears, how three elder brothers had submitted—not always silently, but submitted nevertheless—to their father's silver-handled whip?

One by one. Year after year, until they were old enough or smart enough or strong enough to leave. Or ashamed enough. One by one by one. The sequence had become as predictable as the seasons. Harsh winter giving way to spring, again and again. Louis first. Then Edgar. Then Jerome.

But always there had been Charles Ian Hazard. Earl of Bridgewater. Beautiful. Father. Monster. The man who had showered his attentions, and his unholy love, on one son at a time. Louis. Then Edgar. Then Jerome.

And then there had been only Jack.

## Chapter Fifteen

Despite the warmth in the lobby, a chill rippled along Madelaine's spine. She had worn the veil to conceal her identity, but now she was grateful that it concealed her tears as the memories she'd tried so hard to banish came flooding back.

She could picture Jack so clearly. He'd been such a handsome little boy, with his black hair always combed just so and his shirts tucked in and his fingernails clipped and clean, just in case Father ever checked, which of course he never had.

She had been Jack's tagalong, his perpetual shadow, in those early, good years in Sussex, where Hazard House lay close enough to the chalk cliffs for the wind to bring them daily whiffs of the sea. Like Jack, Madelaine had been lonely. But unlike him, she had been happy that their father ignored them and let them have the run of the place, especially the stables and the green meadows where Jack had taught her to ride.

He hadn't seemed to find his little sister's companionship altogether burdensome or unpleasant. Perhaps he had even prized it. He had never said, one way or the other. So much had gone unsaid at Hazard House. There had been so many secrets. Louis. Then Edgar. Then Jerome.

"I'll tell you a secret, Maddie," Jack had said one day, while they were rubbing down yet another horse they'd nearly run to death. "It's about why Father never looks at us or speaks to us. It's because we're not his actual children."

"Don't be a goose, Jack," Madelaine had snapped. "We look exactly like him. Everyone says so."

"Nevertheless, I'm going to pretend my real father is Admiral Nelson. Or better yet, Napoleon. I'm dark. I could easily be French."

It had been such a simple wish, Madelaine thought now. A boy yearning for his father's mere regard, if not his love. Madelaine hadn't wanted either. Jack had. Desperately. And his simple, childlike solution had been to slip into fantasy more and more, fashioning fathers who cared, and imagining himself a beloved son. Little wonder he'd become a master spy, able to change personae quite convincingly at the drop of a hat. He'd perfected that talent early. He could easily be French or Swiss, or the son of a Portuguese wine merchant. How easy it was for him to seem happy or whole when he wasn't, to persist dreaming dreams in which he was worthy of a father's interest and affection. Like Louis. Then Edgar. Then Jerome.

And then Jerome had been gone. Though she had tried to forget it for years, Madelaine remembered that day as clearly now as if it were yesterday, as if it were happening here and now—not an ocean and more than two decades away.

It was spring—April to be exact—and Hazard House that afternoon was as damp and chilly as a tomb. The servants hadn't yet lit the lamps, so all the rooms were grayed by the oncoming dark. Except for Father's study. Except for that private and mysterious place where she and Jack had never been, but where the door that afternoon was ajar. Just enough for the light from Father's fire to burnish a swath across the corridor floor.

She and Jack had been on their way to the kitchen to filch a tea cake when their father's voice called out. She could hear it even now, golden and warm, as beguiling as the firelight pouring through the open door.

"Is that you, Jack?"

Her brother stopped as if a stone wall had suddenly sprung up before him or an invisible net had dropped down from the ceiling. Even after twenty-six years, Madelaine could still picture the expression on his face and see that odd twist of his smile that seemed to register both hope and fear, to signal both victory and defeat.

"Is that you, son?" their father had called again.

Madelaine had tugged at Jack's sleeve. "Ssh...
You mustn't answer."

He had looked at her a long moment then, while
the firelight from Father's study flickered in the
depths of his blue-gray eyes. When he spoke, he
sounded years older than just moments before. "You
go on, Maddie," he told her, easing out of her grip.
"Father wants me now. I'll be along in a while."

"No. Please. You mustn't go in there. He'll...he'll
hurt you. Like our brothers. And then—oh, God,
then you'll leave."

"Don't cry, Maddie. And don't be afraid. I
promise you I won't leave." That odd smile twisted
even more before it split into a dazzling grin. "He
*can't* hurt me. Father loves me now, you see."

She wanted to scream—"No! That isn't love!
Don't go Jack! Please!"—but instead she only stood
there in desolate silence, afraid to even breathe, as
she watched her brother walk through that golden
slice of light.

"I must punish you, son," their father said.

"Yes, sir. I know."

"There's a good boy. Close the door, Jack. And
then undo your breeches."

Madelaine blinked now, beneath her veil, as she
had that day when the door clicked closed, leaving
her in the dark corridor. Alone. Afraid for her
brother to stay. Terrified that he, too, would leave.
But he hadn't. And to this day, she still didn't know
whether Jack had remained at Hazard House all

those years for her sake, or for his own. That was the final secret she didn't dare explore, for if the answer was that he had done it only to protect her, Madelaine didn't believe she could bear the guilt.

She could, however, do everything in her power to ensure that her brother never came under the influence of a brutal and beguiling monster again. And that was precisely what she intended to do.

After wiping her tears and readjusting her veil, she rose and crossed the lobby to the quiet corner where Anna Matlin had taken a seat.

"Mrs. Matlin, we met yesterday." Madelaine raised her veil a few inches, trying not to look desperate or to sound urgent, both of which she felt. "I'm Jack's sister, Madelaine. I need to speak with you."

The little blonde's eyes widened behind her spectacles. "Yes, of course. It's nice to see you again. Jack will be downstairs any moment, if you'd like—"

"No. I need to speak with *you*. Alone. About Jack." Despite her efforts to remain calm, Madelaine's voice began to tremble. "You must help my brother. You might be the only one at this point who can save him."

"Save him?" She sat up straighter, frowning. "Do you mean from drink?"

"No, Mrs. Matlin, I don't. I mean save him from the Baroness Von Drosten. And perhaps . . . perhaps even save my brother from himself. May I sit down, please?"

"You look pale, mouse." Jack took the seat his sister had fled and angled his head toward the hotel's front door, where the dark-veiled woman had just vanished. "What was that Gypsy hoyden doing?" he asked with a chuckle. "Reading your palm and telling you to beware of tall, dark men?"

Anna blinked. It was too late for that, she longed to say, but instead she summoned up a lie. "She was inquiring about my dressmaker," she said, smoothing her skirt over her knees. "The woman was quite taken with my dress."

Jack's gaze was warm, appreciative and—thank heavens—utterly credulous. "I'm not surprised. You look lovely. But pale. Are you sure you're feeling up to this outing? We don't have to go, you know. Especially since Mrs. Bissell doesn't intend to accompany us." He leaned back and crossed his arms. "Rather like two actors playing to empty seats, don't you think? I can't see much point in continuing the charade without an audience."

Oh, but there was! And Anna suddenly knew why.

Even if she hadn't quite been able to comprehend everything Madelaine had whispered to her.

Even if she hadn't yet been able to fit together the pieces of Jack's past, or to fathom how a man's notions of love and pain could become so twisted that they were virtually inseparable.

Even if she still had absolutely no idea what she herself could do once she had puzzled it all out. But Anna knew she had to do something to reach out to Jack, to clasp him to her and keep him safe. And what better place to reach out to an inveterate pretender, to someone who had spent a lifetime hiding in his own imagination—to a consummate actor—than alone with him, onstage so to speak.

"We *have* to go this afternoon, Jack."

He raised an eyebrow. "Why?"

Why? Because she felt an urgency she couldn't explain. Because she wanted to take him away from everyone and everything that might tempt him and do him harm. Because... She lifted her chin and met his stubborn gaze with one of her own. "Because I promised Mrs. Bissell."

Jack sighed, throwing up his hands. "God forbid you break a promise, mouse." He shook his head. "I don't suppose there's anything in the stickler's handbook about breaking promises, is there?"

"No, there isn't," she replied coolly. Nor was there anything in that handbook about breaking all the rules, which was exactly what Anna had in mind right now.

She stood up and then peered down at Jack over the rims of her spectacles. "Shall we go? I expect Mrs. Bissell's carriage and driver are waiting for us."

The mouse was up to something, but for the life of him Jack couldn't figure it out. A promise might be a promise in her book, but still, her willingness to carry on with the house-hunting charade surprised him.

She was quiet on their ride through the country-side north of the city. Not quiet as a mouse, though. More like a dreamy tabby, wearing a smile that struck him as similar to the Mona Lisa's. Even now, while Mrs. Bissell's driver moved the matched pair of grays along at a brisk clip, that smile was still perched on Anna's lips. Secretive. Slightly seduc-tive. Wholly uncharacteristic of his little stickler. And thoroughly unsettling to one Jack Hazard.

For a woman with little or no imagination, she seemed to have a great deal going on inside that pretty head of hers. He slanted her a glance. "What are you up to, Anna?"

"Up to?" She blinked, all innocence behind her silly lenses now. "Nothing. Nothing at all."

The driver pulled the carriage to a halt and called over his shoulder. "That'd be the place. Up there on the hill."

Jack looked up the long green knoll to the right of the road. Good God! It wasn't a house at all. It was a deuced wedding cake.

"Isn't it beautiful?" the mouse squeaked. "Oh, Jack, isn't it perfect?"

For what? he wondered bleakly while he helped her out of the carriage and tried to disregard the warmth of her waist and the delicacy of her rib cage.

He tried, as well, to ignore the rather impish expression on her face as she stood there looking up at him.

"Perhaps we should send the driver off for a while," she said then.

And said it, blast her, loud enough for the fellow to hear and to offer immediately and oh-so-gallantly that he wouldn't mind one bit whiling away an hour or so at the cheery inn they had passed a mile back. The fellow's hands were already twitching on the damn reins in his eagerness to be off to the "cheery inn" which was a swill shop if ever Jack had seen one. It had caught his eyes, too, when they drove past it. A rummy always knew.

"You folks just go on and take your time," the driver—damn him!—suggested pleasantly.

"Tip him, Jack," Anna whispered, nudging an elbow into his ribs.

He stared at her in disbelief. Who was this stranger standing beside him? Surely not the little fusspot of a file clerk he'd brought to St. Louis with him. Certainly not the skinflint who a mere week ago would have driven the carriage herself to save a paltry gratuity. Or, even worse, would have walked the whole ten miles, out and back.

Before he could reply, though, Anna was rummaging in her handbag, then smiling brightly as she produced a silver dollar and offered it up to the driver.

"Kind of you, ma'am. Enjoy your tour of the place." With a wink and a flick of the reins, he turned the horses and set off the way they had come.

Back to the bloody tavern, leaving Jack high and dry and utterly bemused, with a wedding cake of a house on the hill behind him and a suddenly incomprehensible woman—a woman who only days before had given him the very devil about this house-hunting business, who had accused him of playing a cruel charade, who had berated him for toying with peoples' hopes and dreams in a thoroughly shameful way—and who was, at this very moment, hurrying up the hill.

Glowering at the white gingerbread confection that sat atop the knoll, Jack gave a sigh and followed along the flagstone path. Ahead, Anna's petticoats winked at him and, each time she turned to beckon, sunlight twinkled on her spectacles.

"Hurry, Jack," she called from beneath the spun-sugar eaves of the veranda. "Isn't our house wonderful?"

Our house? Jack stopped as if his boots had just been bolted to the paving stones. Our house?

"Jack," she called again, urgent as a little girl who couldn't wait a second longer to tear into a gift.

He lifted a hand to gesture her on, and then just stood there watching as Anna produced a key from the depths of her handbag, twisted it in the lock, then punched her skirts through the doorway and disappeared inside.

Our house? Was that what she had said? God in Heaven. His little stickler had gone around the bloody bend. Like as not, she had swilled the remnants of that champagne this morning, while he was gone. He couldn't think of anything else to account for her odd behavior.

The musty odor of the house engulfed Anna the minute she came through the door. To her left, the draped furniture in the parlor looked more like snowdrifts than sofas and chairs. To her right, the covered side chairs in the dining room appeared to be a party of mute ghosts, gathered for a long-overdue feast. The grandfather clock that towered before her in the vestibule was silent, stuck at 2:16.

She wasn't sure just what she'd been expecting, but the sad reality of the place slapped her like an invisible hand, and the smile she'd been wearing all afternoon evaporated from her face.

What had she been thinking? She wasn't a Pinkerton agent. She was a file clerk. She wasn't Mrs. Jack Hazard. She was and always would be Anna Matlin. And no matter how deeply she cared for Jack, his problems were far too complicated for someone as inexperienced as she.

*I don't know if you can do anything, Mrs. Matlin, but at least you're aware of the enemy now.* Madelaine's words sounded in her head, as if spoken by one of the straight-backed ghosts in the dining room. *If you care for him, Mrs. Matlin—and I believe you do—then you must help him.*

"I can't." The dust-covers seemed to swallow up her forlorn little cry.

"You can't what, mouse?"

Anna turned to find Jack leaning in the doorway, arms crossed and one hip cocked at a cavalier angle. The smile on his face was the one that always took her breath away, and it was succeeding with a vengeance at the moment.

"I . . . I can't breathe," she said, one hand fluttering to her glasses, while the other fumbled with the tight collar of her dress.

"I'm not surprised." Jack's gaze made a quick circuit of the draped furniture. "All this bloody dust," he muttered as he shouldered off the door frame and took two long strides toward her. "Are you still so determined to have a look around the residential wedding cake?"

"Well, I . . ." Actually Anna had been about to say she'd just as soon give it up—all of it, really—but Jack swept her up in his arms before she could utter another word.

"The parlor, Mrs. Hazard, is on your left." He swung her in that direction. "Rather small, actually, but our friend Mrs. Bissell would probably describe it as intimate."

He swung her to the right then. "And this, my love, appears to be the dining room." He narrowed his gaze and crimped his forehead. "Again, small.

But perfectly suitable for newlyweds who undoubtedly won't be inviting large numbers of guests to dine."

When he shifted her higher in his arms, that dazzling smile was just inches from Anna's face. "Have you seen enough, my dear, or would you care to explore further?"

"Well, perhaps— Oh, this is silly. Put me down."

"Say no more." Gripping her more firmly, he strode down the hallway, pushed a door open with a boot and angled her through. "Ah... The kitchen. Every house should have one."

He made an exploratory circuit of the room, shifting her this way and that in his arms while he opened cupboards and slammed them closed, while he tested the pump handle and found it "somewhat balky," while he peered into the black depths of the oven and shuddered dramatically.

And suddenly, in spite of all her good sense and innate seriousness, Anna found herself laughing. Gaily. Giddily. There had been so little laughter in her life. So little joy and delight. This man gave her that so effortlessly. He made her feel so alive. She wanted to feel this way always. So happy and so...so desperately in love.

Pretend, she ordered herself. *Do it. It's the only way to reach him, to hold him fast, to keep him safe from harm. From her.*

*Pretend! You can do it, damn it. Step out of your small, safe self and into Mad Jack Hazard's daz-*

*zling and dangerous imagination. Join him completely. Be his wife. Imagine it. Just imagine.*

"There you have it, mouse." He came to a stop in the middle of the room. "I'd say it's adequate for a kitchen, wouldn't you?"

"More than adequate." She linked her arms around his neck and nestled more closely, more warmly against his chest. "I love our house, Jack. And if there's not quite enough cupboard space, we'll simply build more. For the Haviland, you know."

He was quiet for a moment, as if her reply hadn't completely registered. Or perhaps as if it had. Anna saw a little muscle jerk in his cheek, and she could feel his chest expand as he drew in a breath, then let it out, almost quizzically. "The Haviland?"

"Hmm." She snuggled more closely, threading her fingers through his hair. "You remember. Our best china. The Haviland, with the family crest in blue."

"I remember—" he said softly, although there was more bewilderment than certainty in his voice, and it seemed to catch deep in his throat. "What are you doing to me, mouse?"

Anna tipped her face up, letting her lips drift along his jawline, feeling his heart hammering against hers and watching his blue-gray eyes deepen to pewter. She whispered then, and was only half surprised by the sultriness and certainty in her own voice. "Let's go upstairs, darling. Please. To our bedroom. Now."

## Chapter Sixteen

Jack climbed the staircase slowly with one hand on the banister and a cautious tread, as if at any second a stair might collapse and send him hurtling backward. Like a practiced drunk, he thought dismally. Like somebody who knew from long experience that the staircase, and the entire world, could slide out from beneath him. Above him, he could hear the whisk of Anna's skirts as she moved from room to room.

He felt slightly drunk now. And there had been that moment in the kitchen when he wasn't sure he wasn't once more under the influence of opium. That moment when reality and make-believe blurred and he wasn't able to blink them back to their proper places.

Shaking his head now, he decided he had merely heard Anna wrong. It had to be that simple. Anna Matlin didn't know how to play the seductress. The woman didn't know how to play, period.

She had the imagination of a bookend. A solid, stable prop. That was one of the reasons he was drawn to her, if not damnably in love with her. In a different life, she could have been his anchor. In a different life, this wedding cake of a house could have been their home.

He could picture it so easily. Too easily, damn it. Those simple pleasures and uncomplicated joys weren't meant for him. If he hadn't learned that as a boy, then certainly Chloe had driven the lesson home.

Only sometimes—as now—he wished . . .

A bitter oath crossed his lips. He wished he'd gone back to the cheery inn with the thirsty driver. He wished he was pouring sour mash down his throat and obliterating the very ability to wish.

Wishes seldom came true. When they did, it was with a vengeance.

He found Anna in the last room down a long hall. She was standing at a window, gazing out, looking prim and serious and self-contained, with her arms hugged about her. And if somewhere in an old, hopeful corner of his heart, he'd imagined her greeting him from the drawn-back linens of the bed, Jack felt more relief than disappointment now. He bade the image go as he moved to stand behind her, letting his gaze drift with hers over the untended lawn below, and a garden gone mad with leggy phlox and daisies.

She sighed and lifted a hand to give her glasses a nudge. "The gardener's drinking again, Jack. We really ought to fire him, only—"

"Stop it." Jack blinked to separate the here and now from the preposterous fantasy, the impossible future.

"—only the children love him so. Perhaps if you had a word with him. Or I could, if you like."

Closing his eyes now, he clenched his teeth as a wave of dizziness went through him, along with a tide of wanting so strong it nearly buckled his knees. This was what he wanted—house, home, the invisible children, the drunken gardener. This house. This home. This sweet shelter. Her.

It wasn't until Anna leaned back against him that he realized his arms had moved to enfold her. Her head came to rest on his shoulder, and Jack dragged in a breath of her fragrant, bewitching hair.

Dear God, if this was dementia, he didn't care. If this was a dream, he never wanted to wake. He wasn't meant for heaven, but somehow he'd inadvertently stumbled in. And how he longed to stay.

A shudder racked him. Anna turned in his arms. Her cool hands came up to cradle his face, so tenderly he wanted to cry. Instead, he buried his lips in the palm of her hand.

"Oh, Jack," she whispered. "My darling Jack. Let me show you how sweet and gentle loving can be. Please. Let me teach you. Now."

She continued to whisper—murmuring words of which he hardly comprehended anything, other than their softness and sweetness—soothing him with her voice while she unknotted his neckcloth and pulled it slowly, sinuously, away, then moved her hands to the buttons of his vest and shirt. She kept whispering while she slipped button after button through, while he stood there, mute, mesmerized, unable to move, even though every nerve in his body was on fire and every inch of him was burning with desire.

When she parted the halves of his shirt and her fingertips just skimmed him, his eyelids twitched before they sank closed in sensual submission. He could hear the sound of his own tattered breathing, and then the rustle of Anna's skirts as she moved closer. He felt the exquisite warmth of her breath on his bared chest. And then her lips, warm and moist, kissing him, moving over him.

Ah, God... It had been so long, an eternity since— A vision of Chloe streaked through his brain, and Jack winced in anticipation of the pain when Anna's soft lips would disclose sharp little teeth to test his flesh to the limits.

He groaned when her tongue touched his hardened nipple, but instead of biting she laved him gently, then suckled so tenderly he thought he might weep from the sheer sweetness of it, from the rush of sensations he had never known before.

"You...you don't know what you're doing to me," he whispered, barely recognizing his own broken voice, but needing to warn her that he was dangerously close to losing what little control he still possessed. "Stop now, love, unless you want..."

"I want." Her lips grazed across his chest, burning him while they caressed him. While they blessed him. "You."

Anna had never wanted anything, anyone, more. During her marriage, she had experienced desire, but this was more than mere desire. Her attempt to salvage Jack by means of a tender seduction had turned into something altogether different. What had begun in tenderness had turned fierce and urgent now. What had started as a gentle, wavering flame was burning through her now, wild and hot and not to be denied.

It wasn't supposed to happen this way. But now, as much as she wanted to shower this man with sweetness and cover him with gentle kisses, she wanted, as well, to consume him like a fire, and to be consumed by him. To go up in flames beneath him.

She lifted her face to his and saw the raw hunger in his eyes. Before she could beg him to kiss her, he lowered his head and laid claim to her mouth. Ravishing. Ravaging. Turning the fire inside her to liquid heat.

"Hurry," she breathed as his fingers fumbled with the buttons down her back and she tore at the tiny ones on her sleeves. Moments later, she stepped out of a pool of castoff silks, wearing only her thin chemise and drawers. Then she yanked the dustcover from the bed, barely aware of the little cloud of dust she raised, and slipped between the cool sheets.

Dust motes danced in the late-afternoon sunlight, surrounding Jack with a golden aura, glittering around his dark hair and exquisitely handsome face, falling softly on his muscular shoulders as he sat on a corner of the bed to take his boots off. Anna closed her eyes a moment, thinking this man was too beautiful to be true, certainly far too beautiful ever to be hers. And then she remembered that beneath all that masculine grace and perfection, there was a heart so wounded she might never be able to heal it.

She opened her eyes on the hard-carved musculature of his back, then found herself staring at the fretwork of scars that ran from his shoulders to his waist. A network of terrible lines, some of which were a pearly, antique white, but many of which were a newer, pinker hue.

Jack was unbuckling his belt, but when she drew in an audible breath, he glanced over his shoulder.

"What, mouse?" he asked.

Unable to say a word just then, Anna reached out and ran her fingertips delicately over the warm, scarred ridges of his skin.

"Ah. The stripes." He sighed and turned his attention back to his buckle. "Not to worry, love. Those are just a few souvenirs from my years in Castle Thunder, during the war."

His tone was so convincing, Anna thought she probably would have believed him, if Madelaine hadn't told her the truth. She wondered what excuse poor Jack had used before his imprisonment in that Rebel hellhole. She wondered if he had ever told anyone the terrible truth of how a little boy came to believe that love always came with pain, like a rose with its natural complement of thorns. Had he confessed to Chloe Von Drosten? Anna wondered as she looked at the newer lash marks on Jack's back.

There were more, she noticed as he took off his trousers and drawers in a single motion. His body was as perfect as any marble statue she had ever seen—all taut skin over hard muscle, beautifully male—and so indecently abused it made her want to weep. Suddenly, then, the heat of her passion cooled. Now, instead of wanting to take pleasure, Anna wanted only to give it. She wanted only to gift Jack Hazard with the sweetest and the gentlest of pleasures and, if she could, to give him peace—utter peace—of body and mind and spirit. His body first.

When he turned to gather her in his arms, she slid out of his embrace and got to her knees.

"Lie down," she said, suppressing the urge to laugh at his bemused expression. "Lie down, Jack. Close your eyes. Please."

With a sigh that suggested he was trying to be a gentleman and cope with a lady who had just changed her mind *in medias res*—not to mention *in flagrante delicto*—he dropped his head back onto the pillow, then closed his eyes, less like a man expecting gratification than like one struggling for control. This was one particular battle she had no intention of letting him win, however. She took off her glasses and leaned to place them on the dusty table beside the bed. Leaning back, she skimmed her fingertips across the perfectly molded planes of his chest.

The little moan that broke from his lips was part pleasure and part surprise. His eyes snapped open and he gripped her wrist, hard, flattening her palm over the hammering of his heart. "This isn't a game anymore, Anna. You know that, don't you?"

"I know."

"We're not playing now, love. Don't—don't ask for more than you want. Do you understand?"

"Completely," she whispered, lowering her head to kiss the hard fist that restrained her and feeling his heartbeat surge beneath her hand. "I'm not asking for anything. I only want to give you sweet, sweet pleasure."

Oh, dear, if I know how, she thought. Being brazen and bold would only get her so far. She wasn't a seductress, despite the fact that she'd been married. Even then she'd never been more than a willing recipient of her young husband's attentions. Billy Matlin, she suspected now, had had a very limited repertoire when it came to the grand opera of lovemaking.

Anna drew in a deep, calming breath while gently disengaging her wrist from Jack's grip. Then she guided his hand toward the headboard, where she curled his fingers around one of the iron spindles.

"There," she said, then proceeded to do the same with his other hand. "Now just close your eyes and let me be sweet."

Sweet! It was like lying in a field of clover, only instead of the sting of bees, Jack felt as if he were covered with the sunshine of Anna's golden hair, the warmth of her kisses and the honeyed stroke of her tongue on his chest, his belly and his thighs. It was an ecstasy he had never known.

When she straddled him and took him inside her, he couldn't stifle a moan of pleasure, and then, when she found her own perfect rhythm to match the thrust of his hips, it went beyond ecstasy to a realm of sheer heat and pure light where he was absolutely lost. Where he was totally drunk and unaccountably blind.

He could hear the iron bedpost battering the wall, and the wild creak of the ropes beneath the mattress, and his own strangled moans. He could feel the arch of his neck and the sudden spasms from his fingers all the way to the soles of his feet. And finally he heard Anna's name and God's name both break from his throat in the groan of a man who was dying the sweetest, most lingering death imaginable.

"I love you, Jack," she whispered when she moved to nestle against his side. Her hand splayed over his heart and her breath shivered over his damp skin. "Hold me, please. Would you?"

Jack blinked like a man just awakened from a deep sleep, if not revived from a brief death. "What?"

''Let go of the bedpost, please, and hold me.''

He shot a glance over his head to where his fingers were twisted in the iron spindles. Sweet Christ! He'd imagined—no, he'd been sure—his hands were bound there, as they had been so often in the past. And now he didn't know whether to laugh for joy or to cry with shame as he unwound his stiff fingers, then brought down his arms to enfold Anna and draw her even closer against him.

His breathing smoothed out and his heartbeat slowed. The circulation prickled back into his arms, and elsewhere, as well, to Jack's amazement. Desire flowed through him again, only this time not hot and wild and ungovernable, as before, but warm and slow and self-contained as a river of honey. He gazed at the pale hair straying across his chest, at the fragile alabaster hand resting on his darker skin, and suddenly found himself wondering how an intoxicating angel could have appeared in the guise of this sober little stickler.

He edged up on an elbow. ''Where the devil did you learn to send a man to the farthest edge of paradise, mouse?''

''Here,'' she said. ''Just now.'' She tipped a tiny grin his way. ''I only listened to your body and did what it was telling me to do.''

''Oh.'' Jack sighed and dropped back. Then he chuckled softly. ''Praise the Lord for my unintentional eloquence.''

Anna slid a cool foot along his calf and murmured, "Loving can be sweet, Jack."

"Apparently so, darling."

"So sweet. Oh, I do love you so." She drew back her head to meet his gaze. "Does that surprise you?"

No, he wanted to say. So many women had claimed to love him. And yes, he felt like shouting. The fact that this woman said she loved him was astonishing, and without a doubt the best thing that had ever happened to him. Or ever would.

"Everything you do surprises me, little mouse," he whispered, tucking her head into his shoulder and letting his fingers drift over the smooth skin of her arm.

Outside, the day was mellowing to dusk. The light coming through the window was drenched with the crimson of a setting sun. Jack had never felt such peace. It was more than sexual release, although God knew that was part of it. It was being here, in this house—*our house*—with Anna in his arms. It was wanting to stay here always. Like this. With the sun sliding toward another day of loving. And another. It was the prospect of life and love and children and even—yes, even the drunken gardener who required a dressing-down.

Why not? he thought suddenly. He could buy this residential wedding cake with the purse from the Carondelet Stakes. This house, and additional acreage for Madelaine and the horses she would be asked to train. Why not make it more than mere make believe?

But as quickly as that bright inspiration came, it was tarnished by the truth. Why not? Because he wasn't worthy of Anna Matlin. He was no match for an angel. Jack Hazard's sole religion, thanks to dear old Papa, was whiskey and pain. The day would come when he'd be drunker than the gardener ever dreamed. And then some midnight—some, dark damnable midnight—when all the gentle love Anna could bestow on him wouldn't be enough to convince him that he deserved it and he'd cry out, begging like a dumb wounded beast for...

Chloe. The ceiling blurred for a second. Jack closed his eyes in defiance of the tears. So much for angels, he thought bitterly. It was time to find the devil and drive her out of every dark corner of his heart. After that, it would be time to curl up with a bottle in one of those dark corners and be done with it. Done with angels and devils both.

"It's getting dark, love," he said softly. "It's time for us to go."

It was dark. Moonless. Starless. Anna heaved a forlorn sigh at the black sky overhead, then punched her spectacles farther up on her nose—for all the good that did. They'd already walked at least half a mile, and the lights of the cheery inn still seemed ten miles ahead.

"I'm sorry. It's all my fault. I shouldn't have told the driver to leave."

Jack laughed, and his hand tightened on hers. "Or paid the old rummy a whole dollar to do it."

"What in the world was I thinking?"

"As I recall, you had seduction on your mind, mouse. I can't imagine any other reason for your incredible lapse in frugality, or your loose purse strings. Can you?" He laughed again.

"Now you're making fun of me." Anna jerked her hand from his and walked faster. Not fast enough, though, because a second later Jack caught her in a solid embrace.

"I'm not making fun of you," he said adamantly, using a knuckle to lift her face to his. "I'd be making love to you right this minute, if it weren't for the damn dark. And as soon as we get back to civilization, Anna, I intend to give you at least as much pleasure as you gave me. Consider yourself warned."

There was barely time to smile before his mouth slanted across hers for a possessive kiss. She reached on tiptoe, eager for more, but he broke the kiss and took up her hand once more.

"Let's go." He tugged her along in his wake, surprised that she wasn't more truculent than she was, considering she'd given so much and received nothing in return. But that was a situation he had every intention of rectifying as soon as they closed the door of their suite.

The carriage was parked—hastily, judging from the angle of it, and from the dangling reins—in front of the tavern, and just as Jack had expected, the bloody driver wasn't in sight. Now he was going to have to go into that reeking swill shop and haul the man out by the scruff of the neck.

"Wait here," he told Anna, but when he started for the door, she didn't let go of his hand.

"I think I should be the one to retrieve the driver, Jack. I was the one who sent him away. You wait here. It won't take me a minute."

Now it was Jack who was pulling her back. Yanking her, in fact, and rather more roughly than he had meant to. He let her go just long enough to rip his fingers through his hair, then growled, "What the devil are you thinking? That I'm such a craven weakling that I can't walk into a tavern without falling irrevocably from grace? Is that what you believe, Anna?"

She shook her head so vehemently her glasses slipped. "No. I just— I only wanted to be kind. To help you."

"Don't help me!" he bellowed. "I don't need it!"

Her chin snapped up and her pretty face hardened with determination, but behind their lenses her eyes shimmered with tears. "Why are you so angry, Jack?"

"I'm not angry." Oh, God, yes, he was, and suddenly he knew exactly why. *He* was the one who wasn't sure he'd be able to walk in and out of the tavern without that perilous slip. He was the one who ought to be protecting her, and yet here Anna stood, like a bespectacled guardian angel, convinced she needed to protect him and somehow knowing that ultimately he couldn't do it himself, because he *was* a craven weakling. She was right. And it shamed him beyond endurance.

He caught her in his arms and crushed her to him. "Let me at least try to be a man, Anna. Despite the risks." His voice softened to a whisper then as he told her why she couldn't go into the tavern with her hair in a wild tangle and her dress in less-than-pristine condition. "You look like you've just been tumbled, quite frankly, and there won't be a man in there who wouldn't be tempted to try it again. It's been years since I've taken on a mob, darling, and I'm not in any condition to do so tonight. So stay here. All right?"

While Anna watched, Jack disappeared into the smoke-filled, dimly lit den of temptation. He was right, of course. She had feared that if he went in there he might never come out. Once again, she felt overwhelmed by his problems and her inability to solve them. But he had wanted to protect her. That had to be a good sign. And he'd been much more keenly aware of the situation than she. It hadn't even occurred to her that she probably looked like a woman who'd just climbed out of bed.

She dragged her fingers through the knots in her hair and made a few adjustments to her hastily donned corset. She was tending to the misdone buttons on her sleeve when the tavern door burst open and Jack walked out with a man slung over his shoulder.

He dumped the driver's inert body in the passenger seat.

"What happened?" Anna asked.

"We exchanged unpleasantries," he answered calmly, while brushing off his coat.

It was then that Anna noticed the dark specks on Jack's lapel, and the trickle of blood at one corner of his mouth. She gave a little gasp. "You hit him!"

"Only once, love."

He cocked an eyebrow, and then his mouth flared in the most dashing and dazzling of grins. Anna thought that if she lived to be a hundred years old she would see it as clearly then as she did this moment. No matter what happened. No matter how long she lived, she would forever see Mad Jack Hazard proud and victorious and in his glory.

She was a bit mad herself, Anna thought, on the carriage ride back to the city. Jack kept one arm around her and the other on the reins, while they sang every sweet and foolish song they knew. Or didn't know, in Jack's case. The fact that he didn't recall half the lyrics didn't prevent him from blending his rich baritone with her surprisingly bold soprano.

They were like youngsters in love for the very first time. While the driver remained insensate in the back, Jack stopped the horses every half mile or so to take her in his arms, to kiss her senseless while apprising her—shamelessly, explicitly, thrillingly—of his every amorous intention once they were back in their suite.

It couldn't be soon enough, she thought, as she stood on the sidewalk in front of the hotel while Jack arranged for the return of Mrs. Bissell's carriage and its unfortunate passenger. She didn't even blink when he overtipped the reluctant doorman by half. She nearly giggled when it occurred to her that an amount that would have sent her reeling two weeks before was now merely a sum necessary to expedite their loving.

"Mrs. Hazard." Jack's warm smile and firm hand on her back had her fairly dancing through the Southern Hotel's front door. And then, only a few yards into the lobby, Anna stopped dead still.

Standing across the room was the most beautiful woman she had ever seen or imagined. Tall and slim. Statuesque, really, with her perfectly molded body barely disguised by the silken sweep of a black riding habit that echoed the color and sheen of her hair. The word goddess flickered in Anna's brain, but when she opened her mouth it came out differently. "The baroness," she breathed.

# *Chapter Seventeen*

No sooner had Anna spoken than a vicious oath ripped through Jack's teeth. She realized now that he had come to a standstill at the same moment she had. His hand remained on her back, but his fingers had tensed. In fact, his whole body seemed to stiffen as with an electric jolt, while his dark eyes fixed on the woman in the black riding habit. His breath rattled in his throat, and then he seemed to stop breathing completely.

Oh, Lord. Not knowing what to do, Anna gave her glasses a brisk two-fingered poke and let her panicky gaze skitter around the lobby, as if help were available—somewhere—if only she could find it. And then a miracle—she did. At the far side of the lobby, in front of a bank of windows, Anna caught a glimpse of wheat-colored hair. Freddy! Thank God. Relief coursed through Anna like a spring river going over its banks. Then she watched the lanky agent lean down to aim a polite ear toward a small, gray-haired and oddly familiar woman who was tugging at his sleeve.

It wasn't. It couldn't be. The relief Anna had felt dried up like a creek in a heat wave when she recognized little Miss Richmond. A second later, big Miss Richmond hove into view, just to Freddy's right. All three of them then—Freddy and the Misses Richmond, in terrifying unison—smiled gaily in Anna's direction and eagerly began to wave.

Out of a corner of her eye, Anna could see the woman in black start to move—slither, really—across the lobby. It was like being caught between a trio of chirping finches and a snake. Between chaos and the plague. The baroness could ruin Jack—perhaps. But Anna's landladies would certainly bring their whole plan to ruin, unless...

"I'll be right back," she whispered frantically to Jack.

He caught her hand. His palm was wet and his fingers quaked. "Stay. I need you here."

Oh, God, she knew that, but there wasn't time to explain. She went up on tiptoe and kissed the rigid line of his jaw, then wrenched her hand from his and rushed away.

"Jack."

The cat purred while she circled him. Darker. Sleeker than he'd ever seen her. More beautiful, if that was possible. More dangerous than his worst fears.

Jack felt like a drowning man whose last grasp at a lifeline has proved futile. It was all he could do to stand there without sinking to his knees while she drew the circle tighter, tapping her damn quirt in her black-gloved hand. Relentless as the tick of a clock. A little like the crackle of pine wood in his father's study. More like the maddening drip of cool water in a Chinese torture—and the sweat that had begun to trickle down his sides.

"It's good to see you, Jack," she purred. "I've missed you, darling."

She smelled like a cat just come from a saucer of brandy. Jack lifted his gaze from the whip in her hand to her amber gaze. The pupils were huge and black, and he found himself wishing for a drop or two of whatever was pulsing through her veins.

"I imagine you have missed me, Chloe." He angled his head toward the pair of hulking idiots she'd left in her wake. "But I see you've acquired a suitable replacement. Or should I say replacements?"

She laughed. "Perhaps. Viktor has your stamina, and Constantine, well . . ." She shrugged. "Nobody has your style."

"Poor Chloe."

"No. Poor Jack." The baroness smiled as she touched the tip of her gloved finger to the corner of his mouth. She stared at the drop of blood that came away, her own mouth twitching a little. For a second, she looked almost human. Then her cat's eyes flicked up to his. "Damn you. Why did you leave me?"

He pulled a handkerchief from his pocket and dabbed at his cut lip, eyeing her all the while. "To put it quite simply, Chloe, you were killing me. I decided suicide was preferable."

Her fist curled around the whip. "Did you? I heard otherwise." She sniffed. "I heard you'd married a pale little nobody with a great deal of money, and that you're running a horse in the Carondelet Stakes. Is it true?"

"Some of it." He jammed his handkerchief back in his pocket. "My bride is a very generous woman, but she's hardly a pale little nobody. She's Mrs. Jack Hazard, isn't she?" He smiled as he crooked a finger to draw her closer. Then his voice lowered to a croon. "And my horse runs like the bloody wind, Baroness. Chloe's Gold is through."

Her head snapped back. "Is that a threat?"

Jack shrugged.

"There isn't a horse alive," she hissed, "that can take a race away from mine."

Now he laughed. "That's because you withdraw from any race you might lose, Duchess. Oh, pardon me. I meant Baroness. Or—" Jack stopped laughing suddenly, and his voice roughened "—you send some damn lackey to dope the competition."

"Some damn lackey more than willing to give a horse a little laudanum to assure himself of his own, don't you mean?" Chloe contemplated his face for a long moment. Her crimson mouth softened, and her expression came so close to being wistful that it sent a chill skidding along Jack's spine as he remembered—no as he *felt*—the touch of her cool hands on his hot skin.

"How long have you been sober, Jack?"

Too long, he wanted to say. Not nearly long enough. "Since the day I left you, Chloe."

Whatever wistfulness had been on her face hardened to fury, and she gripped the riding crop in both hands, very nearly snapping it in two. "Nobody walks out on me."

Jack laughed again. "No, I daresay you're right, darling. If I remember correctly, I crawled."

"And you'll crawl back to me, too, God damn you."

Looking into her fierce, feline eyes just then, Jack wouldn't have bet his life that Chloe Von Drosten was wrong. It was a dark and distinct possibility. It lurked in the bass thrum of his heartbeat even now. It pulled tight in his heart, like an ancient scar. It was the reason he'd needed a Pinkerton wife as a shield. For all the good that was doing him now. Where the devil was she?

He took his wary eyes off Chloe just long enough to scan the lobby and to find Anna deep in conversation with two old biddies.

"So that's the pale silk purse who's captured your noble heart." Chloe's gaze had followed his. "I'd like to meet her, Jack. I really must congratulate her for keeping you on the straight and narrow. For now, anyway.''

''Sssh ... Here they come. Now, remember everything I've told you. Both of you. It's absolutely crucial.'' Anna lowered her voice ominously. ''It's a matter of life and death.''

Her warning probably wasn't all that far from the truth, she thought, and it had the desired effect on her landladies. Little Miss Verna Richmond blinked rapidly, and big Miss Dorothy nodded slowly and somberly. Their separate gestures reassured Anna that their plan—hers and Jack's—wasn't going to come crashing down. At least not in the next ten minutes.

Thank God, she thought, Freddy had rushed back to his paperwork the moment she took the two elderly spinsters off his hands. The Misses Richmond had descended upon him at the Pinkerton office late that afternoon, and Freddy—bless him—along with calming their fears, had fed them and secured them a room and then had waited with them until Anna's arrival.

Anna was grateful for what the agent had done, but she was still relieved that he was gone, because Freddy would never approve of what she had just done. Not that Anna exactly approved of the deception herself, but it was the only thing she had been able to think of at the time.

The second Freddy walked away, and while she kept one eye on Jack and the baroness, Anna had deputized her landladies.

"Don't look right now," she had whispered, "but that's the Baroness Chloe Von Drosten over there."

Of course both women had promptly whipped their heads in that direction.

"The jewel thief?" Miss Verna had gasped, nervously fingering the cameo at her throat. "I've read about her in the newspaper."

"You rarely read anything but the recipes, sister," Miss Dorothy said with a snort. "And I don't think the baroness will look twice at your brooch. Really."

"Well, we did bring Mother's—"

"Hush," Miss Dorothy snapped, cutting her sister off. "Let's listen to dear Anna. It's obvious she needs our assistance."

"Yes. All right, Dorothy." The smaller sister peeked across the lobby again. "Is that elegant man a jewel thief, as well?"

There was no doubt about the elegant man to whom Miss Verna was referring. Anna peeked now, and her heart clenched when she saw Jack smiling one of *those* smiles at the baroness. How long, she wondered, before he came under her spell again? If he hadn't already.

"He's not a jewel thief, Miss Verna. He's—he's my husband." While both women clasped their hands to their hearts, Anna continued. "I know it's a shock.

It was a shock to me, too. The suddenness of it all. He's a Pinkerton agent, you see. We were supposed to be just partners, but, well . . . we fell in love." She snapped her fingers. "Just like that. So we were married. Last week. See?" She held out her left hand in order to display her last-minute ring.

"I've heard it can happen that way," little Miss Richmond said, rather breathlessly. "Two people meet, and—"

"Balderdash." Big Miss Richmond removed her hand from her heart and flapped it in front of her sister. "You don't know the first thing about it, Verna. Do be quiet and let Anna speak."

Anna had spoken then—had lied through her teeth, actually—about the simple wedding ceremony that had taken place amid the more complicated task of bringing the infamous baroness to justice. "That's one of the reasons I'm so delighted to see you both. I doubt Mr. Broome told you, but we're extremely shorthanded at the moment. I need your help desperately, and I'd be so grateful if you'd be willing to act, for a short while, as deputy Pinkerton agents." Despite the fact that she was lying, Anna's eyes had filled with real tears. "Would you? Please?"

"My dear child," Miss Dorothy said, "you can count on us implicitly." She pressed Anna's hand between both of her own liver-spotted hands. "We've cared for you deeply these last six years, you know."

"You're like a daughter to us," Miss Verna chimed in.

"More like a niece," Miss Dorothy said.

The sudden display of affection from her landladies left Anna nearly speechless. "I never realized..."

"Well, you never gave us a chance, dear." Miss Dorothy clucked her tongue. "You took your meals out, and when you came home you went straight to your room."

It was true, Anna thought. She'd never really given anyone a chance. She'd lived like a ghost after Billy's death, coming and going silently, invisibly. She had lived as if she were already dead herself, inside a sort of translucent and protective shroud of her own making. Until Mad Jack Hazard happened to her and turned her life inside out, upside down, and altogether visible. Until love happened to her heart and urged her to reach out, instead of constantly withdrawing.

"I'm so sorry," she said through trembling lips. "I never knew."

Big Miss Richmond sniffed, more from indignation than from sentimentality, but even so, she squeezed Anna's hand more tightly. "Well, now you know. Let's not dwell on it."

Edging a finger beneath a lens, Anna caught a tear that was about to spill, telling herself tears would only make her brain soggy and dull right now, when it needed to be as hard and sharp as steel.

"If we're to be assistant Pinkertons," Miss Verna said, "oughtn't we to have some means of identification, dear? Just to make it official?" The little woman smiled and blinked expectantly. "A silver badge would be ever so nice. What do you think, sister?"

"They're tin," Miss Dorothy snapped, but then she, too, gazed at Anna with fond hope.

Was everyone in the world a stickler for symbols and badges of office? Anna wondered. She sighed and rummaged quickly through her handbag, then handed Miss Dorothy her railroad pass, with the wide-open Pinkerton eye clearly displayed. That seemed to please her large landlady, for she made a small mewing sound deep in her throat.

"And for me?" her little landlady chirped.

Anna dug into her bag again and produced her small bound expense booklet, in which she'd barely made a notation for the past day or so. Why not? she thought. This wasn't Pinkerton business for her anymore. It was personal. "Here," she said, putting the booklet in Miss Verna's hand with a definitive little slap. "Now it's official."

So much for her own career as a stickler, Anna thought suddenly. How Jack would laugh to see her giving up her expense sheets without so much as a whimper—and without a loaded gun held to her head.

He wasn't laughing now, though. He appeared as grim and haunted as she'd ever seen him as he walked across the lobby, half a pace behind the woman in black, his eyes locked on Anna's all the while. There was a cold warning in those blue-gray orbs, and something close to icy fear.

"Ssh... Here they come. Now remember everything I've told you. Both of you. It's absolutely crucial. It's a matter of life and death."

"Darling, I'd like you to meet my aunt Dorothy and my aunt Verna. They've come all the way from Chicago to surprise us." The mouse nudged her glasses, then linked her arm through his. "Isn't that sweet?"

Sweet Christ! All he needed right now was another bloody surprise, Jack thought. And more women! He ran his damp palm down his trouser leg and attempted to conquer the tremors there, then shook each eager, gnarled, liver-spotted hand, while Anna beamed happily on his left and, on his right, Chloe looked down her narrow nose with a sigh of undisguised irritation.

Whatever the mouse was up to now, it was too late not to play along. "I'm pleased to meet you." Somehow he dredged up a smile for each of the elderly creatures. "Anna speaks of you so warmly." Under his breath then, and for Anna's sole benefit, he added, "And so often."

"Allow me," he continued, "to introduce the Baroness Chloe Von Drosten."

After a brief exchange between the she-devil and the twittering aunts, Jack sucked in a fortifying breath, while he shifted Anna in front of him so that she stood between himself and Chloe. Where she bloody well belonged, damn it. He linked his arms around her waist and summoned up what he hoped would pass for a grin.

"And this, Baroness, is my lovely bride."

Half an hour later, his lovely bride preceded him into their suite. Before he was even across the threshold, Jack had ripped off his cravat and wrenched off his coat, dropping them on the floor as he walked to his customary chair. He swore at the bottle of sour mash, which had never looked so appealing as it did this moment.

His lips ached from smiling—first at Chloe, whom he'd wanted to strangle, then at the mismatched aunts, and finally at the two stevedores, Viktor and Constantine, whom Chloe had introduced to the happy little group in the lobby.

He had even smiled at Anna, who had reassured him on their way upstairs that the aunts, who turned out to be her landladies, wouldn't be a problem. "You charmed them utterly, Jack. But then, I was sure you would. They think you're an absolute darling."

He was a darling, all right, he thought as he glared at the tempting bottle. That Hazard charm ran bone-deep. Just one more reason to thank the old man for the glittering shards of his life. For a while today—with sweet Anna—he'd almost forgotten. He'd had a brief glimpse of heaven, before the sight of Chloe reminded him of his permanent residence in hell.

Anna was moving around the room now, picking up his discarded jacket, brushing it before she hung it up carefully, then beginning to work the buttons of her sleeves. Despite their tryst this afternoon, there was an innocence about her still, a sweet glow that warmed him all the way across the room. More than warmed him. It burned through him. He wanted her more than ever before. Especially now. He wanted to bury himself in that sweet glow, and lose himself completely in her soft and generous warmth. So much so that he didn't dare touch her at all now for the violence of his need to do just that.

The thought brought a wry quirk to his exhausted lips. Here sits Jack, with all his legendary stamina and style, scholar of the intricacies of the kiss and the whip, master of the netherworld of love. Here sits Mad Jack Hazard, about to renege on all those sensual promises he'd made in the carriage coming back to town, because he couldn't keep them. Not sweetly, the way Anna deserved. Not tonight. His need was too fierce.

She was struggling with her blasted buttons now on the other side of the room.

"Come here, little mouse."

When she perched on the arm of his chair, he lifted a hand to unfasten the rest, careful not even to brush his fingers against her skin. He could hardly breathe, for wanting her. His throat tightened, just like the rest of him.

"There. All done. Go on to bed now. Sleep well."

She was silent for a moment, her gaze fastened on the darkness outside the window. He couldn't fathom what was going on behind those lenses of hers, or beneath those tumbled golden curls. Disappointment, perhaps. Need. A tangle of emotions, not the least of which had to be confusion. She was his little stickler, after all, and he'd given her no reason for this abrupt and callous rejection.

His fingers clenched on the arms of the chair now, and he gritted his teeth in preparation for a gentle plea, if not an argument. Bloody hell. How did you tell a woman you needed her so much you might break every delicate bone in her body? And, yes, that out of habit—hellish habit of a lifetime—you might suggest she do the same for you? He didn't want to be cruel and cold, but better that than burning her.

"You ought to have a good night's rest," he said, less cool than gruff, because of the constriction in his throat. "Tomorrow our plan begins in deadly earnest."

She bent to kiss his cheek, her touch as innocent and undemanding as the brush of a butterfly's wing, then whispered, "No, love. Not tomorrow. It's already begun."

# Chapter Eighteen

Judging from his name, Anna had expected Chloe's Gold to be just that. Gold. But as the sleek stallion raced past her and Jack and the Misses Richmond, Anna had to admit she wasn't at all surprised that he was glossy and black, and just as beautiful as his owner.

Jack clicked his stopwatch and muttered an oath.

"Was that fast?" Anna asked, looking up into his dark face.

"It appeared quite fast to me," Miss Verna said, only to be told by her sister that she didn't know the first thing about horses.

But Jack did, and he was glowering at the time-piece in his hand. "Two minutes and forty seconds. For a workout, that's comparable to lightning down a rod." He ground out another oath, then levered himself off the white-painted rail and stalked away.

"Oh, dear." Anna frowned as she watched him walk toward the paddock, where a reed-thin boy was preparing Polaris for his own turn on the track. Was

Jack truly worried about the speed of Chloe's Gold, she wondered, or was this—like so much else in Jack Hazard's life—just for show?

His tenseness this morning, however, was legitimate. Of that, Anna was sure. He'd barely slept a wink the previous night, after sending her off to bed. She knew that because she'd barely slept herself. She'd lain there for hours, aching for the loss of the glorious night they had been planning, worrying that all her efforts to clasp this man so tightly to her had come undone the moment Chloe Von Drosten appeared on the scene. Was he still so captivated by her? Was he still so shackled to his dreadful past that there was no hope for escape? Or, worse, had he lost the will to escape the moment he saw Chloe again?

There hadn't been time to ask him this morning. He had left their suite early, and by the time Anna got down to the lobby, Jack had already had her landladies in tow and been anxious to get to the racecourse. And whether that had been to see Polaris, or Chloe's Gold, or Chloe herself, Anna still didn't know.

All she knew was that he hadn't touched her since introducing her to the baroness. Not last night, as he had so amorously promised. Not this morning. Every time their hands brushed, she had felt Jack draw away, as if touching her were decidedly unpleasant. Unbearable, even. She couldn't help but wonder if he'd spent the evening dreaming of touching Chloe, instead.

"Good morning, Mrs. Hazard. He's a stunning piece of flesh, isn't he? Or perhaps you don't appreciate such physical things."

Anna turned to encounter Chloe Von Drosten's glittering topaz gaze. The woman was dressed as she had been the evening before, complete with leather whip and silken air of superiority.

"I'm afraid I don't know much about horses, Baroness." If, indeed, that was what she had been referring to. Considering the malicious smile on her crimson lips, Anna wasn't all that sure.

"That's unfortunate." As she spoke, Chloe's eyes drifted again and again toward the paddock where Jack stood. He had taken off his coat, and beneath the warm May sun the muscles of his back were rippling under the saturated cotton of his shirt. "Horses," the baroness continued, "particularly stallions, are a lot like some men. They need a firm hand on the reins. Sometimes they require a Spanish bit between their teeth. And frequently they need..."

Her voice faded, and her gaze intensified on Jack, while she tapped the quirt in the palm of her hand. "Tell me, Mrs. Hazard—how is Jack, now that he's sober?"

"How *is* he?" Anna blinked, only half pretending she didn't comprehend the baroness's meaning.

"In bed, of course." Chloe looked down her narrow nose. "He does sleep with you, doesn't he? I can't imagine Jack Hazard agreeing to a marriage of convenience, no matter how much money the woman has.''

Anna's urge to tap her glasses was overriden by the need to curl her hands into fists. Jealousy wasn't an emotion she was accustomed to feeling, but it blazed through her now. She couldn't bear the thought of this woman touching Jack, gently or otherwise.

''Our sleeping arrangements are none of your business, Baroness,'' she replied, only to see the woman's red lips rise in a smug curve, as if Anna had given her precisely the answer she sought.

''It's just that poor Jack appears so, well... unsatisfied. So unrelieved. And you seem so demure, Mrs. Hazard, it's difficult, if not impossible, to imagine your doing anything to excite him.''

Smiling as demurely as her seething temper would allow, Anna said, ''I wonder if it would excite him to see me strike you and remove that vicious expression from your face.''

''Probably.'' The baroness smiled, just as demurely, while her eyes sparked with challenge. ''Why don't you try it, dear?''

Anna might have, too, if her landladies hadn't chosen that particular moment to greet the baroness and pepper her with questions about Chloe's Gold. Miss Verna kept nervously fingering the cameo pinned at her throat, as if she expected it to be snatched away any second. Miss Dorothy was fidgeting with something, as well, and when Anna looked closer, she was amazed to see the large ruby-

and-diamond brooch that had appeared, as if by magic, on her landlady's ample bosom.

The baroness had noticed it, too. Well, it would have been impossible to ignore, the way big Miss Richmond kept repositioning it and turning the brooch this way and that in an apparent effort to find the proper angle for the summer sun to set each stone on fire. What in the world did she think she was doing, waving a prize like that under the very nose of a thief?

Oh, Lord. Had the silly Pinkerton deputization gone straight to Miss Dorothy's head? Anna was about to draw her aside when a deep voice sounded at her back.

"Ladies, may I direct your attention to the track?"

Jack jammed his thumb down on the stopwatch just as Polaris took off. "My horse, Baroness," he said, not taking his eyes off the mahogany bay whose hooves were tearing up the first furlong. "Behold the future winner of the Carondelet Stakes."

The watch ticked like a living thing against Jack's damp palm, while the cautions he'd given the jockey ticked inside his brain. Hold him back, damn it. Sit on him. Don't give him his head. Bring him in at two minutes and forty-six seconds. No more. No less. No more. No less.

Yes. One-twenty at the six-furlong flag. Right on the mark. No more. No less. Hold him.

"Yes." Jack's breath hissed out of him as Polaris's hooves thundered past.

Chloe glanced at the watch in his hand. Then she laughed. Exactly as he had planned.

"Runs like the bloody wind, does he, darling?" She lifted her sharp little chin to look into his face. "I'd call that a breeze, at best."

Jack let his gaze flit to the watch again. As if the horse's time hadn't quite registered. As if he hadn't already calculated the six-second difference between Polaris and Chloe's Gold, or hadn't translated the lag into the several lengths of horseflesh flying across the finish line, or didn't know the difference between winning and losing. He coaxed the flicker of a frown across his forehead and set his lips in a worried line before he gave her a foolish and hopeful grin.

"He's faster when he races, actually." He looped an arm around Anna's waist. "Isn't he, love?"

There was no questioning the sincerity of the frown that creased her pretty forehead. "Much faster," she said, trying hard, but—bless her honest little heart—failing to sound at all convincing.

"I'm sure," the baroness said with a shrug. "There's probably still time to redeem your entry fee, Jack. Unless, of course, you like throwing your wife's money away."

Jack hugged his rich wife closer. "To tell you the truth, Chloe, I had something else in mind. With my bride's permission, I'd like to suggest a wager."

"A wager?"

The same words sounded from all the females assembled around him. The aunts gasped them. Anna fairly choked them out. But Chloe—ah, Chloe—the devil love her dearly—purred, while the glitter of greed lit up her tigress eyes.

"What sort of wager?" she was quick to add. "Just how much did you have in mind, Jack? You'd have to make it worth my while."

"Ten thousand dollars! Ten *thousand* dollars!"

Every time Anna said it, she felt dizzy and a little sick, which meant that she'd spent most of the day in a queasy condition, ever since Jack had proposed the amount that was worth Chloe's while. That staggering sum, and its attendant risk, had driven all other concerns from Anna's brain.

She sagged onto the bed with barely enough energy to slip off her shoes. "Ten thousand dollars," she moaned.

Across the room, Jack shrugged off his jacket and draped it over a chair. "You're beginning to sound like a bloody parrot, mouse."

He seemed more amused than irritated, and blithely unconcerned. He'd behaved that way all day, much to Anna's consternation. "But what if you lose, Jack?"

"I'm not going to lose," he said cheerfully. "That's the whole point."

Anna let her shoes thunk on the carpet, then leaned back on an elbow. "Do you even have ten thousand dollars?"

"Today?"

"Yes, today."

Jack clucked his tongue with soft derision. "You're such a stickler."

"You don't have it." Anna dropped back onto the mattress and raised her hands heavenward. "He doesn't have it," she muttered through clenched teeth. "Oh, Jack. I'm beginning to believe you *are* mad."

"Only a little, darling."

The truth was, Jack thought, that he hadn't felt quite this sane in years. If ever. And it wasn't because his plan was falling into place so perfectly or because he had the black cat right where he wanted her. Rather, it was because all that didn't seem quite so important anymore.

And neither did that, he thought as his gaze slanted to the bottle of sour mash on the table. For the first time in a long time, his gut didn't twitch at the mere sight, and the back of his throat didn't quicken with need. A different need suffused him now, driving out all else. But unlike the night before, when his desire for Anna had left him nearly paralyzed by its violence, tonight that blazing fire seemed to have burned down to a bed of glowing coals.

"Ten thousand dollars." She sighed again. "I've never seen that much money all in one place. Whatever will you do with it if you win?"

"When I win," he told her.

"All right, then. *When* you win. Will you spend it?"

"Flagrantly."

She elbowed up, smiling dreamily for a moment, until her glance strayed to the bottle. Then her pretty mouth turned down at the corners and her eyes narrowed with suspicion. It didn't take a scholar to know that behind those silly lenses she was calculating the cost of a drunken binge.

It was something Jack had calculated more than once himself. It had been his raison d'être and his driving force. That last lethal binge had been the sole bright light at the end of his dark tunnel of sobriety. But it wasn't anymore. If he hadn't known that completely, he knew it now. He could feel it, bone-deep. In every nerve. Mostly he could feel it in his heart. The emptiness was gone. The darkness had somehow disappeared.

"Not to worry, little mouse." He picked up the bottle, amazed that it even felt different in his hand. It seemed inert now and cool, just glass, rather than a warm and vital vessel containing a blessed genie. Still, he wasn't fool enough to believe that after all these years the genie had simply evaporated. Perhaps it never would.

"That may have been my intention once. Spending the winnings on a last liquid spree." He laughed a little sheepishly while he moved toward the bed, where he lowered himself to the edge and sat with the bottle in his hands. "It is what drunks do. That's what I am, Anna, and always have been. I had my first taste of this when I was ten years old, you know."

"So young," she murmured, her hand rising to smooth across his back.

"My father..." Jack's voice caught in his throat. He was unused to so much truth, unwilling to speak it even now, though he remembered so clearly that first time, in the old man's study on that spring afternoon. After his father had his pleasure, he'd exchanged his silver-handled whip for a cut-crystal decanter.

"Have a sip, son," he'd said so affably. "Takes some of the sting away."

Jack had gulped instead, then coughed and nearly vomited, much to his father's displeasure.

"Run along now, Jack. Take the whiskey with you, if you like. And you might want to dab a bit on those welts while you're at it. There's a good little fellow."

He remembered slinking off to the stables, stripping off his clothes, then dousing his bruised body in the cool liquid. Slowly, then and over the years, he'd doused his soul.

Shaking his head now to dislodge the vision, Jack said, "My father encouraged me. I was too young, of course, to appreciate the addictive qualities." He traced a thumb over the label. "And it helped. It helped enormously. But it doesn't anymore."

Anna's hand was still on his back. "I'll help you," she said simply.

"You already have." He leaned forward, placing the bottle on its side beneath the bed. Then he sighed. Out of sight. Someday—please God—out of mind, as well.

Her arms curled around him then, and her sweet, warm, distracting body pressed the length of his back. Desire flicked like fire in the pit of his stomach, and suddenly he wanted to make a million outlandish, far-fetched promises, and to make a thousand heady pledges of love. Words that had never tempted his lips before were fairly itching there now. Words he couldn't say yet. Not yet. Not until he knew he could live up to them.

So he said nothing, only whispered warm endearments while unfastening Anna's dress and loosening the ties of her corset. Love, if that was truly what he was feeling, nearly struck him dumb, even as it set up a trembling in his hands. He could *make* love. Just love. While his body knew exactly what to do, his heart was foundering, unaccustomed as it was to hope.

It was only later, with Anna's body so soft and urgent beneath his, and with her whispered pleas like hot silk at his ear, that Jack's heart forgot to be wary. He was drunk on her now—having sipped from her lush mouth, having tasted every honeyed, hidden part of her—and he forgot all the reasons he shouldn't make promises and made them anyway, as he entered the warm heaven of her. And when he came—when that sweet and exquisite release ripped through him—he cried out her name and then couldn't stop crying—deep in the wet crook of her neck—for utter, unfathomable joy.

Anna held him, stroking his scarred back, crooning softly while his heartbeat slowed to a normal rhythm, continuing even when his breathing eased to that of a man deeply and peacefully asleep.

She, on the other hand, couldn't sleep at all, for the thoughts that kept tumbling through her brain and the remnants of electricity that still thrummed through her body. It shouldn't have surprised her that a man with Jack Hazard's experience could make her feel things she'd never felt before. Never felt, or even dreamed. Sensations that had been mere flickers during her marriage to Billy had turned to uncontrollable flames with Jack. He had set her on fire, with his hands and his kisses and with each wet flick of his tongue. He had made her blaze. Then, when all those wild flames had gathered deep inside her, he had somehow coaxed them even higher—impossibly and achingly high—to an exquisite peak, a hot pillar of flame before it burst apart in a brilliant shower of sparks.

She had wept, too, then. Afterward. From unspeakably sweet release. For sheer joy. It was a bit like being drunk. But Jack hadn't been drunk. Or, if he had, it had been on her alone.

In a far corner of Anna's brain now, the baroness's question echoed again. *How is he when he's sober?* The answer was apparent.

He is unsure, Baroness, she might have said. He is afraid the habits of a lifetime have corroded his ability to feel anything but pain. He wants something so simple—only love—but he believes it is a difficult, hurtful thing.

He is wrong.

And, Baroness, he is magnificent.

Jack woke with a smile on his lips and the mouse curled in his arms. He brought her closer, inhaling her sweet fragrance, treasuring her satin warmth. What miracle had brought her to him? he wondered. How in bloody blazes had he survived so long without her? Badly, he answered himself. And barely. By all rights, he should be dead right now, instead of lying here feeling full of life and blessed with hope.

Judging from the brilliance of the sunlight knifing between the drawn drapes, it was late. Nine. Perhaps even ten o'clock. Time to get to the racecourse, to oversee another of Polaris's workouts, and to draw the noose tighter around the black cat's neck.

Or not. Why not be done with it? If that part of his life was over—and it felt over, if not miraculously healed—why not let it go? He cast about inside for the hot spark that had driven him to seek revenge against Chloe, for the painful scars and the burning need to bring her to ruin for the part she had played in his own near destruction. Hard as he tried, though, he couldn't find a glimmer of that former all-consuming need.

All he needed, right now and always, was the woman in his arms. He slid his hand along her supple flank, then between her thighs, where even now she was wet with their loving. With him. Jack's heart held still, centered around the sweet possibilities of their meeting.

A child. Children. Sons and daughters to shower with love and affection. Sons and daughters through whom he could live again, the way he should have lived all along. He felt his mouth curve in a slow smile, imagining prim little sticklers in pale dresses and dark-haired little boys with killing grins and wet-combed hair.

A light tapping on the door ended his reverie, and the mouse woke, blinking, when the tapping intensified to rapping. Anna flung a hand out for her glasses, while Jack muttered a curse, as much for his obliterated fantasies as for his interrupted lovemaking, then tugged on his underwear and went to the door.

The mismatched aunts stood there, pale and paler, aghast and more aghast. Speechless and not quite.

"She's done it," the little one twittered. "The baroness has stolen my sister's brooch."

# Chapter Nineteen

Anna sat bolt upright in bed, clutching the sheet around her, less disturbed by her own nakedness than by the startling news. By the time she had aligned her spectacles, the Misses Richmond had jammed their skirts through the doorway and bustled into the suite.

Miss Verna looked quite pale. "We went downstairs this morning for a bite to eat—" she began breathlessly. Then, true to form, Miss Dorothy cut her off.

"It's my brooch, Verna. Mother left it to me. I'll tell this, if you don't mind." Big Miss Richmond sucked in a breath. "We went downstairs for a bite to eat, and when we returned to our room, my brooch was gone."

"It was the baroness," Miss Verna chirped. "You saw how the woman was ogling Dorothy's bosom yesterday."

"She was ogling my brooch," her sister said sternly.

"Damn it, Dorothy." Little Miss Richmond stamped her foot. "It was pinned to your confounded bosom, wasn't it?"

Anna sat forward, eager for more information and less bickering. "You can't be absolutely certain it was the baroness, can you?"

"Of course they can." The deep, clipped statement came from the door, where Jack was leaning against the frame. His face was a glowering mask.

"There—you see," Big Miss Dorothy said. "Your husband is experienced in these matters, Anna. He knows who the culprit is."

Miss Verna, fingers clasped prayerfully, turned to the door. "You will help us, won't you, dear Jack?"

"Not to worry, love." Jack's dark mask split to reveal a white and glorious smile, and then he levered off the door frame. "I'd suggest you have a cup of hot tea and give Anna and me time to dress and discuss this. In the meantime—" he put a finger to his lips "—don't breathe a word to anyone else."

Anna watched as Jack herded the distraught women toward the door and then out into the hallway. They obeyed so docilely, he might as well have been carrying them in the palm of his hand. She sat there a second, staggered by that innate magnetism of his, recalling a few magnetic moments of her own from the night before, until the consequences of this recent theft suddenly dawned on her.

They had her! All they had to do was find Chloe Von Drosten in possession of the brooch, and they could send the woman to jail for the next few years. If the theft had occurred just this morning, she surely hadn't had time to fob the jewel off on anyone else.

With her heart beating wildly, she scuttled off the bed, and she was already in her drawers and chemise by the time Jack came back into the room.

"We've got her, Jack," she said, plopping onto the bed to tug on a stocking. "We'll telegraph Mr. Pinkerton immediately. Oh, and there's the request for police assistance to be filled out. We can get one of those from Freddy. The baroness will be behind bars by sundown, if not before."

"No, she won't," he snapped.

Anna's gaze jerked up from the heel of her stocking. "Tomorrow, then." A frown creased her forehead and edged her brows together. "When were you thinking of making the arrest?"

"I'm not." His face had assumed its earlier dark expression. His jaw had hardened, and that magnetic smile had disappeared.

"Oh." Anna gave her glasses a tentative poke. "Well, what are you thinking, then?"

He was thinking he had yet another reason to see Chloe going up in hellfire—her part in interrupting his plan to make love to Anna this morning. Filching the old lady's brooch must've been like snatching a peppermint from a toddler, and she'd done it for no reason other than to twit him, to remind him of her existence. As if he needed a bloody reminder.

And he didn't need a bloody arrest, either, one that would be likely to implicate him. His memory of his time with Chloe was sodden, rather like a swamp, but it was reasonable to assume that he'd been a willing, if not eager, participant in whatever crimes had taken place during those months. With the baroness, nothing was free, and Jack had paid dearly for his habits. But he *had* paid, damn it—with the coin of his soul and the currency of his self-respect.

"There won't be any arrest, Anna," he told her sternly. "At least not before the race."

"But—"

"No buts." He strode to the wardrobe, and after jerking a suit from a hanger he stabbed his legs into the trousers. "I want you to stay here with your landladies today and keep a tight lid on them. They're not to say a word about the theft. To anyone. Is that clear?"

It was clear judging from the sharp angle of her chin that she didn't like it. He could practically see her fingers itching to be filling out forms. When she stopped gnawing her lip to reply, her voice was brittle.

"I see. I'm to stifle Miss Dorothy and Miss Verna. We're all to behave as if nothing has happened, as if no crime has taken place. And while we're all practicing such ignorance and quietude, Jack, may I ask what exactly you intend to do?"

He had his shirt on now and proceeded to stab in the tails. "While you're cooperating, darling, I'm going to get the bloody brooch back."

He was going to get the bloody brooch back if he had to turn Chloe upside down and shake it out of her. She'd have it on her somewhere. Jack knew that. After all, it was bait.

Bloody hell! It was working, too, he thought as he gazed around the racecourse, hoping for a glimpse of black. The bait had drawn him here. Alone. The whole reason for pretending Anna was his wife had been to avoid being alone with Chloe, because he hadn't been sure of his ability to resist her. He told himself he was a fool, confronting her like this, tempting fate, or whatever it was that had allowed her such influence over him.

A cold sweat prickled his skin, and that familiar ache blossomed at the back of his throat. His gaze skimmed the crowd that had gathered to watch the horses work out, and Jack realized he was searching for sunny golden hair, a sweet face lit by the glint of glasses. Dear Lord, how he needed her. Here. Now.

The face that emerged from the crowd just then was anything but sweet. Her red mouth was a cruel, knowing curve, and beneath the raven wings of her brows, Chloe's amber eyes glowed with carnal recognition as she came toward him. Closer. Closing in. The quirt in her black-gloved hand made a terrible ticking sound. To Jack, just then, it sounded like a watch that had slipped its gears and was now grinding backward. His heart jammed in his throat, nearly choking him.

What a bloody fool he'd been to think he'd ever be free—of her, or of himself.

He might not even have noticed the diamond-and-ruby brooch clasped to the black satin just above her breast, if the sunlight hadn't glanced off it just then. A blaze of pure, almost heavenly, light. A white-hot ray that pierced his daze and burned an image on his brain of silly spectacles on a serious, sober and oh-so-sweet face.

As quickly as panic had seized him, it seemed to let him go. Jack's heart centered in his chest again, and he drew in a deep lungful of air. Clean, fresh air, barely tainted by the musky fragrance of the cat. The jeweled cat.

"I'll take that pin, Baroness." He opened his hand—steady—palm up. "Now."

While Jack was at the racecourse, Anna did indeed keep a lid on the Misses Richmond. Her own lid, however, was rattling and jittering like the top of a boiling pot. For all Jack's expertise, she couldn't help believe that he was terribly wrong to rely on a horse race to do the baroness in. It was much too personal with him. She, on the other hand, was able to maintain a certain professional distance where the baroness was concerned. And even though she was merely a file clerk, she knew a thing or two about apprehending criminals. Well, perhaps not. But at least she knew where to go to find out. So, when she suggested an afternoon constitutional to her landladies, it wasn't surprising that their stroll took them past the Pinkerton office, or that Anna proclaimed a sudden and very urgent need for forms.

"I'll only be a moment," she told the Misses Richmond, who seemed quite content to peer through the window of a millinery shop while Anna rushed up the stairs, where she discovered Freddy Broome buried in paperwork again. He seemed happy enough to see her, but answered her questions with an air of harried distraction.

"To suspect someone of theft," he said, putting his signature on another document, "isn't enough, Anna. It might suffice for an arrest, but to guarantee a conviction, proof is absolutely necessary. You would either have to catch the thief in the act or, failing that, you would have to prove that the person was in possession of the stolen articles."

Anna smiled innocently. "Or, I suppose, locate those articles on the suspect's premises."

He nodded as he dipped his pen into the inkwell, preparatory to signing another paper. "That's true. There's a form for that. You're familiar with the items recovered list, surely."

"Yes, I am." She had probably filed hundreds of them, Anna thought, but until today they had all seemed quite abstract. Now that she was planning to recover a few items on her own, however, she wanted to make certain she was dealing not with abstractions but with facts. Hard facts. Ironclad ones. For, once she had the evidence, she wanted the baroness nailed down tight. Tighter than any horse race would accomplish.

She asked Freddy a few more questions before she said as casually as she could manage, "Oh, before I forget, Freddy, may I borrow a set of lock picks? Jack seems to have misplaced his."

The sneer she had expected twisted his lips. It was accompanied by a brisk cluck of his tongue. Then he put his pen down and opened a desk drawer. He handed her a small leather case. "Tell him I'd appreciate it very much if he didn't lose these. If he does, he can fill out the dratted requisition form himself." He lofted one sarcastic brow. "Anything else I can do for Mad Jack?"

Anna sucked in a breath and gave her spectacles a pronounced tap. "Well, yes, actually. You don't happen to have a pistol you could spare, do you? Something small, and easily concealed?"

Jack was sitting in the Southern Hotel's lobby when they returned from their stroll. Anna saw him instantly, and her heart gave a little lurch, as much from the unexpected sight of him as from the guilty knowledge of what she carried in her handbag. If anyone had told her three weeks ago that she'd shortly be the possessor of a set of lock picks and a nickel-plated derringer, she would have laughed. But this was no laughing matter.

Not that you could tell from Jack's expression as he approached them, though. He looked positively, even sublimely, carefree, so much so that Anna was tempted to check his breath for traces of whiskey when he kissed her in greeting.

"Hello, darling."

No. No whiskey. Only his usual wonderful blend of shaving soap and bay rum and essence of male. She took in an additional whiff of it, hoping she smelled half as appealing despite her walk in the warm sunshine and her nervousness over the contents of the handbag currently weighing so heavily on her arm—not to mention her conscience.

"How was the racecourse?" she asked him.

"Fine." He reached in his pocket, then beckoned Miss Dorothy closer. "I believe this is yours," he said, opening his hand to reveal the diamond-and-ruby brooch.

"Oh, my, yes," Miss Dorothy breathed.

"I suggest you deposit it in the hotel's vault for safekeeping," he told her.

Like the sisters, Anna stared at the pin in his open palm. Unlike them, however, she continued to gaze at Jack's hand after Miss Dorothy had scooped up the jewelry. At the base of his thumb, there was a small bubble of dried blood, centered in a purplish bruise that appeared to be quite fresh.

After the Misses Richmond had showered him with thanks and bustled away toward the front desk, Anna asked him quietly, "What happened to your hand?"

"Nothing." He shrugged.

"It didn't look like nothing." Anna reached for his hand and peeled the fingers back, exposing the wound.

"Oh, that. Well, let's just say the baroness was a bit peevish this afternoon, and somewhat reluctant to give up the brooch." He shrugged again and smiled crookedly. "When she finally did, she mistook me for a pincushion."

"She stabbed you?" Anna exclaimed.

"Just a little, darling."

"Poor Jack." Behind her lenses, her eyes filled with tears. Then she bent her head to touch her lips to the palm of his hand. "I'm so sorry," she whispered. "It must have hurt terribly."

It had, Jack thought. When Chloe jammed the pin into his flesh, it had hurt like the very devil. But he wasn't sorry. Not at all. He was thrilled beyond belief because—after all these years—there had been no pleasure—none!—in the pain.

# Chapter Twenty

The night before the race, while Anna was sleeping, Jack rode to his sister's. The moon, full and bright as a newly minted coin, washed the road with silver. A better night for lovers than for spies, Jack thought as he approached Madelaine's farmhouse, and a terrible night for a man who needed the cover of darkness to exchange one mahogany bay for another.

All his nights would be perfect for lovers from now on, no matter the shape of the moon. A smile twitched across his lips. Happiness kept bringing him up short, and he had to remind himself that he still had to use his head, rather than his heart, if he was to see this plan through. His reasons for winning the race might have changed—it wasn't about Chloe anymore—but the race still had to be won. He'd made promises, after all. He was keeping happy secrets.

The mouse had peered at him across the dinner table just this evening. "You have a yellow feather poking out of one corner of your mouth, Jack," she'd said.

"I beg your pardon?"

"You're looking like the cat who just swallowed the canary. Would you like to share your secret?"

He had reached across the table for her hand, and kissed each fingertip. "Tomorrow, my love."

Later, after their loving, she had looked up at him and whispered, "You're smiling that secret smile again." Her attempt to sound lighthearted had been belied by the wrinkle of worry that appeared between her sapphire eyes. "You didn't by any chance have a little nip of something while I wasn't looking, did you?"

Cradling her sweet face in his hands, he had whispered, "Haven't you ever seen a man intoxicated with love?"

She had sighed softly. "I wasn't accusing you, Jack. It's only that I worry sometimes. I know it's still very difficult for you."

"Not so difficult, little mouse." He had kissed that stitch of concern between her eyes. "And anyway, if I had, you wouldn't have to ask. You'd know, because there is no such thing as a little nip in my vocabulary. Remember? It's rather an all-or-nothing proposition for sots like me."

*All or nothing.* Jack said it aloud to the moon overhead. His all was Anna now. And he hadn't lied. It wasn't that difficult not to drink. Now that sweet Anna had filled him with happiness, there didn't seem to be room for liquor. And now that she tempted him, those other temptations had lost their power over him. Thank God.

He hadn't told her that, or told her what lay behind his secret smile. He should have, perhaps, but all his plans and promises still hinged on the bloody race. Their future, or at least his vision of it, would be secure tomorrow, once Southern Cross blazed across the finish line. First.

But there was still tonight, this too-bright night. Even a coating of moonlight couldn't redeem the dilapidated farmhouse that he was now approaching. The front porch canted even more precipitously than on his last visit, and when Jack climbed the rotten stairs, he discovered little Samuel curled up on a blanket there. With a gentle tug, he moved the blanket farther away from the edge of the porch, so that the sleeping four-year-old wouldn't tumble into the weedy yard.

The boy stirred, then tucked his thumb in his mouth and fell back to sleep while Jack stroked his dark head. Hazard dark. The child bore no resemblance to his father whatsoever, and Jack had been thankful for that these past four years. He hadn't wanted to be reminded of his partner, but now, sitting here cold sober and gazing at Samuel Scully's son, the memories that the whiskey had held at bay came rushing back.

Samuel. He'd been big as an ox, and brave as any man Jack had ever known, but the moment they were captured behind rebel lines, Samuel had changed. The minute the cell door slammed on them at Castle Thunder, the big man had seemed to wither, in the grip of a silent, dull terror. Their death sentence had only pushed him deeper. He hadn't eaten. He hadn't spoken. He'd seemed paralyzed by the prospect of death.

Jack, on the other hand, had rather enjoyed the prospect of his own hanging. He had thrived in the shadow of the noose, and prison had bothered him only when he wasn't able to bribe the guards for sufficient quantities of booze.

It occurred to him now, as his fingers drifted over little Samuel's dark hair, that the reason the boy's father had buckled under the death warrant was that the man valued life so much.

Not Jack. He distinctly recalled the flicker of disappointment in his gut when Madelaine had arranged his English pardon, when it had become clear that he would be set free, that he would have to live.

"Go in my place," he'd pleaded with his partner. "We'll tell the bloody Rebs that they got our names wrong. Take my sister and give her the happiness she deserves. Go on, Samuel. Go and don't look back." Jack had taken Samuel's big ham of a hand in his own, then, and gripped it tight. "To tell you the God's honest truth, partner, I've had all I want from this life, but I'm too much the bloody coward to end it myself."

Samuel had shaken his head and smiled grimly. "Mad, maybe, but not a coward, Jack. Thanks, but no thanks. I'll get out, too, but my own way. I have to."

He had, but it had cost him. To have his death sentence commuted, he'd had to tell the Rebs everything he knew—names, places, safe houses. Four Pinkerton spies had hanged in his place. Then Samuel Scully, who valued his own life so highly, had learned the bitter truth, which was that he treasured his honor more. He'd been unable to live with that burden, and its shame.

Jack smoothed a damp lock of hair from young Samuel's forehead. Funny—he'd always thought of himself as weak, but it occurred to him now that perhaps he was the strong one after all. The one who could carry any burden. The mule under the lash. The one who had been able to endure anything—everything—to survive any shame.

Sudden tears stung his eyes, and his vision broke apart in moonlit shards. He *had* survived! All of it. He'd spent decades courting death in every way imaginable, and it turned out that—all the bloody while—it had been life he was pursuing. Jack Hazard had come through. Battered, by God, but whole. And so full of hope now it nearly choked him.

If he hadn't quite believed it before, in the shine of Anna's loving gaze, he believed it utterly now. He was whole and happy. It didn't matter anymore whether or not he deserved such happiness. He had *earned* it—bought it and paid for it with his blood and his tears—and he would hold fast to it for the rest of his life.

Jack knuckled the tears from his eyes, drew in a deep breath, then winked at the moon. The rest of his life was due to begin in a matter of hours, compliments of a fleet horse and a fat, if slightly felonious, purse.

Madelaine was pacing back and forth in front of Southern Cross's stall when Jack entered the lantern-lit barn. "You're late," she said. "I was worried."

"Everything's fine. Only a few more hours and this will all be over." He angled his head toward the big stallion. "How's our magnificent beast?"

"Ready," Madelaine said. "At least I think so. I didn't run him yesterday. And if you don't let him have his head on the road tonight, he'll be anxious to tear up the track tomorrow."

"He'll have to." Jack dragged his fingers through his hair. "He'll have a lot more riding on him than just a jockey. And Chloe's Gold looks good, Maddie. Damnably good."

His sister stepped closer and gazed into his face. Jack saw the little tic of surprise at one corner of her mouth, and heard that same surprise as it registered in her voice.

"So do you," she said. "You look better rested than I've seen you in months. Perhaps even in years.'' A small smile teased her lips, and one of her dark brows arched curiously. ''Dare I say *happy*, Jack?''

He laughed. That wasn't a word normally associated with him. Not from Maddie's lips, at least. But his sister knew him so well he wasn't surprised she could read what was in his heart.

''Well, just whisper it, love. We wouldn't want to tempt fate, would we?''


''Ssh . . .'' Anna hissed, and aimed another menacing glare at her chattering landladies. Good Lord. She should never have enlisted the two of them in this scheme, but she needed someone to stand watch while she searched Chloe Von Drosten's room before the baroness and her two hulking companions returned from the prerace gala that was taking place downstairs in the grand ballroom.

As soon as Jack had left her, Anna had shot from the bed and into her clothes, as if the hotel were on fire. Then, after she'd knocked on their door and awakened them, the Misses Richmond had dressed with the same desperate speed, while still managing to find time for their endless bickering.

They were going at it now, as a matter of fact, Miss Verna having decided that she should stand watch at the staircase and Miss Dorothy claiming the same lookout post for the sole and simple reason that her sister wanted it. They were making enough noise to wake the ancient dead.

"Hush," she said. "I don't care where you stand, but you'll have to do it quietly."

"I was being quiet."

Miss Verna's lower lip slid into an indignant pout when her sister snapped, "No, you weren't."

"Wherever you post yourselves, just be sure to warn me if the baroness or either one of her friends appears. All right? And do be quiet."

Anna marched down the corridor, clutching her borrowed set of lock picks in her hand. Not that she had a clue about using them, but then, how difficult could it be? It was undoubtedly a process of trial and error, and if she was lucky, the errors would be few and she would discover enough stolen jewels to send the baroness to prison for the rest of her nasty life.

Why Jack refused to follow Pinkerton procedure in this was beyond her. His plan was brilliant, true, but to place all one's hopes on a dratted horse struck Anna as foolish, if not quite mad. But she had stopped arguing with him. Let him win his silly race. Or lose it. When it was done, Anna would have an official list with which to put Chloe Von Drosten away.

She knocked softly on the door, an excuse on the tip of her tongue and the lock picks ready to be jammed into her reticule just in case anyone responded. When no one did, she stared at the knob a moment, then sighed and gave it an optimistic, though probably futile, little twist. The knob turned and—Lord, have mercy—the door swung inward.

With her heart wedged in her throat, Anna stepped into the dark room. All she could hear was the soft ticking of a clock. "Is anyone here?" she whispered.

Something bumped in the blackness on the far side of the room. Someone stifled a curse. Anna gasped, uttered a quick curse of her own, and was grabbing up her skirts to flee when an oddly familiar voice rasped, "Anna? Is that you?"

"Yes, but who—?"

A match flared, illuminating a shock of wheat-colored hair above a pale face.

"Freddy!" For a second, Anna thought she would faint from relief. "What are you doing here?"

"I've already done it," he said matter-of-factly as he touched a match to a lamp wick, suffusing the room with amber light. "Have a look at this." He reached into his coat pocket and produced the longest, fattest rope of pearls Anna had ever seen. "Reported missing last summer in Saratoga by Mrs. Roswell Burt. Her initials are on the clasp. And this." From his other pocket came a diamond necklace that glittered in the lamplight for a moment before he put it back.

"Stolen, as well?" Anna asked, a little breathlessly.

"Quite." A rather wolfish grin crossed the agent's lips. "Last September in New York City, from a Miss Henrietta or Hermoine DePew. I forget the exact name, but I remember the description of the necklace down to the last carat.''

''Then we've got her? We've got the baroness?''

''We've not only got *her,* Anna.'' Freddy rubbed his hands together. ''We've got him, too.''

''Him?''

''Hazard, of course. Who else? He was with her last summer in Saratoga, and later in New York. Thick as thieves, the two of them. Thicker.''

The notion that Jack was a thief was so absurd that Anna could only laugh.

Freddy raised a brow. ''You think it's funny, do you? Well, I thought it was funny that Hazard kept playing at being a horseman when he should have been working as a Pinkerton and gathering evidence. It's obvious the man never had any intention of apprehending the baroness. It wouldn't surprise me if he plans to let her get away after the race tomorrow.''

Did he? Anna wondered. Was that why Jack had forbidden her to take any action, using the race as a convenient excuse? Was it because he was guilty, too? She thought about the secret smile he'd worn all evening, and it took on an entirely new and insidious meaning.

''There's no proof,'' she said, giving her spectacles a rather adamant poke.

Freddy patted his pockets. ''This is enough proof to put the baroness behind bars. And I doubt very much if she'll want to go alone.'' With an almost demonic chuckle, he added, "I'm sure she'll want to take her playmate with her."

"Over my dead body." Anna reached into her reticule and gripped the derringer. "Or yours." She pointed it directly at Freddy's heart.

The agent stared at the little gun a moment. Then his eyes jerked to Anna's face. "What are you doing, Anna?"

She smiled. It was a knowing tilt of her lips, not so different from Jack's secret smile, and meant to convey the impression that she did indeed know what she was doing, when she didn't have a clue. The only thing she knew was that she had to buy time for Jack. He had to get away. And if that meant Anna would go to prison in his stead, then so be it. She knew how to cope with loneliness and dreariness. The Lord knew she'd had ample practice.

Freddy took a step toward her now, and Anna waved the gun menacingly. She had no intention of using it. She didn't even know how, but Freddy didn't know that. The sweat that beaded on his forehead was a fair indication of his ignorance. So was the tremor in his voice when he said, "Look. Put the gun away, will you? I'm willing to forget this entire incident. I won't even file a report. That blackguard Hazard's obviously turned your head, and—"

"Hush, Freddy. Please." She was probably the first person ever to use the word *please* while holding someone at gunpoint, Anna thought bleakly. But she couldn't think while he was babbling. And now that she had him at gunpoint, just what was she going to do with him? Oh, Lord... Oh, help...

Help! That was it! "Stay right where you are, Freddy," she warned as she stepped backward toward the door, then hissed down the corridor, "Miss Richmond, hurry, please. Both of you. I need you."

The women bustled down the hallway immediately, Miss Verna getting a step or two on her older, larger sister. "What is it, dear?" Miss Verna glanced at the gun and let out a tiny gasp. "Oh, my stars. Is that what they call a knuckle-duster?"

At her shoulder, Miss Dorothy snorted. "Knuckle-duster, indeed. You've been reading too many dime novels, sister."

With the gun still aimed at Freddy, Anna gestured her landladies into the room. If she'd learned anything about deception from Jack, she told herself, this was the time to put that lesson to the test. "I've suspected all along that Mr. Broome was a rogue agent," Anna said, in her best and most sober Pinkerton voice, "and now I've caught him red-handed trying to steal the baroness's jewels."

Across the room, the accused rogue rolled his eyes toward the ceiling and muttered, "Balderdash."

"I'm shocked," Miss Verna chirped, sounding more thrilled than appalled. "He looked like such a sweet boy. Didn't you think so, sister?"

Big Miss Dorothy snorted. "Looks are deceiving more often than not."

"Oh, and I suppose you knew he was a criminal all along, Dorothy."

"I had inklings, Verna."

"Inklings! Dorothy, you are full of—"

"Ladies!" Anna was briefly tempted to turn the gun on the quarreling crones. Their nattering made it nearly impossible to think. And she had to think. "We're Pinkertons. We must be about our business. And quickly. Miss Verna, please see if you can find a scarf with which to gag Mr. Broome." What else? What else? Think! "Miss Dorothy, I believe one of those drapery ties will suffice for binding his hands. Then we'll take him back to my room and detain him until Jack returns."

Oh, Lord. Let that be soon. How long could it possibly take to exchange one horse for another?

In his stall, Southern Cross snorted and stamped an impatient foot, reminding Jack that he was truly tempting fate by delaying any longer. "It's time to get going, Maddie." He laughed softly. "We don't want to let all this unaccustomed happiness go to our heads."

Madelaine's expression changed then. Her eyes darkened and her lips assumed a somber curve. "No, my dear," she whispered, "we wouldn't want to do that. Happiness is a dizzying prospect, especially for the children of Hazard House."

For a heartbeat, then, Jack was ten and Maddie was eight. It seemed as if they were standing together in a different barn, in a different country. An ocean and a lifetime away. Jack knew that if he closed his eyes he would be able to breathe in the faint salt air of the Channel right here in the middle of the United States, so he kept his eyes open. He didn't want to return to Hazard House, even in his imagination. His sister linked her arm through his, and leaned her head on his shoulder.

"You deserve happiness, Jack." Madelaine's voice was little more than a wisp of breath. "You always have. Even then."

"It's done, Maddie," he said, lifting a hand to stroke her hair. "Whatever that nightmare was, we're both awake now. It's over."

She lifted her dark, shimmering eyes to his. "Almost over. I need to know... I've never had the courage to ask you..."

"Then, don't." He pressed a finger to her trembling lips. "Let it go, little sister."

"I have to, Jack. I have to know. Our brothers all left. But you stayed. Why?"

"Oh, Maddie." Jack let out a long breath and lifted his eyes toward the rafters of the barn, as much to seek an answer as to avoid one. Why? Sweet Christ, there had been a thousand reasons, beginning with love and ending with pain. Hope and horror had been mixed until they were indistinguishable. He had been savior and sinner both. Because if it hadn't been him, it would have been Maddie. Because he'd waited so bloody long to be loved.

When he finally spoke, Jack's voice was thick and his answer was part truth, part lie, a blend of absolution for them both. "I wasn't a hero, if that's what you've been imagining all this time. They call me Mad Jack, remember, darling? Not Saint Jack."

He tipped her chin up. "Look at me, Maddie. Mad Jack. That's all. Not Saint Jack. And if all this time you've believed I was some sort of martyr, the last and best of the brothers, the noble boy who laid his body down like a bridge of flesh and bone so his little sister could cross the abyss of those years unscathed, you're wrong."

Jack dragged in a breath. "I stayed, Maddie, because . . . God help me—I *wanted* to."

"You're lying," his sister said softly.

"Only a little, love." Jack smiled and thumbed the tears from her wet cheeks. "But after the race tomorrow, I'll be an honest man. Sober and utterly sincere." He laughed. "You'll probably find me damnably boring."

Madelaine shook her head, and was about to protest when a voice snapped from the doorway, "I find you damnably boring right now, Jack."

A dark shape separated from the shadows to stand silhouetted in the door. There was, as always, a whip in her right hand. But tonight, in her left hand, there was a bottle. And it glittered like liquid gold in the moonlight.

Madelaine gasped. It was a sickening little sound that conveyed Jack's own feelings as he watched the black cat straddle the path where, mere moments from now, he had planned to lead Southern Cross out of the barn. A black cat, and the worst of luck— a too-bright moon and a man who should have been looking over his shoulder instead of gazing foolishly at the heavens. A man who'd traded his past for his future, incautiously and too soon. Too bloody soon.

He could feel his heart—that hopeful, foolish, battered thing—shrink a size or two within his chest. But even as it did, Jack reached past it to dredge up the best, and perhaps the last, of his weapons—a disarming grin. He flashed it like a saber as he stepped away from his sister to meet the devil head-on.

''Baroness.''

## Chapter Twenty-One

Chloe stepped farther into the barn. Unsteady. Lantern light glossed her too-black, too-big eyes. Laudanum, Jack thought, and a lot of it. But what made her unsteady also made her dangerous. Who knew that better than he?

"Boring, am I, Baroness? I'm surprised. You've always relished a good hunt, haven't you?" He raised an eyebrow. "Riding your quarry down in the moonlight? Isn't that what you've done?"

"Have I, Jack?"

She came closer. Behind him, Jack heard Madelaine's ragged breathing. Southern Cross gave a nervous snort and launched a solid kick at the slats of his stall.

Chloe's black-and-amber gaze cut to the horse and then back to Jack. "That was an ambitious plan, darling. Did you really think you'd bring it off?"

He shrugged. "I was doing my damnedest, Chloe."

"You still could, Jack," Madelaine whispered urgently. "It's not too late. You could—"

A burst of harsh laughter from the baroness cut her off. "Oh, by all means. I believe you should carry through with your little deception. Truly I do. There's no one who would like to see you succeed more than I. I'll even help you." She held up the bottle. "I insist we begin by drinking a toast to your success."

"Help him?" Madelaine took a threatening step forward, her hands clenched into fists. "Haven't you *helped* him enough already? Aren't you satisfied with the damage you've done?"

Chloe only laughed. "I don't know. You'll have to ask your brother." She raised her face to Jack's, pursing her red lips for a moment and blinking innocently. "Are you satisfied with the damage, darling?"

"Quite."

Then, while his sister and the baroness heatedly debated the condition of his body and the relative merits of his soul, Jack considered his options. With his plan exposed, he had already given up tomorrow's race as a lost cause and shunted that bitter disappointment to the back of his brain. He'd deal with that particular wound later. Right now, though, there was Chloe to be dealt with, but not until he knew where her two brawny lackeys were. She might be as sleek and wily as a cat, but she was also as cunning as a wolf. And wolves always hunted in packs, surrounding their helpless prey.

A cold, sickening fear seeped through him, chilling Jack's blood, as he realized who the only truly helpless one on the premises was.

"Bitch!" his sister was shrieking now. "Leave my brother alone!"

Madelaine raised a fisted hand to deliver a blow, but Jack caught her wrist. "Go get Samuel, Maddie."

"What?"

"Go get Samuel." He lowered his voice ominously as he took his sister by the shoulders and turned her toward the door. "Go get him. Now."

"Dear God," she breathed.

"Oh, is that what his name is?" Chloe's voice rang out almost sweetly. "That precious little boy who was sleeping on the porch?"

Madelaine whirled around. "What have you done with my son?"

Chloe shrugged. "I haven't done anything. My friends are merely keeping the little dear company for a while. They're teaching him to play a game. Mumble-the-peg, I think. Some game with a knife."

While a curse ripped from Jack's teeth, Madelaine rushed to the door. "It's true," she called back. "There are two men on the porch with Samuel. They've got a knife. Oh, Jack. What are we going to do?"

Nothing, he wanted to shout. Bloody nothing. It was over. He thought of the million things he'd done wrong and the one thing he'd done right—Anna. And none of it made any difference now.

"It's all right, Maddie." He tried to keep his voice level and calm. Tried to believe the words of reassurance he was giving his sister. "Samuel will be all right. Chloe wouldn't hurt a child." His gaze snapped to the woman in black, piercing her. "You like your victims bigger, don't you, Baroness? More capable of bearing pain."

Her lips tilted viciously, and she tapped the quirt against her skirt. "I can't speak for Viktor or Constantine, though. But, unlike some people, they will obey me."

Jack didn't doubt that for a second. And even though he didn't believe Chloe would sink so far as to harm a child herself, he couldn't be sure how far her accomplices would go to impress her or to earn their abominable keep. And he wouldn't gamble with little Samuel's safety, no matter the cost.

He walked to Madelaine, put his arms around her, drawing her close, and whispered in her ear.

"Go see to your son, Maddie. And don't worry about me. Nothing's going to happen to me here tonight that hasn't happened before, believe me."

"But there must be some other way to..."

Jack held her tighter. "There is no other way. It's too late. Listen to me, love. I was bound to slip back into the bottle sooner or later, anyway. If sooner helps Samuel, then there's some good in it, don't you see?''

She shook her head.

''Just trust me. And do me a favor. When this is done, whatever happens, find Anna and tell her...'' *Oh, Christ, tell her loving her was too good ever to be true.* ''Tell her I meant well, will you? That this was inevitable, and that she's better off without me. Will you do that for me?''

''I'll tell her,'' Madelaine whispered brokenly, ''but I doubt if she'll believe me. God bless you, Saint Jack.''

He tried his best to laugh. ''Mad Jack, love. Remember?'' Then he kissed the top of her head and gave her a gentle but deliberate push in the direction of the house before turning to face the baroness.

''You win, Chloe. Let the boy go, and I'll do whatever you want. I'll be whatever pleases you.'' Jack bent one knee to the hay-strewn floor and bowed his head, in part for dramatic effect, in part because he needed a moment to compose his face, to retrieve the mask of arrogance that seemed to be melting away. ''I am, ma'am, your humble and obedient slave.''

''I'm glad,'' she purred, coming toward him. ''And you'll be glad, too, darling, very soon. Then, when you're more like your old self, I'll send Viktor and Constantine away. I won't be needing them anymore, will I?''

He didn't look up, but stared at the black hem of her skirt and the pointed toes of her boots while he listened to the ticking of the whip against her leg and the click of her long nails against the bottle.

"I want you back, Jack. The way you were." She held the bottle in front of him. "Here. Have a drink. Let's celebrate old times together."

Don't think, Jack told himself as a dozen desperate strategies occurred to him, all of them ending with a little boy's death. Don't think. Just drink. Remember how you wanted this once.

Unwilling to let Chloe see how fiercely he was shaking, he grabbed the bottle with both hands, ripped off the cork with his teeth and spat it at her feet. He lifted his gaze to her black eyes and spoke what would probably be the last coherent words in his life.

"Here's to you, Baroness. Here's to both of us, as we slide toward the fires of hell."

Then he tipped the bottle to his lips and drank deep, letting the whiskey blaze down the back of his throat and burn its way into his brain and turn his heart inside out, like an empty pocket.

Anna glanced at the clock as she paced from the window to the door, once more avoiding Freddy's outstretched, bound-at-the-ankles legs and ignoring another of his muffled oaths.

"You're wearing out the carpet, dear," Miss Verna said.

"Oh, do be quiet, sister," Miss Dorothy snapped. "Anna knows what she's doing."

Anna knew precisely what she was doing. Nothing. She had walked a mile or two in the hotel suite, worrying, accomplishing absolutely nothing, while Jack was out there somewhere, shuttling horses as if they were knights on a chessboard, unaware of the danger he was in. They couldn't keep Freddy tied up indefinitely, and the minute he was free he was going to arrest the baroness, who would then be only too happy to implicate Jack. When the baroness was arrested . . . *if* she was arrested . . .

Halting in the center of the room, Anna gave her spectacles a decisive push, then announced, "I'll be going out for a while."

Miss Verna gave a little gasp. "But it's the middle of the night, my dear."

For once, Miss Dorothy didn't disagree. "Perhaps you should wait," she said.

"I can't." Anna snatched up her handbag and gloves. "I'll leave the gun with you, Miss Verna," she said briskly. "Keep an eye on Mr. Broome now, both of you, and do be careful. We're merely detaining him, you know. We're not authorized to shoot him."

Her landladies nodded enthusiastically, and when their captive made a whimpering sound behind his gag, Anna aimed a helpless shrug in his direction before hastening out of the suite and racing down the stairs.

She was out of breath and her heart was beating wildly when she arrived at the grand ballroom on the second floor, where the party was obviously breaking up. She had to shoulder her way against the tide of chattering guests who were streaming out of the doors, all the while keeping an eye out for a woman dressed in black.

People kept greeting her—"Good evening, Mrs. Hazard." "Lovely to see you, Mrs. Hazard"—and Anna couldn't help but think how accustomed she'd become to the name that she would soon be relinquishing. She wondered if she'd even respond now if someone called her Mrs. Matlin.

Just as she emerged into the ballroom, someone snagged her sleeve. She jerked away, thinking Freddy had gotten loose somehow, and was enormously relieved when she discovered it was Mrs. Bissell who had latched on to her arm.

"I'm sorry, dear," the big woman said. "I didn't mean to startle you. Why, you look as pale as a sheet."

"I was looking for the baroness." Anna scanned the scattered clusters of guests remaining in the room. "You haven't by any chance seen her, have you?"

"That dreadful woman." Mrs. Bissell puffed out her already ponderous bosom. "She was here earlier with those two Gypsy consorts of hers. I believe she mentioned something about taking a ride in the moonlight."

Anna breathed a soft curse.

"My feeling exactly," Mrs. Bissell said with a sniff. "Good riddance to bad baggage." Her sour expression sweetened then. "You must be so excited, my dear."

"Excited?" Desperate was closer to the truth, Anna thought bleakly. Or desolate. "Oh, about the race, you mean?"

"Well, that, too. But I meant about the house."

"The house?" *The house.* Anna blinked. "What house?"

"Why, the one your darling husband is buying for you. He signed the papers yesterday, for that adorable house on Bellefontaine Road, and an additional fifty acres just to the west." She paused to smile like a big, cream-fed tabby. "It's virtually yours. Your Jack said he merely needed to settle some affairs first, but that he would be handing over a check right after the race."

If she'd appeared pale as a sheet before, Anna thought, she must look absolutely bleached now, as she felt the blood drain from her face. Her heart seemed to be collapsing in upon itself as she realized the meaning of Jack's sweet, secret smile. He was planning to use Southern Cross's winning purse to buy the residential wedding cake. He meant to make their fantasy real.

"Oh, dear," Mrs. Bissell said. "I can see from your face that this was apparently meant to be a surprise. I believe I've let the cat out of the bag, Anna. I am so sorry."

Not half as sorry as she was, Anna thought. Jack had been planning to make their dream come true, and she had just done her level best to turn that dream into a nightmare.

"It's not your fault." Anna couldn't even muster a smile to reassure the woman. "I don't much care for surprises, anyway."

The half-dressed man in the livery stable apparently didn't much care for surprises, either, when he finally answered Anna's insistent rapping on the door.

"I need to rent a buggy," she said, using what little breath she hadn't expended rushing the four blocks from the hotel. When he didn't reply, but merely stood in the doorway, blinking sleepily and rubbing his bristly chin, Anna added, "Right now. Tonight."

"Lady, do you know what time it is?"

"Yes, I do." It was time to find Jack, since it was obvious she wasn't going to be able to find the baroness. "I need a buggy right away." She shook her handbag at him and uttered four words she never dreamed she would ever say. "Money is no object."

The man straightened up and hauled his suspenders over his shoulders. "Don't make no difference. All my buggies is gone for the night. All's I got left is that little chestnut mare over there.'' He jerked his thumb toward a stall.

Anna stood on tiptoe to peer around him. The little mare didn't look all that little to her. She tried to remember the last time she had been on a horse. It had been so long that the answer might just as well have been never. ''Is she docile?''

''Regular kitten, that one. I don't have no ladies' saddles, though. If you want her, you're gonna have to fork her.''

Anna gave her glasses a shove. ''Excuse me?''

''Fork her. You know.'' He made an inverted V with his fingers and clamped them over his hand. ''Ride her astride.''

''I see.'' Actually, that was probably the best news she'd had all evening, Anna decided. At least that way she'd be able to hang on to the animal with her legs, as well as her hands. ''Well, saddle her up, please.''

## Chapter Twenty-Two

"What's wrong with Uncle Jack, Mama?"

"Nothing, Samuel."

"But he fell down."

"I know," Madelaine said softly. "Hush now."

There was gruff laughter behind her on the porch from both of the baroness's henchmen before one of them said, "He's stinking drunk, kid. That's what's wrong with him."

Madelaine shot the man a murderous glare, then smoothed her face again for the benefit of the child she was rocking on her lap.

"What does *drunk* mean, Mama?"

"It means Uncle Jack is very sick, Samuel. But he'll be all right soon. Now you put your head back and close your eyes again. It's too late for little boys to be awake." She tucked his head onto her shoulder, then returned her gaze to the man who had just stumbled in the middle of the yard.

Four bottles. Bloody four. That wasn't right. Jack blinked them back to two. One was empty. The other was half-full. Or half-empty. Depending on one's point of view. Which in his case wasn't a *point* of view at all but a dull perspective amid the weeds in the middle of the yard. He kept wanting to laugh— to throw his head back and bloody howl at the moon, or to look down and chuckle softly while he contemplated the creases in his boots—and kept having to remind himself it was entirely inappropriate under the current circumstances. Crying, however— that other tempting alternative—wouldn't do. He was a man, after all.

Well, a reasonable facsimile thereof, despite what the black cat had hissed a short while ago, when he was unable to rise to her occasion. He gazed at the red gashes between the halves of his unbuttoned shirt and couldn't remember now whether she'd scratched him before or after the failed attempt. Not that it made any difference.

Not that anything made any difference anymore.

He'd just shucked off sobriety in a headlong dive to the bottom of the first bottle. Because that was Chloe's price for little Samuel's life. Because, after the first jolt hit his body, he had craved more. As he had known he would. And because he didn't care anymore. The only thing left to want was to get to the place where there was no pain. No sense of regret or loss. No bloody sense at all.

But he wasn't there yet. He grabbed for the half-full bottle, missed it, and grabbed again.

Then, out of the corner of his eyes, Jack was aware of a quick glint of light. He turned his head toward the road, blinked, and brought the approaching rider into focus. Moonlight shimmered on golden curls and winked on two round lenses. He squeezed his eyes closed, praying he'd only conjured her up, like the other creatures he'd often imagined after he'd rounded the bend of dementia. But there she was again, sliding down from the horse and rushing toward him, her sweet face all crumpled with worry.

Jack lurched to his feet and greeted her with a sloppy and woebegone smile, the best he could fashion under the circumstances.

"Hello, mouse." He did his damnedest then not to buckle when she raised her face to his, bewilderment turning to bitter disappointment in her eyes.

Anna tried to keep her mouth from twisting while she fought down the surge of anger inside herself. He was drunk! Every inch of him besotted, from the hair that fell across his forehead to the tips of his clumsy boots. In between, the crisp white shirt he had put on mere hours ago, was now as rumpled as a bedsheet and hanging unbuttoned from his slumped shoulders. And on top of it all, that dazzling grin was a mockery of its former self.

How dare you? she wanted to scream. How dare you do this to yourself? To us?

"Oh, Jack." Love welled up in Anna, along with the anger. She wanted to embrace him and at the same time to strike him again and again.

Like her fists, her teeth were clenched so hard she could barely speak. "I don't understand," she said. "Why this? Why now?"

Jack shrugged, losing his balance briefly before straightening up again. "Sorry, love," he slurred, lifting his hand to trace a finger down her cheek while his gaze, dilated and as dull as pewter, seemed to go in and out of focus.

"Sorry!" Anna stepped back, out of reach. Then, just as she was throwing up her hands in helpless dismay, a voice called out urgently from the dark porch.

"It's not his fault, Anna."

She had thought they were alone, but now she whirled in the direction of the house to see Jack's sister standing there. Behind Madelaine, in the shadows, Anna could distinguish two hulking and familiar shapes. Suddenly she felt as disoriented as Jack.

"What's going on here?" she asked.

"The baroness," Madelaine said. "She threatened to harm my son unless..." Her voice altered, then diminished in a sigh.

"Jack?" Anna turned back. "Is it true?"

He mumbled an oath in reply, head down, his fingers fumbling unsuccessfully with the buttons of his shirt. It was then that Anna glimpsed the long, raw scratches on his chest.

"My God," she breathed. "She's here, isn't she? The baroness. What has she done to you?"

His head jerked up, and for just a second his eyes were clear and fierce. "Nothing. Go back to the city, Anna. And then go home to Chicago. It's over. All of it."

"But the house," she whispered. "I know about the house, Jack." She reached out, gently brushing his hands aside to take the halves of his shirt between her fingers and begin fastening the buttons he couldn't manage. "Mrs. Bissell told me. It's a lovely surprise."

Jack swore savagely, his breath hot on the backs of Anna's hands. "Don't you understand? Can't you see anything but good through those damn lenses of yours? She knows. Chloe knows about the bloody horse. It's over."

He stilled her hands by pressing them against his chest, and Anna could feel his erratic, whiskey-driven heartbeat against her palms. How long could a heart continue to endure such abuse? she wondered. Or the flesh that covered it?

"It's over, mouse."

"Maybe not." She eased out from Jack's grasp. Then after she had poked the final button through and given it a decisive pat, she lifted her chin and set her jaw stubbornly. "I need to have a word or two with the baroness. Where is she?"

"She's right here."

Chloe Von Drosten leaned against the barn's door frame, swatting her quirt at bits of hay on her black skirt. The dark wings of her hair had drooped onto her forehead. Her red mouth was a thin slash. Displeasure seemed to radiate from her every pore.

Good, Anna thought. She had every intention of displeasing the woman even more, but before she could say a word, Chloe snapped her whip and pointed it at Anna.

"Mrs. Hazard," she snarled, "you must be so pleased with yourself. Did Jack tell you?"

"Tell me what?"

Chloe clenched her skirt in one fist and strode forward. "Surely you inquired about his state of—" Her black eyes swung to Jack, and her mouth curved slightly. "Well, how shall I put it, darling? Your state of disrepair? Your disreputable current condition?"

Muttering a curse, Jack bent to snatch up the bottle at his feet. He tilted his head back and swayed as he swigged from it. "Leave her out of this, Chloe," he warned.

"I will not. This is all her fault. All of it."

Anna edged back from the wild sweep of the whip in the baroness's hand. She had meant to reason with the woman, to trade her knowledge of her imminent arrest for Jack's and his family's release, but she could see that Chloe Von Drosten was beyond reason now. She was teetering on the edge of madness.

Her huge black eyes glittered like obsidian in the moonlight as they homed in on Anna's face. "Mrs. Hazard," she hissed, "don't be concerned with your husband's disarray. He was completely and utterly faithful to you. He couldn't, or wouldn't, break his sacred vows. That should please you to no end."

Anna didn't know what to say. She might have been enormously relieved to know that Jack hadn't succumbed that way, but under the circumstances, she couldn't summon up anything remotely resembling pleasure. "What do you want from me?" she asked. "From us?"

"I want you to know just what you've done," the baroness said, taking a threatening step toward Anna, then pointing her quirt at Jack. "Damn you. Damn you for ruining him. Jack Hazard was mine, and he was wild and magnificent before you turned him into something dull and domestic."

"I'm sure I don't know what you're talking—"

"Shut up!" Chloe shrieked. Her dark eyes blazed with tears and her taut mouth trembled. "I loved him! I understood him! I gave him what he needed! He was mine, and you took him away from me!"

"I didn't take him away, Baroness," Anna said, trying to sound as calm as possible, in the frail hope of reasoning with her. "Jack chose to leave you. He chose life over certain death. Love over pain. He left you in order to survive. And if you loved him at all, then surely you'd realize that."

"He chose *you!*" Chloe screamed, swiping furiously at her tears.

Anna nodded her head. "Perhaps. Perhaps he did." She looked at Jack now as she added softly, "I love him, too."

"You love him?" A wet and bitter laugh broke from Chloe's throat as she gestured toward Jack. "Well, you can have him, then. Behold your husband, Mrs. Hazard. The man who chose you. Dull. Domestic. Disgustingly drunk. You're welcome to him. But you owe me for him, and by God, you're going to have to pay a very high price." Her head jerked toward the porch. "Constantine, bring me your knife. Right now."

Jack's hand flashed out, catching the baroness by the elbow and gripping her savagely. "What the devil do you think you're doing, Chloe?" he growled.

"Oh, look who's with us suddenly, in body if not in mind." She wrenched her arm out of his grasp and glared at him. "Go away, Jack. Climb back into your bottle and leave us alone. Your wife and I are negotiating."

"Leave her out of this. She's not my—"

A brawny shoulder came between them just then. "Here's the knife, Chloe. Take care. It's sharp."

"Good. Thank you, Constantine." Chloe smiled, almost lovingly, at the weapon before she turned toward the barn, calling back over her shoulder, "Be a darling now and keep the Hazards occupied for a moment, will you? I won't be long."

"Bloody hell," Jack ground out from between clenched teeth. "Damn her to hell, the bloody, maneating bitch."

Constantine's lips pulled back in a grin. "That she is, fella. That she is."

Anna looked from one man to the other. From Constantine's cruel smile to Jack's expression of helpless fury. She didn't understand what was happening, or why all of a sudden Madelaine had begun a low and mournful keening in the shadows of the porch. "What, Jack?" she asked frantically. "What is she going to do?"

It was Constantine who answered. "The baroness is going to *do* your horse, Mrs. Hazard. She figures, since you ruined her prize lover here—" he jerked his thumb toward Jack, "—she'll do the same to that fine stallion of yours."

"What?" Still not understanding, Anna appealed to Jack once more. "Jack? What? What about Southern Cross?"

Jack's voice was low and harsh. "The bitch is going to castrate him."

"Dear Lord!" Her hand flew to her mouth. "Someone has to stop her."

She jerked up her skirt, preparing to run to the barn, but Constantine grabbed her by the arm. "I don't think so, lady," he warned, just as Jack took a faltering step forward, then halted abruptly, swaying and blinking.

The brawny man laughed. "Now, your husband here is a different story. You think you're up to it, Hazard? Be my guest. Go ahead." He gestured toward the barn. "After all the whiskey you've knocked back tonight, I'd wager those rubber legs of yours won't even get you as far as the door."

But they did. As Anna struggled in Constantine's tight grip, Jack made his way to the barn. He lurched forward, stopped to swig from his bottle, as if it would fuel his progress, then moved forward again. When he reached the barn door, he stood there a moment, gripping the frame to keep himself upright, before staggering into the lantern-lit interior.

What followed was less a confrontation than a grisly ballet played out in golden light on a hay-littered stage, when the baroness turned, knife in one hand and whip in the other, to meet him. Drunk and unsteady though he was, Jack's sheer size and strength allowed him to shoulder her away from the stall where the nervous stallion had begun to rear up on his hind legs, slashing at the air with his lethal hooves.

Chloe screamed, lashing out at Jack, slicing his sleeve with the sharp blade of her knife. She came at him again and again, while he tried to keep his feet beneath him and parried her lunges with the bottle. Whiskey streamed in wild golden arcs around them, and Chloe's black skirts swung furiously, stirring up bits of straw and dust.

Then, after fending off the knife yet another time, Jack managed to knock it out of her grasp, but the effort cost him his already precarious balance and he went down heavily on his knees. The baroness stood above him, shrieking. She raised her black whip high, intending to bring it down with savage force, but the tip of the whip caught the lantern instead and sent it crashing to the floor, where its kerosene exploded in a burst of orange flame.

In the yard, Anna was too stunned to move, despite the fact that Constantine had released his grasp on her arm. All she could do was gape in horror at the flames that raced along the trails of spilled whiskey, igniting the hay-strewn floor. In a matter of seconds, Jack and the baroness were barely visible in a rising pall of smoke behind the fiery waist-high pickets of flame.

"Jack!" Anna screamed and lurched forward, but Constantine grabbed her again.

"Don't be a fool, Mrs. Hazard," he said harshly. "There's nothing you can do."

Nothing she could do except stand there screaming Jack's name again and again, until it felt as if the fire were burning her own throat.

Bloody hell. It took a moment for Jack to comprehend that the flames were real and not some hellish apparition seething in his brain. Then, as much as he had relished the notion of Chloe caught in hellfire, his natural instinct was to save her when the first tongue of flame licked up her long black skirt.

The fury was gone from her face, replaced by stark, staring terror. The whip fell from her hand, and she began to shake her skirts furiously, but her panicky efforts to put out the flames only fanned them until Jack swung his arm to knock her down, then covered her body with his own.

Once her fiery skirt was smothered, the stunned woman lay limp beneath him, fighting for breath and whimpering incoherently.

"S'all right, Chloe..." Jack slurred as his head sagged forward onto her shoulder. The haze in his brain seemed to be mixing with the smoke around them, befuddling him. He was so damn tired. Sick and tired. The temptation to stay right where he was—to let go, to give it all up—was so overwhelming for a moment that Jack's eyes drifted closed.

Dark. It was a little like drowning, he thought. Surely it wouldn't take long, or be more painful than he could bear. How lovely, how deuced lovely, it would be to stop struggling against the terrible tide of his life. He wouldn't miss that. He wouldn't miss anything, really, except golden hair and bright sapphire eyes behind a pair of silly lenses.

Suddenly Anna's face, lit with love and lined with worry, emerged from the mists in Jack's head. He imagined he heard her calling his name. He wanted to go to her, to hold her one last time. Ah, God, if only he could move.

Just opening his eyes and raising his head seemed to take a century. Chloe stared up at him, her glossy black eyes empty of everything but fear. He'd forgotten she was there. He'd forgotten everything, but now—with Anna's desperate calls, and the wild screams of Southern Cross, still locked in his stall— it all came roaring back.

He got to his feet, pulling Chloe with him, then blundered through the smoke until he collided with the front of the stallion's stall. Southern Cross's eyes were huge and red with reflected flames. He had already kicked several slats from the door, so when Jack managed to release the latch, the splintered barrier quickly gave way.

"Run, you devil!" he shouted, shouldering Chloe backward and out of the way.

The big horse nearly exploded out of his stall, but he immediately shied away from the wall of flames between him and the open barn door. Instead of racing toward the safety beyond it, Southern Cross wheeled and ran deeper into the dark recesses of the barn.

And just as he did, Chloe wrested out of the loop of Jack's arm. Wild-eyed, terrified, she turned in the direction in which the horse had gone.

"Not that way, damn it!" Jack tried to snag her back with a handful of black satin, but she whirled on him.

"Let me go!" she screamed, cursing him viciously again and again. Her arms flailed wildly and uselessly a second, but then, with a startling strength born of desperate fear and madness, she shot both hands flat against his chest, breaking his hold on her, stunting his breath and sending Jack reeling and staggering backward through the orange curtain of fire.

## Chapter Twenty-Three

Dead. That was the only explanation Jack could grasp in the aching recesses of his brain. He had been consigned to the fires of hell for a while, but apparently Satan wouldn't have him, so now he was being transported to some other, unknown place, in a vehicle designed for mobile punishment—a creaking, springless wagon that unerringly sought out every bump and crevice in its path.

Of course, how he had managed to die with a hatchet buried in his skull was a damnable mystery, not to mention a bloody embarrassment. And why his head still ached from the lethal wound long after he'd expired was much too difficult to fathom. When he reached his destination, he decided, he'd see to having the bloody hatchet removed. He'd do it himself right now, if he could move anything more than his eyelids.

"You're awake," the angel said.

She was lit from on high by a blaze of light, making it nearly impossible to distinguish her features.

Except for the sweet curve of her smile and, poised somewhere above that, a pair of silly spectacles.

"He's awake, Madelaine." Anna looked over her shoulder at the woman driving the wagon. "That's a good sign, isn't it?"

Although Jack's sister didn't reply immediately, Anna read her answer in the deep sigh that expanded her back and straightened her spine. In spite of her obvious relief, however, when Madelaine spoke there was a note of caution in her voice. "It's a very good sign," she said. "But you must keep talking to him now, Anna, so he doesn't slip away again."

Slip away. It sounded so harmless, even pleasant, like floating on a warm current down a quiet stream, yet Anna knew it wasn't. What Madelaine meant was death, or some living form of it, in which Jack would keep breathing but slip away so far inside his head that he might never find his way back to consciousness. Or so the doctor in Louisville had warned Madelaine last winter.

"You're awake," Anna said again, trying to let her happiness at that hide her grave concerns as she gazed down into Jack's lusterless, red-rimmed eyes and ashen face. "Welcome back, my love."

One side of his mouth crooked upward in a fragile smile, but then, when he attempted to move, the smile gave way to a wince.

"Lie still. You've had a seizure, Jack." She brushed a damp lock of hair from his forehead, doing her best to banish the memory of the convulsion a few hours ago, when Jack had slumped to the ground and his body had gone rigid as a board. The terrible contortions had continued until Anna thought his every muscle must be tearing away from his bones, and she and Madelaine both had sworn during those agonized moments that, if the baroness hadn't perished in the barn, they would have killed the woman themselves for what she had done to Jack.

"Madelaine says you'll be fine," Anna murmured reassuringly.

"You *will* be fine," Madelaine proclaimed over her shoulder, "once that poison is out of your system."

"Bloody hell," he groaned as his eyes sank closed. "Everything hurts, mouse. Even my hair. I need—"

"Rest," she said, knowing full well what he was going to say, but cutting him off before he could voice that need. "But try to keep your eyes open, so you don't fall back to sleep." Then, in an effort to ensure that he remained conscious and to distract him from thinking about whiskey, Anna began to chatter—about the weather, mostly, and about the passing landscape as they neared the city.

It wasn't what Jack wanted to hear, however. What he wanted and needed to hear was the soft thunk of a cork coming loose from a bottle, the sweet music of a metal cap twisting against glass. His throat was parched, and there was only one liquid that could quench his monstrous thirst. His head was reeling, and only a jolt of whiskey would set it right.

He struggled to sit up, clenching his teeth while every muscle and tendon in his body punished him for moving more than an inch. Once upright, he sagged back against the side of the wagon, breathing hard, sweat beading on his brow.

The pain in his head dulled to an ache. The spinning slowed and then stopped. His memory cleared.

"Chloe," he said, in a voice as gritty as sandpaper. "Tell me."

"She's dead," Anna whispered.

"She ran the wrong way," he said dully. "Ah, God. They both did. Chloe and the horse. They ran the bloody wrong way, and I couldn't—"

"You did everything you could to save her, Jack. You tried to go back in the barn, again and again. It was all Madelaine and I could do to stop you from getting killed yourself."

"What about her two companions?"

Anna clucked her tongue. "They were no help. They disappeared as soon as the fire started."

Jack nodded. That made perfect sense. Chloe had inspired many things, but loyalty wasn't one of them. His own vain efforts to save her had come from blind instinct, if not from the false courage of the liquor he'd consumed.

"How's Samuel, Maddie?" When his sister smiled over her shoulder, Jack added, "I'm sorry about Southern Cross."

"Samuel is fine, thanks to you. And there will be other horses, Jack," she answered. "I'm much more worried about you right now, quite frankly."

Anna laid a gentle hand on his arm. "We both are."

"Ah, mouse..." He closed his eyes a moment, hardly able to bear the sweetness of her gaze when he was so gripped by the need for a drink. Still, there was that other need to recapture the happiness he'd felt such a short time before. His heart felt ragged and ripped down the middle, because he knew he couldn't have both, and the whiskey was easier, even more necessary, now. Crucial.

He thought he might scream, at the very least, or the top of his head explode, at the worst, if he didn't think of something else. But what else was there? Then, sadly, he remembered. "I was going to buy you that house, Anna. That spun-sugar fantasy where you loved me so sweetly." He lifted an unsteady hand to coax her spectacles a notch before she could do it herself. "It would have been our house after the race, if everything had gone the way I had planned."

"I know," she answered softly. If there was pain or disappointment in her eyes, Jack was glad he couldn't see them for the shine of her glasses.

He turned his palms up, empty. "It was a dream, Anna. That's all. Only a dream. You'll have more." He tried to grin, but his lips felt numb. "Now that you know how to dream, my serious, sober little mouse."

"*We'll* have more," she told him. "It isn't about the house, Jack. It never was. It's about us."

He nodded in glum agreement, letting his eyes drift closed once more, battling the fierce need that was only his. Not hers. His torture, and—dear God, yes—his cure. He had to swallow the lump in his throat before he could speak. "I don't think I can beat it this time. God. I'm not even sure I bloody want to."

Anna's throat squeezed tight at that admission. *Do it for me,* she wanted to scream. *Do it for all the dreams that can still come true for us. For the dreams I never even knew existed until you taught me how to dream them.*

She reached for his hand and gripped it tight in both of hers. "Listen to me, Jack Hazard. You bloody well better want to, because I need you. You changed my life. The instant you walked into my existence, you changed it."

"For the worse," he muttered.

"No. For the better. For the best. I was hiding, and you found me. I was living in the dark until you brought me into the light. I was afraid, and you made me brave. In these last few weeks, you've taught me how to live, Jack. And how to love. You most of all."

He shook his head in denial.

"It's true," Anna insisted, and then, with a little laugh, she added, "I was a skinflint, remember? A pinchpenny? But it wasn't only with money. It was my heart, too. I was afraid to open it and spend my emotions. But I'm not afraid anymore. I love you, Jack Hazard. I've given you my whole heart, and I will not take it back. So...so..." Her voice faltered as tears began to slide down her cheeks.

"So?" he whispered.

"So you owe me, damn it!" she shrieked.

"You've made a bad bargain, little mouse. You know that, don't you?"

"No, I don't know anything of the sort."

"I have nothing to give you now, Anna, other than hard times." He sighed. "You have my heart, love. You always will, but I'm afraid it isn't going to do you any more good than having some pickled specimen in a glass jar."

Anna pressed her hand over his damp shirt, where, beneath the hard curve of his chest, she could feel the brooding heart.

"This is all I want, Jack. Just your heart. It's good and it's strong. It's all I need. Will you try? Please?"

He closed his eyes wearily to blot out the sight of her earnest, tear-streaked face while he lied through his aching teeth.

"I'll try, mouse." Tomorrow. Or the day after that. When it isn't so bloody hard. When every nerve stops burning from thirst and begging to be quenched. When I can think again. And hope. Maybe next week. Or next year.

"There they are!" Mrs. Bissell's voice carried across the crowded lobby like a cheerful blast from a calliope. "Helloo, Mr. and Mrs. Hazard. Hello, you two."

"Damn." Anna and Jack swore in unison as they ducked behind a potted palm. Madelaine had dropped them off at a rear door of the hotel in order to avoid just such an encounter, since Jack was in no condition to face the lofty racing set—or anyone else, for that matter.

He had been ill only a short while before. So violently and viciously sick he'd thought the soles of his boots had been dredged up through his body and heaved along with the contents of his stomach. When there was nothing left, he had begun to sweat so profusely and to shake so prodigiously he thought he must look like a man who'd just climbed out of an icy river into a brisk, chill wind.

He wanted to die. He wanted a drink. Whichever came first was fine, he decided.

"Hurry, Jack. This way." Anna gripped his arm tighter and steered him toward the elevator, which, with a lurch, turned into a torture chamber of the most exquisite proportions. He would have thrown up again, if there had been anything left inside him.

Poor mouse. Her face was pale but her expression valiant as she ushered him down the corridor under the hopeful but mistaken impression that she was guiding him to the haven of their suite, where, away from prying eyes and clucking tongues, he could crawl into bed and then sleep off the aftereffects of his binge. And Jack was allowing her to do it—being meek as a lamb, in fact—because he had other ideas. One other idea. One shining, all-consuming goal. The bottle of sour mash he had stashed under the bed.

A little taste was all he needed to stop this infernal sweating, to stop his hands from shaking and to obliterate the shadows that were beginning to impinge on his field of vision. The shadows that would soon take horrific shapes, dead center in his sight. The monsters that would make him cringe. Or cry. Or both, as likely as not.

"Here we are," she announced, then fumbled in her handbag for the key—endlessly, terminally—until Jack thought his jaw would crack from biting down on a scream.

"There." Anna opened the door and was greeted by the lethal end of a little gun. "Oh, good Lord." She had completely forgotten about the Misses Richmond. And Freddy! The poor man was still bound and gagged, in the exact spot where she'd left him the night before. It seemed like a century now.

"We were so worried, dear," Miss Verna squeaked.

Miss Dorothy merely sighed, appearing almost too tired to speak much less contradict her sister.

"I am so sorry." Forgetting about Jack for the moment, Anna bustled across the room and knelt beside the hapless agent. While she untied the drapery cords around his ankles, her gaze strayed to the stain on the front of his trousers. Poor man. Of course he had wet himself. He'd been trussed up this way for—what?—fifteen or sixteen hours. Long enough for a barn to burn, for a woman and a horse to perish, and for a man to slide from sobriety to perilous addiction.

"Freddy, I truly regret this," she said as she whisked the bonds from his red, bony wrists.

He jerked the silk scarf from his mouth, then sputtered and spat and finally croaked, "Regret it? Regret it! You'll know the true meaning of the word *regret* once I've filed my reports, Mrs. Matlin." Shoving her away, he clambered to his feet and stood unsteadily, all the while attempting to cover his damp pants with both wrinkled halves of his coat.

"Freddy, I..." Anna's voice diminished to a sigh that the agent promptly cut off.

"I'll have your job for this." He sounded less like a frog now, and more like a baying, abused hound. "You'll never work as a Pinkerton agent again. Never. And as for you, Hazard—I'll have you rotting in jail just as soon as I can get my hands on that whip-wielding, larcenous lover of yours." His angry gaze flicked around the room. "Hazard? I saw you come in. Where the devil did you go?"

"Hello, Broome." A bottle rose in a loose-fingered salute above the far side of the bed, then sank out of sight.

Before Anna could stop him, Freddy stalked around the footboard and glared down. "You're a piece of work, Hazard. My God, you smell like a damn distillery."

Jack's chuckle drifted up from the floor. "I daresay it's better than smelling like an outhouse, Broome. Had a bit of an accident, did you?"

Anna sat down heavily on the bed. The sight of the whiskey bottle had stunned her into silence, and now the sound of Jack's slurred speech made her dizzy. She had forgotten that that poison was hidden under the bed, but obviously Jack hadn't. He'd gone straight for it. He wasn't going to quit. He wasn't even going to try.

He might just as well have kicked her in the teeth, or launched a boot into her stomach. He didn't love her, or, if he did, he loved liquor more. He had made his choice. Not her. Not her.

Anna's vision blurred, and she didn't even have the strength to adjust her glasses. Her head was telling her it was over, that all those dreams had died before they even had a chance to exist. At the same time, though, her heart was refusing to give up. How dare Jack not even try? How dare he teach her to dream and then leave her to do it alone?

She couldn't think—not with her landladies fluttering and fussing, not with Freddy in such a huff.

She needed to think. To hold fast to the dream that Jack was doing his damnedest to drown.

"Poor dear." Miss Verna's worried face swam into sight as she began patting Anna's hand. "You look exhausted. You had a very long night."

"*She* had a very long night?" Freddy said, fuming. "Spent it hunting down Chloe Von Drosten to warn her of her imminent arrest, I'd wager, then helping the woman get away. Am I right, Anna?"

Anna nodded weakly, only half listening, wishing the man would simply shut up so that she could get her thoughts in order, so that she could synchronize her head and her heart.

"Just as I suspected." Freddy clucked his tongue. "I had hoped for better from you, Anna. I thought you were a true Pinkerton, but instead you've proven yourself a disgrace to the profession. Worse than Hazard, here. At least he has liquor and a weak character as an excuse. But you—"

"Shut up, Broome." Jack's voice snapped like a whip. "Leave her alone. Anna's done nothing wrong. And anyway, you idiot, the baroness is dead."

"What?"

"I said, the bloody bitch is dead."

"How? Who?" Freddy sputtered. "What the devil did you do, Hazard? Kill her?"

"Did I kill her?" Jack leaned back, laughing, and took another swig from the bottle. "It was rather mutual, I'd say. Unfortunately, as you can see for yourself, it's just taking me a bit longer to succumb."

"You killed her to stop her from talking, didn't you? To keep her from incriminating you in her schemes! Why, you—" Freddy lunged forward.

"Stop it!" Anna's scream startled her as much as it did the others. Freddy halted in midstep, while little Miss Richmond put a hand to her throat and gasped audibly.

"Stop it, both of you." After she had lowered her voice a notch, Anna jabbed at her glasses, then shot to her feet. "Get out, Freddy. Just get out. Go back to your office and fill out some forms. Send some telegrams. Go. Everyone, please, just leave."

"Oh, but my dear..." Miss Verna said.

Anna held up a hand. "No. Please, Miss Richmond." Her voice trembled, on the verge of breaking. "Leave. All of you. Now. Get out. Get out. With all this nattering and name-calling, I can't hear myself think." She sagged down onto the mattress, biting her lip to keep from crying, her fists clenched in her lap.

"There, there... Poor dear..." Miss Verna stroked Anna's hair. "You'll feel ever so much better when you've had some rest," she crooned.

"Well, let the child rest, then, sister," Miss Dorothy snapped. "Come along." She snagged Freddy by the arm and tugged him toward the door. "That means you, as well, Mr. Broome. I daresay you'll feel better, too, and much more charitable, once you've changed into some fresh clothes.''

The agent wrenched out of her grasp, repositioned his coat, then stalked to the door. ''You haven't heard the last of this. I'll see you all in jail. Especially you, Hazard.'' He grasped the knob and yanked the door open on several astonished faces.

''Oh, my goodness!'' Mrs. Bissell's bulk shifted back a few inches as she surveyed the rumpled agent. Her nose twitched delicately, after which her mouth crimped in distaste bordering on disgust. ''I believe I must have the wrong room. I was looking for Mr. and Mrs. Hazard.''

Anna moaned. The whole world, it seemed, had congregated to witness her despair. Now there was Mrs. Bissell, and behind her was Henry Gresham, the racetrack official, and behind him stood Madelaine. Smiling. Her face was lit by a wide, white Hazard grin that remained intact even when Freddy shoved past her on his way out the door.

''Oh, Jack!'' Madelaine said as she followed Mrs. Bissell and Henry Gresham into the suite. ''There's wonderful news!''

''Ah, Hazard. I see you're already celebrating.'' Gresham gestured toward the far side of the bed, where Jack sat on the floor. ''Can't say as I blame you. I'd be tipping a bottle, too, if I were in your boots.''

Jack blinked up at the sudden and inexplicable crowd in the room. He was seeing double again, which was almost as amusing as it was disconcerting. He cocked his head and squinted at two Mrs. Bissells. Two Henry Greshams. Four twittering landladies. Madelaine and Madelaine, both of them grinning like village idiots. His lovely Annas, with a multitude of hands prodding their silly spectacles.

Everyone was jabbering. Blearily Jack wondered if any of it made sense.

"...left the other four horses in the deuced dust...and by the milepost..."

"Oh, my."

"...pulled away..."

"You should have seen..."

"...nosed the finish line in two-twenty-six..."

"He won, Jack." Madelaine, just one of her now, with a single brilliant smile, was suddenly kneeling beside him. "He won."

"What?" He shook his head in an attempt to clear the haze. "Who?"

"Polaris. Oh, Jack, listen to me. Polaris beat Chloe's Gold by half a furlong. He won the Carondelet Stakes."

## Chapter Twenty-Four

"Bloody hell."

Jack's shoulders hit the wall with a resounding thunk that nearly knocked the breath out of him, and he couldn't decide whether to use what little breath remained to laugh madly or to cry.

His damn daft plan had succeeded. Not perfectly. A far cry from the way he had imagined. But it had worked. Despite Chloe's malign efforts and his own ineptitude, bloody Polaris—the *slow* horse, the *wrong* horse—had run away with the race.

Henry Gresham cleared his throat. "Your sister informed me that she trained the animal in Kentucky, Hazard, but I've told her there are plenty of Thoroughbreds here that could use the benefit of her skills, if she'd consider the move."

Jack smiled at his sister's radiant face, thinking this was the way she was meant to look—ecstatic and on the verge of a successful career as a trainer. His dream for her had come true.

He took a celebratory swig, thinking that that, too, had been part of his plan. His own personal denouement. It was what had fueled him from the start. Only now...

Gresham plucked at his beard. "Perhaps you can persuade your sister, Hazard."

"Of course he will," Mrs. Bissell cut in. "Stop babbling, Henry, and give the man his check."

His check. Jack sat up a little straighter. The whiskey sloshed in the bottle as he propped it against his leg. In the sheer excitement of winning, he had completely forgotten his prize. The ten-thousand-dollar purse from the Carondelet Stakes that he had all but consigned to the Bissell woman in payment for the house.

Muttering, Henry Gresham made a great show of patting his clothes before he dipped into a waistcoat pocket and came up with a folded bit of paper. "Congratulations, Hazard." But before he could pass it to Jack, Mrs. Bissell snatched the check from his hand.

She eyed it briefly. "Exactly the amount we agreed upon for the residence and the adjacent property. You clever man, if I didn't know better, I'd be tempted to wonder if you fixed the race." She laughed then, waving a hand as if to dismiss such a silly notion. "Well, all we need now is your endorsement on this, and the house is yours."

Jack stared at the paper fluttering back and forth in front of him. It might as well have been a windblown scrap, or the last crisp leaf clinging to a November tree. A chill inched along his spine, compelling him to tighten his grip on the warm glass neck of the bottle.

"You still want it, don't you?" Mrs. Bissell stood there, her mouth slightly askew and her eyebrows raised quizzically, waiting.

Did he want it? She meant the house. She was asking him if he wanted the bloody house. Jack knew that, and yet his own definition of the word *want* was so complex just then that he couldn't even nod in simple agreement.

"You do still want the house, don't you?" she asked again as her stiff petticoat began to tick with the tap of her foot. It reminded him for a second of Chloe's damnable whip. He shook his head.

Want it? The woman might just as well have asked a blind man if he wanted to see, or inquired of a prisoner if he wanted to be free. As it was, she was asking a dead man whether or not he desired to live again.

Did he? He looked toward Anna, but she had moved from the bed to the window, where she stood with her back to everyone in the room, including him. Perhaps specifically him.

From the tilt of her head and a certain wistful slant of her shoulders toward the open window, Jack thought she might have been wishing on a star. But it was daylight. What the devil could she find to wish on in a city sky punctured with chimney pots and smudged with smoke? What in blazes was she forever seeing through those bright bits of glass she perpetually wore?

The better question, of course, and the crucial one, was what did Anna see in him? What glimmer of worthiness had she detected in the dark expanse of his soul? But was it even there anymore for her to see? Or would she even want it now?

Mrs. Bissell tapped her foot one last time. "My dear Mr. Hazard, *do* you want the house?"

With his gaze still fastened on Anna's back, he answered, trying his damnedest not to slur. "You'll have to ask my wife. It's completely up to her."

"All right then." The woman sighed laboriously, but before she could frame another question, Anna answered her with a single softly spoken word.

"Yes."

Mrs. Bissell let out a dignified little whoop then, and everyone started chattering about houses and horses while Jack took several deep, measured breaths and glanced at the golden remnants of sour mash—his courage, his curse, his precious poison and perilous antidote, his pleasure and pain. But not his life, and surely not his love. He set the bottle aside, then got to his feet with as much dignity as any drunk man ever had, and after a bumbling attempt to button the collar of his shirt and drag his fingers through his unkempt hair, he walked to the window.

Standing behind Anna, he circled her with his arms and brushed his lips against the warmth of her hair and held his breath. She had said yes. He was certain his serious little mouse had meant it, and yet still he expected to feel the backlash of her bitter disappointment in him, in a quick stiffening of her spine, a subtle and unforgiving shift of her shoulders, a grudging motion away. But instead she leaned back against him, sighing, drawing his arms more closely around her, blending into him. Warm. Sweet. And liquid. And magical.

Jack crooked his knees a bit and pressed his cheek to Anna's, angling his head in order to gaze out the window through one of her lenses, willing himself to see whatever future she seemed to picture so easily, so clearly, in the distance.

But he couldn't.

Anna nestled even closer against him, and when she spoke, every prim note of the stickler had vanished from her voice. It was a dreamy whisper, meant for him alone. "You need to speak with the gardener, Jack. He's drinking again."

Then, just for an instant, Jack's vision cleared, and the blurred, broken images before him gave way to a sudden sweep of lawn and a white fence and the bright green pastures beyond.

"Ah, God, mouse." He sighed, then closed his eyes against the alcoholic haze that was building and beginning to sully the view, while he tried to summon every shred of strength he had left to see him through the next week, the next day, the next endless minute. "You ought to fire the bastard, darling.

Just boot him out on his drunken backside. You'd be much better off.''

''No,'' she said. ''Never.''

Then Anna turned slowly in the circle of his embrace and fitted her arms around him tight, so tight Jack knew she'd never let him go.

# Epilogue

*Chicago*
*May 15, 1870*

Nora Quillan locked the center drawer of her desk, then slid the key beneath the footed inkwell. She was poking a hatpin through her straw boater, already thinking about the warm beer and the cold pork sandwich that were waiting for her at home, when Allan Pinkerton jerked open the anteroom door, snorted a greeting as he passed her desk, then kicked his office door closed behind him.

The vision of her dinner faded, along with her hopes of catching the five-o'clock omnibus. Nora sighed and took off her hat before unlocking her desk and reaching in for an envelope of headache powder.

She didn't bother to knock, and Mr. Pinkerton didn't bother to lift his head from the cradle of his hands to acknowledge her presence, so she set the murky medication down on his blotter with an authoritative little thump.

"I take it your trip to St. Louis was less than a success," she said, watching to make sure he drank every drop. He might be the head of the country's largest detective agency, but at the moment Allan Pinkerton appeared more baffled than any man she'd ever seen.

He had gone to St. Louis for the express purpose of replacing Frederick Broome, who had resigned just the previous week, in order to begin his own detective agency. The idiot had had the nerve to try to hire Nora away from the Pinkertons in order to help him get his business under way.

"I do so admire your expertise with forms, Miss Quillan," he had said, after which Nora had told him precisely where he could put those forms and never to cast his skinny shadow across her desk again.

Mr. P. was gazing into his empty glass now. "No, Nora. It was not a success. Far from it. It was more like an exercise in pure futility. Damn it. I'm afraid Hazard's lost to us for good."

"Oh, dear." Nora sat and clasped her hands in her lap. "He's drinking again," she murmured. "I had hoped, with the baroness dead and with the help of little Mrs. Matlin, that Jack might change."

"He's changed, all right. And he isn't drinking. At least nothing more potent than water, as far as I could tell." His chair creaked when he leaned back, and his pained expression cheered. "Nora, it's the most amazing thing. Jack Hazard, one of the most urbane and worldly men I've ever known, is living out in the country in a house that looks like a ridiculous white frosted cake. And he's surrounded by women, which shouldn't seem so uncharacteristic, except his harem includes his sister and two old-maid aunts of Anna's who simply dote on him. It's constantly 'Dear Jack this' and 'Darling Jack that.'''

Nora felt a smile inching across her lips. "And little Mrs. Matlin? Is she well?"

"Mrs. Hazard, you mean. Quite well. Quite lovely, actually. And not so little anymore. She's about to have a child."

"Well, that's good news, then, isn't it?"

He nodded. "Except Jack turned me down. Flat. Doesn't want to take those risks anymore, he claims, now that he's a family man."

"I can understand that, Mr. P. What does he intend to do if he doesn't come back to the agency?"

Allan Pinkerton rubbed his temples, and that earlier look of pained bemusement returned to his face. "He says he's going to be a gardener, Nora. Can you imagine that? My best operative is going to be a gardener."

Nora's smile widened.

"I'll tell you one thing, Nora." Pinkerton flattened his palms on the top of his desk, glared at his nails a moment and then scowled at his secretary.

''The next time an agent walks in here and tells me he needs a wife, I plan to tell him in no uncertain terms that it's strictly against company policy.''

\*     \*     \*     \*     \*

## Harlequin® Historical

From the author of HEAVEN CAN WAIT
& LAND OF DREAMS comes another,
heartwarming Western love story

# BADLANDS BRIDE

## by CHERYL ST. JOHN

Keep an eye out for this delightful tale of an eastern
beauty who poses as a mail-order bride and winds up
stranded in the Dakota Badlands!

Coming this August
from Harlequin Historicals!

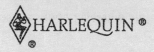

HARLEQUIN ®

BIGB96-6

A baby was the last thing they were

**XPECTING!**

But after nine months, the idea of fatherhood begins to grow on three would-be bachelors.

Enjoy three complete stories by some of your favorite authors—all in one special collection!

**THE STUD** by Barbara Delinsky
**A QUESTION OF PRIDE** by Michelle Reid
**A LITTLE MAGIC** by Rita Clay Estrada

Available this July wherever books are sold.

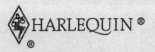

## BRIDE'S BAY RESORT

## UNLOCK THE DOOR TO GREAT ROMANCE AT BRIDE'S BAY RESORT

Join Harlequin's new across-the-lines series, set in an exclusive hotel on an island off the coast of South Carolina.

Seven of your favorite authors will bring you exciting stories about fascinating heroes and heroines discovering love at Bride's Bay Resort.

Look for these fabulous stories coming to a store near you beginning in January 1996.

**Harlequin American Romance #613 in January**
*Matchmaking Baby* by Cathy Gillen Thacker

**Harlequin Presents #1794 in February**
*Indiscretions* by Robyn Donald

**Harlequin Intrigue #362 in March**
*Love and Lies* by Dawn Stewardson

**Harlequin Romance #3404 in April**
*Make Believe Engagement* by Day Leclaire

**Harlequin Temptation #588 in May**
*Stranger in the Night* by Roseanne Williams

**Harlequin Superromance #695 in June**
*Married to a Stranger* by Connie Bennett

**Harlequin Historicals #324 in July**
*Dulcie's Gift* by Ruth Langan

Visit Bride's Bay Resort each month wherever Harlequin books are sold.

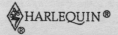

## Harlequin® Historical

Bestselling author **RUTH LANGAN** brings you nonstop
adventure and romance with her new Western series
from Harlequin Historicals

### The Jewels of Texas

| DIAMOND | February 1996 |
|---------|---------------|
| PEARL | August 1996 |
| JADE | February 1997 |
| RUBY | June 1997 |

Don't miss these exciting stories of four sisters as wild
and vibrant as the untamed land they're fighting to protect!

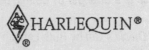

HARLEQUIN®

Look us up on-line at: http://www.romance.net

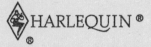

# Harlequin® Historical

If you're a serious fan of historical romance,
then you're in luck!

Harlequin Historicals brings you
stories by bestselling authors, rising new stars
and talented first-timers.

Ruth Langan & Theresa Michaels
Mary McBride & Cheryl St. John
Margaret Moore & Merline Lovelace
Julie Tetel & Nina Beaumont
Susan Amarillas & Ana Seymour
Deborah Simmons & Linda Castle
Cassandra Austin & Emily French
Miranda Jarrett & Suzanne Barclay
DeLoras Scott & Laurie Grant...

You'll never run out of favorites.

Harlequin Historicals...they're too good to miss!

HH-GEN